PEARL'S DRAGON

A DRAGON LORDS OF VALDIER STORY

S.E. SMITH

MONTANA
PUBLISHING

CONTENTS

The single greatest gift for me is to be able to give to others. I am honored to share my talents to bring joy and offer support through the Embrace the Romance: Pets in Space 2 Project.

I would like to thank my husband Steve for believing in me and being proud enough of me to give me the courage to follow my dream. I would also like to give a special thank you to my sister and best friend, Linda, who not only encouraged me to write, but who also read the manuscript. Also to my other friends who believe in me: Julie, Debbie, Christel, Sally, Jolanda, Lisa, Laurelle, and Narelle. The girls that keep me going!

—S.E. Smith

Science Fiction Romance
Pearl's Dragon: Dragon Lords of Valdier Story
Copyright © 2017 by S.E. Smith
First E-Book Published October 2017
Cover Design by Melody Simmons

Summary: When sixty-something year old Pearl St. Claire traveled to a far off alien world with her granddaughters, she never expected to be caught up in the adventure – or in the grasp of a dragon warrior who insists she is his true mate!

SYNOPSIS

Asim Kemark has lived a long, lonely life. It is his pledge to his former king and to Mandra Reykill that keeps him, his dragon, and his symbiot from going mad. He has given up on finding his true mate and devotes himself to caring for the wide assortment of creatures on Mandra and Ariel's mountain retreat. The last thing he expects to happen when he visits the palace is to lose control of his dragon and his symbiot after they sense their true mate. Before he knows it, he has kidnapped her!

Pearl St. Claire is enjoying a new adventure – learning to live on an alien planet. As a mature woman in her sixties, she thought she had experienced just about everything life could throw at her – only to discover she hasn't really experienced anything yet! She is both amused and exasperated when one of the dragon-shifting aliens kidnaps her, believing she is his true mate.

Life is no longer boring or lonely as Asim courts the enchanting and spirited, human woman, but he isn't the only one who has noticed Pearl or the unusual animals under his care. When poachers attack, determined to steal the exotic creatures under his protection – including Pearl and a new clutch of alien eggs from Earth – he will do everything he can to protect them. Can one dragon keep the most precious creatures under his care safe, or will he lose the biggest battle of his life?

PEARL'S RULES FOR LIVING:

1. Use your brain - that is why you have one.
2. Safety is something you take seriously, otherwise you end up dead.
3. If you have expressive eyes, keep them covered if you are going to bluff.
4. Give someone enough rope, and they are bound to get tangled and hang themselves.
5. Always carry a roll of quarters, you can do your laundry and knock out bad guys at the same time.
6. There are rules and there are rules, pick which ones work for you.
7. Don't fuck up unless you are willing to make it right.
8. Mistakes are good, learn from them and move on.
9. Always stay alert and don't let your guard down.
10. Ask yourself, 'Am I ready for this?' If the answer is yes, go for it. If the answer is no, run like hell.
11. If you are going to hit someone, make sure they stay down the first time. You might not get a second chance.
12. Don't trust a man, especially a good-looking one who starts

out with sweet words. Same goes for a woman, she just wants something.

13. A good book and fresh batteries can make your day tolerable.
14. Your word is your honor, be careful what you promise.
15. Humor solves any problem; think in animation.
16. The only opinion you have to worry about is your own, since *you* have to live with it.
17. Be the best possible you that you can be.
18. Your goal each day is to make it a good one.
19. Words can be as powerful as a fist; be careful how you use them.
20. If you or your family/friends' lives are on the line, ignore all of the above except Rule Number 1.

Unbreakable rule: Family and friends come first. Be loyal, be true, and love them like there is no tomorrow.

PROLOGUE

Present Day:

"The last rule I'm going to share is the Unbreakable Rule," Pearl St. Claire stated in a firm tone. She released a sigh and raised an eyebrow at the scarred warrior sitting in one of the two chairs in the room. He was staring at the board she was pointing to with a mutinous expression. "What is it now, Brogan?"

"I told you when you started. I don't follow anyone's rules but my own," Brogan stated, folding his arms.

"And look where that got you! All I can say is you'd better learn if you want to get out of this room - alive," Pearl snapped in a sharper tone than she originally intended before adding the last word under her breath.

"Pearl," Asim cautioned in a low voice from where he was sitting on a bench by the door.

Pearl slowly counted to thirty. She'd already bypassed ten and twenty. Why she was chosen for this exasperating task was beyond her. The only thing she could think of was that she had survived raising Riley and Tina without any casualties.

Surely, I can manage a few lessons in humility for the two men sitting in front of me, she thought.

Unfortunately, she felt like she was starting all over again – only this time during the toddler stage. Being over sixty, she'd thought she was finished dealing with stubborn, defiant, and downright ornery kids. Back on Earth, she'd been a surrogate grandmother to the kids in the neighborhood. During that time, she had seen and heard a lot. She was well aware that she was the kind of grandmother every kid wanted to have – and the one every parent wished they could hide in the closet.

She didn't dress like a grandmother – she preferred leather and boots to dresses and pearls. She didn't go to church; instead, she owned a bar. She never carried a wooden spoon, but hell if she didn't still have a shotgun loaded with rock salt. Her platinum-white hair was cut short and she stayed in shape by doing Yoga, Zumba, and Weekend Warrior trainings with her newly adopted great-grandson.

Jabir, Mandra and Ariel's son, had captured her heart as quickly as her own great-grandsons, Roam and Leo, had. Unfortunately, Roam and Leo lived on the Sarafin home world while she lived on Valdier. Living on another planet wasn't much more of a problem than living across town – well, except for having to use a spaceship to visit. Still, Pearl was able to talk with the two boys regularly and they loved visiting her here.

At the moment, she would rather be with the cuddly little dragonling and his menagerie of unusual pets or her great-grandsons. It sure as hell beat resisting the urge to find a baseball bat and knock some sense into two well-seasoned warriors who had an elephant's hair up their asses.

As it was, there were currently only the four of them – her, Asim, and the twin dragon warriors – in the barn's tack room. Her classroom was not much larger than a ten by ten shed back home. There was just enough room for the table and two chairs that Asim had brought in earlier this morning, plus the bench he was sitting on by the door. Harnesses for the Pactors, leashes for the smaller animals, and maintenance tools hung neatly on two of the four walls. The floor was clean and the room smelled of the sweet warm grass that was used as hay for the animals in the outer stalls.

Pearl shot a heated glare at her amused mate when he smothered a chuckle. Asim raised an eyebrow in response and tried to look innocent. With a shake of her head, she slowly turned back to the twin dragons.

She rested one hand on her hip and tapped her fingers against her side. She was really going to have a private talk with Asim later. She needed to remind him that her personality was not conducive to being a teacher.

Pearl studiously observed her two pupils. She had quickly distinguished the difference between the identical twin dragons known as Barrack and Brogan. Barrack had more patience and control than his brother, Brogan – by about the width of a human hair.

After hours of trying to explain human culture to the brothers, Pearl decided her patience was fast disintegrating to their level, almost nonexistent. While Brogan had questioned or argued every single rule she had tried to explain, Barrack had just released long, drawn-out sighs of impatience.

Raising her chin, Pearl returned Brogan's steely gaze. Time was fast running out for the two men. She was about to open a can of whoop-ass on them if they didn't get their heads out of their asses. She pointed a determined finger at Barrack.

"What is Rule number one?" she snapped.

"Use your brain – that's why we have one," Barrack replied with an uncertain tone in his voice.

Pearl would have felt more confident in Barrack's answer if he hadn't looked doubtful and raised his hand to scratch at his temple. She gave Barrack a firm nod of agreement. Of course, Brogan snorted. She shot the scarred warrior a sharp, reproving look. The fingers of her left hand twitched. Pearl drew in a deep breath. She would not resort to violence!

"Yes, use your brain. You can't use your brain, Brogan, if your head isn't attached to your damn shoulders," she stated.

"Fine, but what has this got to do with our mate? The Curizan takes us to your world, Jaguin and Sara show us where our mate is, and we claim her. Why do we need to learn these... rules?" Brogan demanded with a wave of his hand.

"Because Aikaterina is giving you a second chance at life," a voice dryly replied from the doorway.

Pearl turned to see two tall, lean warriors and a slender, blonde woman standing in the entrance to the tack room. She recognized one of the men and the woman as Jaguin and Sara. For a private meeting, the room was quickly filling up.

"Hi Pearl. Thank you for doing this," Sara said with a sympathetic smile.

"Hi, Sara. I wish I could say teaching these two boneheads was a pleasure, but...." Pearl gave Sara a wink to show she was teasing. "Hi Jaguin, I see you brought a friend. Are you part of this mission, too?" Pearl asked.

Pearl turned her attention to the tall man with the scar running down one side of his face. He positively exuded an air of power and danger. It was a good thing he was obviously a friend because she sure as hell wouldn't want him as an enemy.

"This is Adalard Ha'darra, the captain of our transport to Earth," Jaguin replied.

"Better known as Curizan trash," Brogan added with a heavy dose of disdain.

Pearl had had enough of the twins' attitudes – especially Brogan's. He had a smart retort to just about everything she'd said and an expression of condescension on his face that reminded her of the college-educated Preppies who came into the White Pearl Bar she'd owned back on Earth. He continued to be a pain-in-the-ass from the second he stepped into the classroom. Her patience was on empty.

Pearl decided that some people just needed to learn the hard way and Brogan was one of those people. She slipped her hand into the pocket of her black pleather jacket. She wrapped her fingers around a small but very handy device that she had confiscated from one of her granddaughters. In the background, Pearl heard Asim's loud curse, Jaguin's warning, and Sara's smothered gasp as she stepped forward, pressed the Taser firmly against the dragon warrior's chest, and pushed the button.

"Rule number nine: always stay alert and don't let your guard down," she stated. "That means for everyone," she added with a nod of gratification when he grimaced and hit the floor with a resounding thud.

$$\sim$$

The grunted curses coming from the two men on the floor finally began to fade. Relaxing back against the wall by the door, Asim patiently waited for the men to recover. Studying the sculpture, he blew off some of the loose scrapings from the small creature he was carving before he lowered the knife and the wood figurine to his lap.

Brogan was the first one to sit up – if you could call scooting back against the wall and propping himself up 'sitting'. Barrack continued to lie on the floor, rubbing his chest. Barrack would have fared much better than his brother if he hadn't growled at Pearl. The second he did, she'd shocked his ass and put him on the floor next to Brogan.

Asim warily studied both men to see if they had calmed down. He had to admit it had been hard not to laugh when Pearl asked if Brogan understood the rule of learning to shut up before it was too late. While the two men lay twitching on the floor, Pearl calmly turned to Sara to ask if she would care for a cup of hot tea and a piece of the freshly baked cake that Ariel brought over the night before.

Pride mixed with exasperation. He probably should have warned Pearl about the possible consequences of enraging Twin Dragon warriors – especially those who already had a history of maiming and killing anyone who got in their way.

"What was that?" Barrack asked in a strained voice.

"*That* was my mate being nice," Asim stated.

"That… was being nice?" Brogan repeated in disbelief. "What happens when she isn't being nice?"

"You don't want to know," Asim assured him with a lopsided grin.

"Why did she react so strongly to Brogan's comment? Is she part Curizan?" Barrack asked, confused.

"Strongly?! She almost killed us! I swear I can still smell my flesh burning," Brogan retorted.

Asim couldn't contain the chuckle that escaped him. He shook his head. He knew exactly what Brogan was talking about. After all, he had been in the same position as the two men on more than one occasion when he finally pushed Pearl too far.

"No, she is fully human," he replied. "She was asked to help you. If you don't listen, expect the consequences," Asim said.

"Are all humans like this? If they are, we need more information about them," Barrack demanded.

"Finally! Some information that will be more useful than a bunch of rules," Brogan retorted under his breath.

"Well, I know enough never to underestimate the powers of a human – be they man or woman. I can't tell you about the others, only those who I have met. You will learn more about them on your journey," he replied.

"Tell us about those you've met then," Barrack insisted.

Asim thought about where to begin and decided that telling his story might help the two warriors. A lot had changed over the centuries and Pearl was a good example of what they could expect, he reasoned. He had heard of the original Twin Dragons. The stories he remembered said they died.

Asim had been shocked when Zoran Reykill, King of the Valdier and ruler of all Dragon Lords, had contacted him requesting Pearl and he help with an urgent matter. The next day, Jaguin and Sara appeared with the legendary and highly volatile warriors who were alive and well. The only thing Jaguin and Sara said was the men needed to be instructed in the ways of the humans, and that a very special person whom they had insisted remain a mystery – much to Asim's annoyance – had requested that Pearl be the one to help the twins understand.

Zoran had been a little more forthcoming. He said the Goddess Aikaterina had appeared to both Sara and Jaguin. Worried about Sara after her traumatic experience back on Earth with a group of human men, Zoran had suggested approaching Pearl – after all, he reasoned, Pearl had no problems handling Vox and Viper.

Zoran had felt that Pearl was the only one who could get the twins ready to court their human mate in a timely manner – and teach them a little humility at the same time. Asim didn't know if using that shocking device would count as listening, but it definitely got the men's attention. He just needed to remember to find the damn thing and hide it again – this time in a place where Pearl wasn't likely to find it.

"The story I will tell you will seem incredulous, perhaps no more unbelievable than your – second chance – but this species is unlike any that we have encountered before. When Jaguin and Sara told Lord Zoran about your second chance, he decided it was important for you to understand what you will face," Asim explained.

"Surely it cannot be that difficult?" Brogan asked, wiggling his fingers.

"Shut up, Brogan. My chest hurts enough thanks to your comments. I would prefer to keep my head and my nervous system in working order from now on, brother," Barrack retorted.

Asim released a sigh as he remembered his own struggles with the loneliness and despair when he thought he would never find a true mate. He turned the wooden figurine over in his hands, trying to think of what he could tell the men that would help them understand the difference between a Valdier mate and a human one.

The wooden bird in his hand was a creature alien to their world. It was large, flightless, and smart. In a way, his history with the emus reminded him of the humans he had met. Oh, he didn't think of humans as flightless birds – just that it was easy to misunderstand them, like it had been when he found Jabir's hidden cache of eggs. It was better to have the knowledge before you went into battle – every good warrior knew that.

"Over the last couple of years, my life has become very interesting, more fulfilling than I could ever have hoped – and definitely a lot more complicated. Like you, my dragon felt the emptiness of not having a true mate, but it was my symbiot who grieved the most. It was only my promise to our former king and my sworn duties to Lord Mandra, Lady Ariel, and their young son, Jabir, which gave me the strength to carry on. I never expected to be given the gift of finding my true mate. When I saw Pearl…." Asim shook his head and chuckled. "Shocked would be a mild description of my feelings. To find my mate after so many years… it was a revelation like nothing I could have imagined."

"What do you mean? Your dragon and symbiot would know. The female would immediately recognize what was happening. What could be so surprising?" Barrack asked.

Asim raised an eyebrow. "You assume that Pearl is like a Valdier female, but she is not. Her species do not connect the same way we do. Our dragons and our symbiots recognize our mate even before we do, but we understand what is happening. Humans do not have that same connection. They must be courted," he explained.

Barrack sat up with a confused expression on his face and asked, "Courted? Why should they be forced to go before the council? Are they sentenced to be with another?" he asked.

"No, no. Courted is a term I learned from Lady Ariel. It means you must put your mate first and bring her gifts and spend time with her so that she will accept you and fall in love with you," Asim said.

"Of course, we will put our mate first!" Brogan exclaimed. "As for the rest, once she sees us, she will grow to care for us. How can she resist?" Brogan asked with a skeptical glare.

"Our symbiots will protect her – even from us if necessary," Barrack added, glancing at his brother with a stern expression. "She will not need to fear us. We have learned from our experience before."

Asim shook his head. "You two have a lot to learn about your true mate's species. They are fragile, delicate creatures with a steely will beyond anything you have ever encountered," he replied in exasperation.

"Pearl certainly seems to be," Brogan replied, rubbing his chest. "What is that?" Brogan asked, nodding to the figurine Asim held in his hand.

Asim glanced down and grinned. "This is part of my tale, but first I need to tell you about how I met Pearl," he said, reaching out and handing the odd-looking bird to Barrack. "My story begins just a couple of years ago during a very bizarre Earth ritual called Easter...."

1

T hree years before:

"No more. You've had enough," Asim Kemark ordered in a stern tone.

Of course, the damn creatures ignored him. The mass of small wiggling bodies turned their heads in unison to gaze up at him with dark, soulful eyes filled with a silent plea for more food. The floor of the barn was covered with furry bodies.

If the colorful Maratts weren't enough to drive him crazy, the Grombots swinging from the makeshift lines and custom playset were doing a pretty good job. He and Mandra Reykill had built dozens of the playsets for the six-legged creatures. At the moment, the Grombots were doing a pretty good job of utilizing them.

No have this problem if you let me eat them, his dragon chortled.

Don't remind me!

"Stop! Get out of there now!" Asim shouted in dismay as he tried to carefully navigate his way to the Grombot reaching into the feed sack hanging on a peg in the wall. The damn thing was using its four hands to sprinkle food onto the floor while handing from by its feet.

The Maratts surrounding him turned as one toward the piles of food the Grombot was scattering. His jaw tightened in aggravation when the Grombot looked at him and grinned before it reached into the sack again and dumped not one or two, but four more scoops onto the floor. If he didn't stop the damn beast, it would empty the sack and he would end up nursing several sick baby Maratts!

Lifting his foot, he started to take another step when a stray Maratt darted out from under a bale of freshly cut, warm grass. Asim twisted in an effort to avoid crushing the tiny creature and his arms wildly pinwheeled as he tried to keep his balance. He might have succeeded if another Grombot, hanging upside down from one of the beams above his head, hadn't chosen that exact moment to drop onto his shoulders.

"Ugh!" Asim groaned.

His arms came up to grab the Grombot as he fell. Fortunately, he landed on the warm grass instead of the floor or any critters. If he had landed on the floor, his morning would have ended up going from bad to worse. Some of the little ones were not house-trained yet and the floor was usually a minefield on a good day and a landfill on the bad ones.

Holding the Grombot protectively against his chest, Asim leaned his head back and groaned. Three of the Grombots were now in the upper rafters despite the netting that was fitted across the beams to prevent it. One of the older ones must have figured out how to loosen it.

Asim grimaced when he noticed that one of the three was a juvenile. Lady Ariel would have a fit if she saw them up there, especially the baby. Jabir, on the other hand would probably be sitting up there with them. He had caught the little boy trying to imitate the various creatures on the ranch before. Asim pushed up, still cradling the Grombot against his chest, and gazed down at the mass of Maratts eagerly enjoying their extra breakfast.

"All of you will get sick again and Lady Ariel will be upset," he informed them. Of course, they didn't pay him any attention. He was about to get up when the Grombot in his arms turned its head. "Ouch!

Dragon's Balls! That is my chest hair you are chewing on. Oh no! You are definitely not trying that! I am not your *Dola*! You need to keep your grubby lips off my man nipples."

The Grombot struggled against his grip, trying to suckle. Asim winced when several of his chest hairs were ripped out. He must remember to wear more than a vest when he fed the animals. Some of them were getting a little too attached – literally! He stood up, placed the Grombot on one of the climbing nets, and rescued the almost empty feedbag. He had no doubt that he was going to have a pile of shit to clean up when he returned this evening. He still needed to take care of the Pactor inherited from Lady Melina. He glanced at his communicator and noticed the time.

"*Bloody Sarafin hairballs!*" Asim cursed. "I'm late and none of you are helping. Pokey, get in here!"

The morning feeding was going about the same as it did every day – complete chaos. He ignored the sniggering of his dragon and waited for his symbiot to come help him. Ever since his dragon learned that none of the tasty treats running under foot and swinging overhead were on the menu, the damn thing was having way too much fun – at his expense.

It better than hurting and being grumpy like Pokey, his dragon pointed out to him.

"I know," Asim snapped before he drew in a deep breath and replied again in a calmer tone. *I know, my friend. I thank you for your control. It is obvious I have very little left.*

True. You also have Grombot escaping, his dragon chuckled.

Asim turned to see the Grombot hatchling slowly crawling toward the opened door of the barn. If Lord Mandra didn't set up another run to these creatures' home planet, they would have to build another barn. It didn't matter how hard he tried to keep the boys and girls apart, they always seemed to get mixed up. It had taken him a month – and almost three dozen new babies – to discover Jabir was sneaking out to play with the creatures after everyone had gone to bed and then returning them to the wrong cages.

"Dragon's balls! Don't you care that the Pactor would eat you up if you aren't careful?" Asim demand in exasperation

He was about to pick up the dark gray creature when his symbiot trotted in, snatched it by the back of its neck, and continued past him. Asim turned and raised an eyebrow at his symbiot. The damn thing had been behaving strangely over the last few months.

"What took you so long? You know they get antsy if they don't eat on time," Asim demanded.

His symbiot dropped the Grombot on the bale of warm grass and shook. Its body shimmered for a moment before the glow died. Asim bit back the caustic retort he had been about to direct at the golden creature.

Symbiot like to be called Pokey, his dragon reminded him.

I know, Asim snorted with a shake of his head.

Pokey was the name that Jabir had given Asim's symbiot because he liked a creature his mother told him about called Pokey the Puppy. Of course, his symbiot wasn't the only critter with a name on the vast mountain spread that Lord Mandra, Lady Ariel, and little Jabir retreated to whenever they could. Those visits invariably meant more rescued animals added to the menagerie of creatures now under Asim's care.

"Can you retrieve the three Grombots from the rafters while I take care of the Pactor?" Asim asked.

The symbiot shrugged and began climbing up the thick post. Asim didn't miss that it moved with about as much speed as the Grombots and with a lot less enthusiasm. Concerned, he touched the thin band of gold on his arm to connect with his symbiot. A curse escaped him when the golden creature sent a warning zap of electricity through it. Asim winced and rubbed his arm. It was obvious Pokey wasn't in the mood to communicate.

"How can we help you if you won't let us?" Asim demanded, watching the symbiot climb up onto the rafter.

Asim drew in a swift breath when his symbiot opened to him for a brief moment and showed him the darkness that was dragging it down before it closed their connection again. In that second, it dawned on Asim how much his symbiot and his dragon were hiding from him. While they were all interconnected, the other two had somehow managed to shield his awareness of the slender thread of control they were struggling to preserve.

"What have I done?" Asim groaned, running his hand over the back of his neck in self-disgust. "I think only of my discomfort without consideration of what I've been doing to you."

You protect us – we protect you, his dragon replied in a solemn tone.

Asim stared out the barn door, lost in thought. Beyond the fences that circled the assorted barns was a long meadow. Tall, purple grass swayed back and forth thanks to the breeze flowing down from the mountains that surrounded the valley. At the far end was a large lake fed by the waterfall and streams coming from the ice capped mountains. A thick forest of trees near the west side of the lake sheltered his modest home.

Perhaps it was time to move on to the next life. It was not as if the prince needed his protection any longer. With Lord Raffvin dead, the threat to the Dragon Lords was vastly reduced to a handful of traitors who were being steadily hunted. There were more than enough warriors to carry on the fight. He was just an old, worn out warrior with little left to give to his king and the rapidly growing royal family.

No! We be alright, his dragon snarled. *We find true mate now.*

The snort from his symbiot told him a different story. He had prolonged the inevitable as long as he possibly could in good conscience. That brief glimpse had shown him that his symbiot was trying to absorb his and his dragon's despair. The negative emotion was slowly killing the creature that fed on their essences.

"We are killing our symbiot, dragon. He can only live on our negative essences for so long before he dies a slow and torturous death. What honor is there in that? Once he dies, so will we. Why should we be so cruel as to push all the weight of our despair on him in the hopes of finding a true mate who does not exist? We are old. What female in her right mind would want a dragon warrior like us? No, it is time to do the honorable thing and acknowledge our time is at an end before we lose control – which *will* happen when our symbiot is no longer with us," he said with a deep sigh.

It not time. We find mate who likes old dragons, his dragon stated stubbornly.

"I need to take care of the Pactor before we can leave," Asim said, ignoring his dragon.

Asim's dragon muttered under his breath before pulling away. Asim had to give his dragon credit for not giving up hope. He wished he could believe there was a true mate out there for them as much as his dragon did.

Unfortunately, now that he knew how sick his dragon and he were making his symbiot, he couldn't deny that they had been deluding themselves and each other. No, tonight he would tell Mandra that it was time for him to move on to the next life. He would order his symbiot to return to the Hive, and he and his dragon would die an honorable death in the ways of the ancient warriors. For now, though, he would enjoy the last of their time here in this world.

"Well, maybe not completely enjoy it," he muttered, staring at the huge piles of Pactor dung in the corral that would need to be shoveled before he could leave.

This is something I will not miss in my next life, he thought as he reached for the large shovel leaning against the fence.

Pearl St. Claire gazed around her. A part of her wanted to pinch herself again, while the other part remembered that it hurt like hell when you weren't dreaming. There was no denying that she was on an alien world. If the tall purple grass, unusual plants, and even stranger men running around in the shape of dragons and tigers weren't enough to convince her, nothing would.

"Vox, you…!"

Pearl turned in time to see her new grandson-in-law, Vox d'Rojah, King of the Sarafin cat-shifters, pull her oldest granddaughter, Riley, into the large fountain where their son Roam, along with a small burgundy and gold dragonling named Bálint, and he were cavorting. Pearl swore if she tried to say that out loud, either her tongue would get twisted or she would end up in a padded room.

The sound of laughter echoed through the garden. Pearl shook her head and couldn't keep the soft chuckle from escaping her. For the first time in her life, she felt like everything would be alright for her granddaughters.

"I think they've broken the St. Claire curse," Pearl said in a soft, satisfied voice.

The St. Claire curse was what her mother had called the St. Claire women's long line of bad relationships. Eloise James St. Claire had blamed the curse on Pearl's great-great-grandmother, who was said to have passed down the curse from one daughter to the next. Pearl had never believed in all the hocus pocus until she had her own daughter. The thought of Teri sent a familiar twist of pain through her. If only....

"Remember rule number eight," Pearl said to herself.

Pearl had developed a list of rules to help remind her when she started to lose her way or forget. Some rules had changed over time, and she had no doubt that more would, but some rules had stayed constant. Rule number eight was a reminder that everyone makes mistakes in their life. Mistakes were okay – as long as you learned from them and moved on. Learning from the past was all right but living in it was not. Pearl had learned that sometimes it was hard to distinguish between the learning and the living, though.

That life lesson occurred when Teri passed away. Pearl had woken in the middle of the night with her heart pounding and tears streaming down her face. The shadowy image of Teri hugging her and smiling before letting her go still burned in her mind. The dream had ripped a cry of denial from her and deeply shaken her.

Unable to go back to sleep, she had slipped out of bed to check on Riley and Tina. Fortunately, both girls were sound asleep, oblivious to her panic. The next morning, the sheriff's office had contacted her. Pearl had quietly made the arrangements for Teri's funeral, unwilling to subject her granddaughters to the darkness and grief that had been their mother's life.

Deep down, she had always known the girls would find out. She just wanted them to be old enough to understand. She didn't know she had made the right decision until a few years later. Riley had called her and told her that she knew about what had happened to her mom. When Riley thanked her for leaving them with only the good memories of Teri, Pearl had choked up. At the end of their conversation, Riley had quietly asked her not to tell Tina yet.

"She doesn't remember much about mom. I think it would be better to wait until she is older, like me," Riley had suggested.

Pearl had agreed, never really finding a good time or way to tell Tina. Of course, like Riley, Tina had eventually discovered the truth – thanks in part to her biological father. That, of course, opened another can of worms that Pearl didn't want to think about.

While Teri's death initially left a gaping hole inside her heart, having Riley and Tina had quickly filled her life to overflowing. Pearl had sworn she would do everything in her power to give them the home she had struggled to give their mother. It hadn't been easy, but Pearl had trusted her gut and persevered. Oh, she had to learn a lot of hard and painful lessons along the way. In fact, she reckoned that she had done enough self-reflection over the years to fill several volumes in a self-help textbook.

Her early years were complicated. She had fallen like a ton of bricks for Teri's father when she was barely eighteen. A bad boy on leave, Joe had been in the Army and their short time together produced her beautiful daughter. Her mother kicked her out of the house when she found out, but Pearl hadn't cared. She had faced the world with the defiance that only someone as naïve as a young girl in love could.

It wasn't until after her mother's death that Pearl discovered that she was the product of her mother's own youthful indiscretion. It turned out that the man she'd thought was her father had really been her uncle. He had married her mother to protect his older brother who was married to someone else at the time. The hypocrisy of the situation wasn't lost on Pearl, but instead of being angry, she embraced the freedom of the world around her.

That freedom wasn't easy, but she had never asked for easy. She had worked at any and every job she could find to provide a good home for her daughter, but it hadn't been enough. Teri fell in with the wrong crowd when she was fifteen and while Pearl did everything she could to help her daughter, the darkness continued to draw Teri deeper and deeper into a world Pearl struggled to understand.

There were rays of hope that quickly faded with the drugs. The only time Teri remained clean was when she was pregnant. Those were the only two times in her daughter's self-destructive life that

Teri had found a reason to fight back. Out of the two girls, Pearl had worried the most about Tina. Riley was too much like herself, a fighter, but Tina was a lot like Teri – quiet, introverted, and smart.

The sounds of Riley's laughter drew her back to the present. The glow on Riley's face and the love in Vox's eyes was enough to send a surge of warmth through Pearl. Viper had that same look in his eyes when he looked at Tina. She chuckled when Riley pushed Vox's head under the water cascading from the top of the fountain. Of course, Vox pulled Riley with him, kissing her with a passion that drew groans of disgust from their young son.

"I hope you aren't expecting me to sit next to wet cat hair on the way home," Pearl called out to Riley before turning to shake her head at the couple who were standing nearby. They were kissing as well. "Damn, I swear these have got to be the horniest damn men I've ever seen. How in the hell does anyone get anything done around here?"

Of course, no one answered, not that she was really expecting one. Chuckling under her breath, she walked over to the table where the refreshments were set out. For a brief moment, Pearl wondered if there could be a good-looking, older warrior who might be interested in a more mature woman. With a shake of her head, she pushed the thought aside. Who was she kidding? Even old, these guys looked young enough to be her grandkids!

"What I wouldn't give for a guy with a few lines on his face who spoke to me of fine Kentucky bourbon and messy sheets," she mused.

"Excuse me," a deep voice said from behind her.

I t took Asim longer than he expected to finish the chores scheduled for the day. Two of the baby Grombots had escaped when he was finishing the cleanup of the Pactor's holding pen. They had opened the door to the barn and all the Maratts had run loose. They had frightened the Pactor who, in turn, left him another gift to shovel.

He finally ended up resorting to bribery. A trail of food and the greedy little creatures had followed him, their stomachs practically dragging on the ground because they were so full. Tomorrow morning was not going to be a pleasant day.

He would have to postpone his talk with Mandra tonight. There was no way he would leave the young prince and Lady Ariel with what was bound to be a ton of poop to pick up. He honestly needed to talk to Mandra about shipping the Pactor back to Cree, Calo, and Melina. They had their own spread now. It was about time they shoveled the huge piles of dung.

He was running so late by the time he finished that he almost decided not to attend the function at the palace. It was only his promise to Jabir that he would join the little boy and his parents that compelled Asim to clean up and make the long flight over the mountains. As it was, it was well past the mid-day mark before he soared over the outer wall of the palace grounds.

The guards along the wall raised their hands in a salute of respect for his service and position within the royal family. Asim snapped his tail in response, drawing the attention of some of the young recruits who turned to watch him in awe. He swept past the large towers and curved around to the back gardens.

The sounds of laughter rang out from below. Asim followed the joyous noise, hoping to arrive quietly without Mandra or Ariel realizing how late he was. His gaze skimmed over the families below. Pride and a deep affection swept through him.

Asim understood the feeling of pride. He had been a part of the royal family's lives since the first king, Jalo Reykill, and Lady Morian joined as a mated pair. He had stood guard over each of the princes, but the affection came from the deep bond that he had developed with Mandra.

If anyone had asked, he would have been hard pressed to deny that he thought of Lord Mandra as the son he'd never had. The largest of the Dragon Lords, Mandra had always been self-conscious about his size. It was hard when both the men and women feared you. It was especially difficult for a young dragon coming into his prime.

Asim knew that underneath the huge exterior of the man lay the heart of a true warrior. He was a gentle giant with a tender heart for all creatures large and small. It was one reason the young prince spent so much time at the mountain retreat Asim had helped him to build. Asim, lost in the memories of his time with the young lord, was startled when his dragon shouted with excitement.

I find her!

What? Who did you find? Asim asked, focusing on the present again. He tried to concentrate on what his dragon saw. His dragon twisted in the air, narrowly missing the branch of a tree. *What are you doing?*

I find mate! I find her! His dragon excitedly exclaimed.

What are you rambling on about? Have you gone mad? Asim demanded, trying to rein in his dragon when it lunged recklessly toward the garden.

Asim silently swore when he felt another powerful burst of joyful emotion sweep through him. Confusion struck him as to the source until he realized the emotion was coming from his symbiot. It had lagged further and further behind them on their journey here, as if reluctant to be around others, but was now putting on a burst of speed in its excitement. Asim tried to focus on what could have caused such a reaction in his symbiot. A curse ripped through his mind when he saw the vivid mental image of a woman that his dragon was sharing with his symbiot.

The picture of a slender woman flashed through his mind so fast that he barely had time to see more than a glimpse of white hair and what looked like black leather. The confusion he'd felt a second ago was nothing compared to what was hitting him now. He must be mistaken. Perhaps Lady Cara had dyed her hair a different color, or Lady Riley had cut hers. That was it! That color reminded him of the hair color of Lord Vox's mate. He needed to get his dragon under control before the damn thing started another war. With a mental shake of his head, he snapped at his dragon.

Watch out!

His dragon swerved upward and expanded his wings completely at the last second. If Asim hadn't warned the damn thing, they would have made a spectacular exhibition of themselves. Fortunately, they landed on the back side of a large cluster of shrubbery.

Asim shifted into his two-legged form the moment he landed. Irritation flooded him when he stumbled several steps. He hadn't had such an uncoordinated landing since he was a dragonling!

"What is the matter with you?" he snapped.

His dragon was pacing back and forth inside him, trying to escape again. Scales rippled over his body, and he could feel the bands around his wrists heating up almost to the point of burning his skin. He rubbed at the gold bands.

It our mate! I see her, his dragon insisted.

You have lost control, he silently snapped, glancing around the garden. *The only ones here are the princes and their mates.*

I see our mate, his dragon insisted, trying to push him toward the main garden where everyone was.

You need to get under control before we join the others, Asim ordered.

You wait. You see mate, you not be in control no more, his dragon retorted.

Asim shook his head and drew in a deep breath. He glanced over his shoulder when he felt – more than saw – his symbiot land behind him. The large golden body was in the shape of a WereCat with wings. That was a new addition, since Jabir loved WereCats but wanted one that could fly. It shimmered with more colors than Asim had seen in centuries.

"Don't...," he started to warn, lifting a cautioning hand to his symbiot. "Wait here. I don't want to endanger anyone. I am having a hard enough time trying to control my dragon. I don't want to have to deal with you as well."

His symbiot snorted and paced back and forth behind him. For a moment, Asim wasn't sure it was going to listen to him. It kept glancing in the direction of the main garden. The huge golden body was shimmering in an ever-changing array of colors, and its ears were moving around like small radars turning to analyze the laughter of each member of the royal family.

Asim studied his symbiot with a wary eye when it froze again. He waited to see if it would follow his orders. He grunted quietly when it shook its head and blinked at him.

"Stay here," he repeated in a firm voice.

He was rewarded with a snort and a light shock to his wrists. Cursing under his breath, Asim glared at his symbiot. Between it and his dragon, he was ready for a drink – or a hundred.

No time to get drunk, we have mate to court, his dragon gleefully retorted.

Court? Asim asked, distracted.

Remember what Ariel say? Mandra court her if he make her mad, his dragon reminded him. *I court my mate. She like me then.*

"We don't have a ma...."

The words died on Asim's lips when he stepped around the bushes and onto the path. He jerked to a stop, his gaze immediately locked on the slender figure of a woman standing near a table laden with food. She was turned slightly away from him so all he could see was her profile.

I told you. I find us mate! His dragon gloated.

Asim swallowed, blinked, and nodded without realizing he was silently agreeing with his dragon. From her profile, he could tell that she was older than the other princesses – a fact that sent a wave of relief through him. She was like finely aged wine that a man could appreciate.

His gaze ran over her short hair that was as white as freshly fallen snow. Her hair was spiked on the top but cut close on the sides. The style showcased her delicate features and made him think of what it would look like after he ran his hands through it.

She was wearing a dark blue, silk blouse tucked into the waist of her black leather trousers and a pair of low cut black boots. His fingers itched to pull the silky fabric free so he could run his hands up under it to caress her skin.

A low curse escaped him when his dragon struggled to get out. Asim acknowledged his dragon was right – they had found their mate. Of course, to be absolutely sure, he would need to see if his symbiot agreed. Hope was one thing – all three of them actually agreeing tended to be another. He had met women in the past who he'd thought had the potential to be his mate only to be disappointed when his dragon, his symbiot, or both didn't agree with him.

Where in the vast universe had she come from? He couldn't help but wonder in shock.

He ran a damp palm along his pant leg. He was afraid to test if the Goddess had finally gifted them with a woman who could complete them and fill the empty void gnawing away at them. If the woman wasn't their mate, the disappointment could likely drive all three of them to lose control. But... if she was, he would need to handle this delicately. He would introduce himself, strike up a conversation, and put her at ease. He would make sure that his dragon, his symbiot, and he didn't scare her.

Asim remembered all too well the struggles Mandra and the other Dragon Lords had faced. He would be more controlled, more refined – that should help him in his courting of her. Clearing his throat, Asim took several steps closer to the woman.

"Excuse me," he said in a thick, rasping tone that demonstrated his dragon was close to the surface and he wasn't as in control as he'd hoped.

4

Pearl released a sigh of irritation at being pulled back to reality. She swallowed the sarcastic comment on her lips and turned toward the voice. She needed to watch what she said. After all, she wasn't on Earth anymore.

She had always tended to speak before she thought, especially after working at the bar for so many years. That bad habit had gotten her into trouble more than once. Thank goodness for Tiny, her six-foot-five, three-hundred-five-pound bouncer, and her rock-salt-loaded shotgun. Between the two, she'd seldom been in a situation she couldn't handle. But, that was back on Earth, and she needed to remember that she wasn't on her planet any longer.

Still, whenever she heard 'excuse me', a hundred different retorts popped into her mind. Since she was on an alien planet, she decided it was probably best that she didn't say *'Why? Are you about to have a baby explode out of your chest and need someone to catch it?'* After all, who knew if it might be true?

Turning to face the man, Pearl couldn't help but suck in a deep, calming breath when her gaze locked on a pair of black booted feet spread apart in a stance that spoke of power. She clenched her fingers into a fist to keep from fanning herself as she ran an appreciative gaze up the man's legs. He was wearing black leather trousers that did nothing to hide his long legs, thick thighs, narrow hips, and….

"Someone crank down the air conditioning, I think I'm having a hot flash. Lordy, but I love a man who can make leather look that good," she said under her breath.

Pearl's gaze paused at the opening of the man's vest. She couldn't stop from licking her bottom lip at the tantalizing view of his rock hard abs. She swallowed and breathed deeply, afraid she might have forgotten how to for a second. Her gaze continued up his muscular frame. She hadn't seen muscles like that in… ever.

Fear of disappointment struck her hard – what if she got to the top and it turned out to be a pimply-faced boy and not a hunk like Sean, Sam, Kurt, Liam, or Denzel? Nothing killed a good fantasy like hearing a rough, sexy voice and finding out it is the kid from down at the Dairy Queen going through puberty and taking steroids.

Her eyes followed the path of exposed tanned skin until she stopped at a set of blazing golden eyes and a face weathered by time and life. The instant attraction hit her hard.

How do you say yummy? Over fifty and single, she thought.

Her delight changed to a scowl of shock at her reaction to him. Hell, she had only made a half-hearted wish, not a full-fledged, certifiable one! It wasn't like she was really in the market for a man in her life! She had been on her own for so long, she wasn't sure she would know what to do with one who had actual working parts. She wouldn't call any of the few serious relationships she'd had in her life earth-shattering. They had all been more like shaking the Jell-O bowl – lots of wobble before they melted into goo. Something told her this guy could make the bed shake like an earthquake!

Asim held his breath when the woman turned to face him. The moment their eyes connected, his dark golden with her vivid blue ones, he knew he was lost. Her expression quickly turned from surprised interest to a dark scowl. Dread swelled inside Asim and a sense of panic began to rise up, threatening to choke him.

"Who the hell are you?" the woman demanded, gazing back at him with an intense look.

"Asim," he automatically replied.

She doesn't like what she sees, he thought in dismay.

You think too much. She like us. She say she love man who make leather look good. You a man and you wearing leather, his dragon sighed in exasperation.

That doesn't mean she likes the rest of me! Asim snapped in irritation.

Pearl was flustered by the way the man was returning her gaze, as if she was part of the brunch buffet. True, she might have been doing a bit of eye-candy sampling, but since she had found herself on an alien world in her sixties, she figured, she deserved to sample all the candy she wanted. Hell, at her age, she would throw in the whole damn cake with it – in every flavor, along with the ice cream and whipped topping.

The man said something that Pearl wasn't sure she heard correctly. It sounded like a guttural *'Mine!'* The translator thing they had given her must not be working correctly; because there was no way that this man could mean what she thought he said.

"I beg your pardon? What did you say?" she asked with a raised eyebrow.

"You are mine!" the man repeated.

Pearl blinked and took a startled step back when a golden creature suddenly surged from her right to stand between her and the man. The creature was like the other ones she had seen wandering around the gardens – only this one was focused on her like a starving dog eyeing a T-bone steak.

Panic hit her and her hand automatically reached behind her for a weapon to fend off the large, golden cat-shaped creature. Her fingers curled around the handle sticking out of a bowl and she whipped it around, slinging a creamy pudding mixture through the air. Dismay washed through Pearl. The gooey, cream-colored dessert and spoon were no defense against her attacker. In fact, the damn thing opened its mouth and swallowed the flying mixture. Unfortunately, the man standing behind it wasn't quite as agile. Specks of custard dotted his face. The intense expression on his face darkened into one Pearl wasn't sure she could define. The only thing she could think about when the man said *'Mine!'* was he was a dragon, and dragons were meat eaters.

"Oh, shit! My old hide is too tough to eat. You'd be better off chewing on your pants," Pearl snapped in exasperation, waving the spoon in front of her.

The symbiot paused for a brief moment, opened its enormous mouth filled with large, impressive, razor-sharp teeth, unfolded its tongue, and promptly licked the spoon clean. If that wasn't bad enough, it sat down in front of her, tilted its head sideways, and gave her a silly-ass grin when it was finished.

"Really? You know, that isn't a very intimidating look," Pearl stated dryly, raising an eyebrow.

A reluctant but amused smile curved her lips. The thing looked so damn proud of itself that it was hard not to be amused by its pleased expression. She was about to drop her arm when the man standing behind the golden creature transformed. One second there was a gorgeous hunk of masculinity in front of her and the next there was a massive, fire-breathing dragon with long claws and sharp teeth. Pearl had to check herself when she started to release a wolf whistle. Even as a dragon, the guy was impressive in a turn-you-on, heat-me-up kind of way.

At least, that was her first thought. Her second one was that she was in deep shit when said gorgeous dragon reached out with his tail and wrapped it around her waist. Pearl released a strangled cry when she felt her feet suddenly leave the ground.

A second later, the golden goofball that had been in front of her transformed. Pearl watched in horrified fascination as long tentacles of gold rose up and reached outward from the creature to form an ornate, adult-size bird cage. If watching the creature transform wasn't disconcerting enough, the thin threads of gold that reached out and wrapped around her wrist was enough to send her into panic mode. Pearl released a startled curse and raised her other hand to try to pull away. Before she could break free, new threads wrapped around her right wrist, creating a matching bracelet on each arm.

She had been so focused on the delicate golden bracelets forming around her wrists that she didn't noticed the other change occurring right in front of her until it was too late. Confused by what was happening, she glanced around to see if anyone else was noticing that things were quickly going to hell faster than Satan on a Sunday drive. Her mouth fell open and she stared at the man in front of her in surprise.

Correction – the dragon in front of her was close enough now that she could see every tiny detail of his face. Dark, gun-metal-gray scales lined his face. He had a high brow, long black lashes, and small, white spikes along his cheeks. His eyes had turned to a darker golden color and she swore she could see a bonfire burning in them.

"Oh shit," Pearl whispered in a strangled tone. "To hell with a spoon, I need my fucking gun!"

～

Lost in his dismal thoughts, it had taken a moment for Asim to realize that his dragon and his symbiot were not suffering from the same self-doubts as he was. If he hadn't been so preoccupied, he would have been aware that the two were silently conspiring against him. He smothered a groan when he saw that his symbiot had ignored his orders to stay and was circling around him from behind. It landed on silent feet a short distance from the woman.

Asim uttered a choked snarl of warning. His symbiot did more than land near the woman; it was now scaring the hell out of her! Asim winced when white globs of creamy dessert flew through the air, splattering tiny dots across his face. He raised a hand to wipe at the food particles while he watched with exasperation as his symbiot licked clean the spoon in the woman's hand. This was not the first impression he wanted to make.

He opened his mouth to protest, but quickly realized something else – his dragon had taken advantage of his distraction to seize control of his body – and this time the damn thing was determined to retain it. Asim understood that none of them wanted to lose the woman now that they had discovered her, but there were better ways to do that than by kidnapping her – in front of the entire royal family. He opened his mouth to warn the woman, but promptly made the situation worse, if that was even possible.

"You are *mine!*" slipped from his lips in a barely recognizable voice.

Oh, Pactor's dung, this is not going to end well, he thought as his body shifted to that of a powerful, gray dragon on a mission.

"What the…? Who the hell are you talking about? What the hell is going on? *Riley!*" the woman demanded in a loud voice that held a clear message – she was not happy with her first impression of him.

Asim's dragon and symbiot were totally out of control. Since he couldn't fight them both, Asim decided that he might as well focus on damage control. He would concentrate on planning how he would fix this mess once he regained control.

The woman was staring at him with a look of dismay, and with his dragon in control, all he could do was grunt out like some primitive idiot that the woman belonged to him – not that she could understand what he was actually saying since it was his dragon speaking! He could picture Lady Ariel rolling her eyes at him the way she did at Mandra when he tried talking to her in his dragon form. For now, Asim was consigned to watching in despair as his dragon wrapped his tail around the woman and gently lifted her.

The woman's curse echoed through the air, drawing the attention of the others. His dragon carefully deposited the woman in the golden cage his symbiot had become and waited for the bars to seal around her. It was obvious his dragon and symbiot were going to completely ignore everything and everyone around them except the woman.

You know there is going to be hell to pay for this, as Lady Ariel would say, don't you? Asim informed his dragon in a stern voice.

Yes, I know. All be good. We get our mate. You fix trouble, his dragon chuckled.

Asim released a long stream of mental curses, wishing he could say them out loud as his dragon pushed up off the ground. *Correction,* he thought with a grimace. *...My dragon's large, battle-scarred body is lifting off the ground gripping the cage with a very enraged woman inside.* Asim winced when the woman released a long series of threats.

Yes, they were going to be in big trouble – and most of that trouble looked like it was going to come from the delicate beauty they had just kidnapped. The only saving grace was that none of the royal family appeared to be too concerned about his unusual behavior – especially Lord Vox if the Sarafin king's grinning face was anything to go by.

Correction number two – none of the royal family with perhaps the exception of Lady Riley. She doesn't sound as pleased as her mate, Asim thought with a wince when he heard Riley's frantic yell. *I can just see another Great War about to begin.*

I tell you – you think too much, his dragon replied, releasing a triumphant roar as the small group turned in the air and retraced their flight from a few short minutes before.

"I'm going to cut your wings off and feed them to the buzzards," the woman growled.

Asim snorted in response. She had already threatened that. His least favorite was when she threatened to cut his balls off and use them as a door knocker. Even his dragon grimaced at that promise.

"Where in the hell are you taking me?" the woman demanded.

Asim glanced down. Far below them were the thick forests of Valdier. They would be crossing the North River soon. He turned his gaze to the woman when she muttered under her breath. Concern swept through him when she rubbed her arms. With a swift thought, a section of his symbiot dissolved and formed a thin blanket.

"What...? Oh, thank you," she said with a sigh when the golden blanket wrapped around her. "So, your name is Asim?"

Asim bowed his head and grunted. He mentally ran a hand over his face when his dragon continued to grunt, snort, and speak in *dragon speak*. The damn thing was rambling on about how long they'd been looking for their true mate, how happy they were to find her, how he couldn't wait to share the Dragon's Fire with her...

Enough! She can't understand a thing you are saying, Asim said in exasperation.

"What the hell is the dragon's fire?" the woman asked before she released a long hiss. "Never mind, I think I get the picture."

Yes, she can. Symbiot showing her, his dragon replied with satisfaction.

You are going to doom us. She will run as far and as fast as she can the moment we release her, Asim groaned.

"My name's Pearl St. Claire, by the way. Not 'woman', 'female', or 'she' if you think anything like Vox and Viper," Pearl dryly replied.

Asim closed his eyes when his dragon continued to talk to the woman – Pearl. *Damage control* – he kept repeating to himself – *just focus on damage control.* He didn't even bother to listen to what his dragon was telling Pearl anymore. He had a feeling he was going to be answering a lot of questions anyway, if Pearl was anything like Lady Ariel.

An hour later, they swept through the last mountain pass and into the valley where his home was located. Pearl had grown quieter the closer they got. Normally that would have been a good sign, but the way she was drumming the fingers of her right hand on her knee told him that he needed to be wary.

Take us to the edge of the lake and give me back control, Asim ordered.

Why? What you do if I give control? His dragon asked.

I am going to try to smooth things over. She is sure to be upset about our kidnapping her, Asim replied.

Maybe she not upset. Maybe she like we take her, his dragon suggested in a hopeful tone.

We are about to find out, my friend, Asim dryly retorted.

He wasn't feeling as optimistic. If he wasn't mistaken, her fingers were moving a little faster and the tension in her body was radiating outward. Asim connected with the part of his symbiot wrapped around her wrist and winced.

Yes, she might be just a little upset, Asim thought in resignation.

His dragon circled around and swooped down low over the water. He swerved upward, his powerful wings keeping them airborne while he gently released the cage. His symbiot stretched out, cushioning the cage for a soft landing before it dissolved and reformed in the shape of a large puppy complete with big, pointy ears.

Asim concentrated, focusing on shifting back to his two-legged form. He landed near the edge of the water. His boots sank into the mixture of sand and fine, colorful pebbles. He lifted a hand to run it through his short hair and drew in a deep breath, trying to think of what to say.

"First, I would…."

Asim never had a chance to finish his sentence. The deep breath he had inhaled whooshed from his lungs and he found himself stumbling backwards when a well-placed, booted foot landed squarely in his stomach.

Caught off guard, he lost his balance on the loose gravel under his feet. He barely had time to brace for the icy water that greeted him. He closed his eyes and clamped his lips as the cold water washed over his face. Stunned by the unexpected force of the attack, he lay in the shallow water for a moment before he sat up.

"That is a warning to keep your cotton-picking claws off me unless I tell you that you can touch me. You're lucky I didn't kick you in the balls," she snapped.

Asim blinked up at where Pearl stood on the bank with a large piece of driftwood in her hands. She was pointing the stick at his symbiot and her finger at him in apparent warning not to try anything. Asim ran both hands down his face and shook his head. His symbiot had its butt up in the air, the long tail wagging while its tongue lolled out and its ears twitched. The last time he had seen it behave like this was when he was a dragonling.

"He wants to play," Asim informed her.

Pearl glanced at him and rolled her eyes. "Duh. I think I can figure that out on my own," she retorted, waving the stick.

Yep, just like Lady Ariel, he thought with a grudging smile.

"I guess I deserved this," Asim grimaced, waving his hands at the water he was sitting in. "Though, technically, I did try to stop them from kidnapping you, so I believe my dragon and my symbiot deserve the cold bath more than I do."

Pearl glanced at him again and frowned. "Aren't you all the same thing?" she asked.

Asim pushed up off the ground and stood up. This was his third bath of the day, and it wasn't even late afternoon yet. A shudder of distaste ran through him when he felt the water in his boots as he took a step forward.

"Yes and no," he stated, slowly walking out of the water. "While I can shift to my dragon and we are the same, we still have our own awareness. It is… complicated."

She gazed at him with a skeptical expression. "Obviously," she replied. "So, besides having multiple personalities that can shift into a fire-breathing, mythological beast and having a…." She waved her hand at his symbiot who was now gnawing on the other end of the branch she was holding out. "…whatever in the hell that is, plus a problem with kidnapping the wrong woman, do you have any other psychological issues I should be aware of?" she asked with a raised eyebrow before turning to frown at his symbiot. "Will you knock it off? This is my branch. Go find your own," she ordered in a stern tone.

The symbiot paused and reluctantly released the end of the branch. Asim watched it turn and trot over to several pieces of drift-wood. It tested each piece of wood before picking one and returning to sit in front of Pearl with a happy, sloppy grin on its face, a two-meter branch clenched between its jaws. Pearl released a loud huff, threw a hand up in the air in exasperation, and shook her head.

"You are all crazy," she muttered.

Asim didn't bother to hide his amusement. Part of it was because he was beginning to see the humor of the situation and the other part was the joy his dragon, his symbiot, and he were feeling at finding such a perfect woman for him – one with fire! He quickly adjusted his expression when she shot him the same stern look that she had directed at his symbiot.

"May I formally introduce myself? I am Asim Kemark, protector of the royal family, knight of the Valdier, and your true mate," he stated with a deep bow.

Asim waited for several extra seconds when silence greeted his introduction. It wasn't until he heard the soft sound of footsteps against the loose rocks that he glanced up. Slowly straightening, he stared at the back of the woman as she walked away from him. He released a deep sigh.

"Well, at least she didn't hit me again," he said with a shake of his head.

She going wrong way. Home other way, his dragon pointed out to him.

"*Sarafin hair balls!* Well, what are you waiting for? Help me bring her back!" Asim ordered in aggravation.

He glared at his symbiot who just sat there watching Pearl walk away. He grimly strode after his mate – loud, squishy boots, chafing leather, and low expletives filling the air as he chased her down. He was going to have a serious man-to-man talk with both his dragon and his symbiot later tonight.

We still find true mate, his dragon huffed before he yawned and curled up with a happy sigh. *It exhausting work.*

6

"Would you like some hot tea?" Asim asked nearly an hour later.

Pearl turned from where she was standing on the wide deck overlooking the waterfall that flowed from underneath it. She saw a flash of uncertainty flicker through the man's eyes before it was replaced with the same stubborn, determined expression that had brought her to his home. Crossing her arms to keep from reaching out to smooth away the worried expression on his face, she shrugged and nodded.

"You have hot tea?" she asked in surprise.

"Yes. Lady Ariel enjoys it," he replied.

"I would love a cup," she said.

He nodded, turned, and retreated back inside. The moment he was gone, Pearl uncrossed her arms and fanned herself. A snort from the golden creature watching her made her scowl.

"Hot flash," she lied.

The creature shimmered and she could feel the warmth shoot up her arms. It was obvious it knew better. Turning back around, Pearl couldn't prevent the amused grin that crossed her face.

It would appear her later years in life were going to be filled with firsts. The first time she met an alien. The first time she traveled to another planet. And last but not least, the first time she was kidnapped by a horny, dragon-shifting, alien warrior. She wondered what other firsts were in store for her.

"Hopefully, some hot alien sex," she chuckled.

The sound of dishes rattling told her that she hadn't spoken as softly as she thought. She turned to see Asim standing just outside the doorway. His hands clenched the tray so tightly that Pearl was surprised the metal didn't bend. She lifted her gaze to his face.

Yep, he heard me, she thought with a sigh.

His eyes burned with intensity. He had slipped on a shirt when he changed out of his wet clothes and a pattern of scales was visible under the collar. Vivid images of tangled sheets flooded her with warmth and made her question her sanity. She honestly didn't know if that last thought was hers or his.

"Both," he said in a tight voice. "It has been a long time."

"Honey, if these bands wrapped around my arm are any indication, I'd have to say it has been way too long," she dryly retorted.

"I'm not opposed to correcting that issue," he replied with a grin.

Pearl gazed at Asim for several seconds before she threw her head back and laughed. Damn, but if this man – alien – dragon – warrior – whatever in the hell he was – didn't make her feel young again. Shaking her head, she placed her hands on her hips and grinned.

"I think a cup of hot tea is in order before we jump in the sack," she chuckled.

Asim's face flushed and he returned her grin. "I will hold you to that promise," he said with a matching mischievous grin.

Pearl's eyes widened and she caught herself before she raised her hand again to fan herself. The symbiot knew exactly what she almost did. She shot it a quick glare when it snickered at her.

"Oh, go fetch another stick," she murmured.

Asim's smothered chuckle told her that he'd heard her. It was obvious that these men did not have the same issues with hearing loss that most humans did when they grew older. She would have to remember that – not that it would keep her from speaking her mind.

"So, do you make a habit of kidnapping poor, unsuspecting women with the intention of ravishing them, or did you just start your nefarious career?" Pearl asked.

"I just started," he admitted with a sheepish grin. "Lady Ariel likes sweet crystals for her tea. Would you care for some?"

"Sweet... oh, sugar. No, thank you," Pearl replied, sliding onto the chair he pulled out for her. "This is all very impressive. It looks like something out of a Frank Lloyd Wright design. I saw his Falling Water house in Pennsylvania once. Talk about someone having more money than they knew what to do with."

Pearl pursed her lips together. That hadn't come out quite the way she meant it. Luckily, Asim didn't appear to notice her gaffe. He carefully placed a cup of hot tea in front of her before glancing around.

"My home is modest, but comfortable. If you would like something larger, I can build it. I designed and built this home several centuries ago. If you wish a new one, we could design it together," he said.

Pearl lifted her hand to close her mouth after it had dropped open at his first sentence. He thought this was modest? She'd hate to see what he thought of some of the places she and the girls had lived in.

"I've only seen the decking so far, but I'd hardly call this modest. It is... gorgeous," she said, waving her hand at the woods and the small waterfall flowing from under one side of the deck, and continuing its journey on the other side. "How did you manage this?"

Asim's expression relaxed, and he smiled. "I enjoy working with my hands. Before the war, King Jalo gifted me the land in this valley for saving the life of his son, Lord Mandra. It was a gift I could not turn down. I began building this house. I wanted it to blend in with the natural beauty of the forests and mountains. Each plank comes from the trees that grew here and the rocks from the mountains. I planted new trees to replace those I cut down and over time they have grown tall and strong. The flow of the water and the wind in the trees are soothing to an old dragon like me. Over the years, Mandra has helped me add on to the original structure. In time, he asked if he could build a house on the far side of the valley. I was honored to be able to return all the help he had given me," Asim explained, lost in the memories.

Asim described his original home to her. He elaborated on the special features of what could be seen from their vantage point, adding in bits of knowledge about each one. The wall of large, clear windows looked out over the deck to the lake and beyond to the mountains on the far side of the valley. In her mind, she could imagine the winter snow covering the landscape.

She could see the lake that never completely froze solid because of the water flowing from the waterfall. In the distance, she noticed the small hot springs, dotting the valley. Thin wisps of steam rose from them, sending spirals of heated vapor into the air. Her gaze moved to the mountain when he told her of how the animals from the higher elevations would migrate down to the valley for warmth and food in winter. He explained that just before the spring thaw, the herds of wild beasts gave birth.

"That is the hardest time of year for us now," Asim chuckled.

Pearl frowned. "Why? Are they dangerous?" she asked, placing her nearly empty cup down on the table.

"Nothing is more dangerous than a dragon – except a little boy who loves animals," Asim replied. "Jabir has the touch, just like his mother. Animals gravitate to him. He'd have the whole damn lot of them as pets if Mandra didn't put his foot down."

"What you describe reminds me of a place back on Earth called Yellowstone," Pearl shared, fingering her cup. "I took the girls there one summer when we lived in Colorado. Riley thought the buffalo had the mange. We didn't get out of the city much."

"Would you prefer to live in a city? I have a permanent apartment in the palace. If you prefer to live there, we could move," Asim stated.

Pearl shook her head and leaned forward. "Listen, Asim. I'm not sure I understand everything that is going on. Your offer to build a new house, move to the city, yada, yada, is all very impressive, but you don't have to impress me. You do a pretty damn good job of that by just wearing leather. How a guy like you doesn't have some little woman running around catering to your every need is beyond my understanding, but shit happens. Maybe you had someone and she died or discovered she wanted something else. All I can tell you is that

I'm not the woman you are looking for. I'm too old, too stubborn, and like my freedom far too much to settle down. Now, saying all that, I'm not opposed to enjoying life either, if you know what I mean."

From the expression on his face, he did understand what she was saying and didn't like it. His face had grown dark, his eyes narrowing with the stubborn glint in them the more she spoke. By the time she finished, his lips were pressed into a firm line and she swore his face looked like it was carved from the same rock as the mountains.

"I understand what you mean, but it is clear you do not understand me. You are my true mate. You are a gift from the Goddess – a perfect match for my dragon, my symbiot, and me. There is only one true mate for a Valdier warrior – and you are mine," he stated in a voice that sounded suspiciously raspy. "I will not let you go. You are not too old, you are perfect. I have no desire for a young female like the princes have. I have lived too long. I wished for a woman who would taste like fine wine."

Pearl slid from her seat when Asim stood up and started walking around the table. The fire was back in his eyes along with the determined look. Scales rippled across his neck and up along his cheeks.

She took several steps back, retreating as he advanced on her. Her eyes grew wary and her hand slipped into her back pocket before she remembered she left her pepper spray in the pocket of her jacket. Great! No gun, no pepper spray, no Taser, and no Tiny. It looked like it was going to be a good, old-fashioned form of self-defense if things got rough.

"Asim…," Pearl started to say, stopping and raising her hand.

"I like a mate who is stubborn. She will need to be if she is going to be able to deal with my dragon and me. As for freedom, I will give you all the freedom you desire, as long as it does not endanger you or your dragon," he gritted out.

"Dragon? I don't have a dragon! See, that is another thing, I know that Abby and the other women can somehow change into one now and Riley and Tina can shift into a tiger, but me? I think I'm a little beyond all of that. You know, kind of like going through menopause – no more life changes," Pearl argued.

She froze when Asim lifted his hand and wrapped it around her outstretched one. He pulled her closer, wrapping his other hand around her waist. This was the first time she had felt just how strong he was in his man form. Swallowing, she held back a moan of delight at the feel of his large hand sliding across the thin material of her blouse.

"What... What do you think you are doing?" Pearl asked, pressing her other hand between them.

Asim tugged her forward, his eyes glittering with fire. "Finding out what type of wine you remind me of," he stated before he bent and captured her lips.

Fire swept through Pearl's veins, warming her body as sure as a shot of whiskey. Sliding her hand up his chest and around his neck, she tangled her fingers in the back of his hair. The rush of desire hit her with an unexpected punch.

Forget the wine! This is pure Kentucky bourbon at its finest, Pearl thought, deepening the kiss.

L ife was too damn short to risk not embracing the spontaneous moments that were too good to pass up. Pearl knew she was on the other end of the scale when it came to life, so she needed to be extra vigilant. Following her two granddaughters to another world was one adventure she was glad she hadn't passed up. This was going to be another.

Touching her tongue to his lips, she took advantage when he opened for her. She felt him stiffen before a soft groan escaped him and he wrapped both arms around her and tightly pressed her against his body. She tightened her hold on him and settled down to enjoy the kiss. Holy Venus, Goddess of Love, but it had been a long time since she'd felt this kind of arousal.

She pulled back, pressing small kisses to his lips and the corner of his mouth before running them along his jaw. A silent squeal of excitement raced through her when his hands frantically moved from her waist down to cup her buttocks. This was a man who knew what he wanted.

"Say yes," he ordered in a husky voice. "Say you want me as much as I want you."

Pearl chuckled and slid her hand along his neck, down his chest, skimmed the waistband of his trousers, and continued lower. She felt his response to her brazen touch. There was nothing wrong with his package, and judging by the swelling under the palm of her hand, everything was in working order.

"Oh yes," Pearl murmured against his lips. "You bet your sweet ass I want this."

~

Yes!

Asim could feel his dragon's enthusiastic response reverberating through his body. The fire of his dragon licked through his veins, threatening to scorch him with the heat. His dragon was heating up for his mate just as much as Asim was for his. A soft groan escaped him as his cock throbbed to feel the touch of skin against skin. Behind Pearl, he could see the grinning face of his symbiot, its body shimmering brightly with an assortment of changing colors.

Images flashed through his mind. For a moment, he realized how much pain and anguish his symbiot had endured in order to protect him and his dragon. Reaching out, he sent a wave of warmth and comfort to his symbiot.

We will be whole at last, he assured both his symbiot and his dragon.

I bite? His dragon eagerly asked.

Asim groaned when he felt Pearl pulling his shirt loose from his trousers. He didn't need to answer his dragon. The Dragon's Fire was already driving him to press his lips against her exposed neck.

"I want to share my Dragon's Fire with you, Pearl," he murmured against her throat.

"Dragon's Fire," Pearl gasped as a shiver of need ran through her at his hot breath against her skin. "What... What is Dragon's Fire?"

"Everything I am – everything we can be together," he said.

Asim gazed down into Pearl's eyes. He would give her the choice. He had waited too long for this moment and something told him that Pearl was the type of woman who wouldn't be happy if he didn't. His gut tightened when her eyes narrowed.

"Does this have anything to do with changing me like Riley and Tina?" Pearl suspiciously asked.

Asim scowled and shook his head. "No! You would be a dragon! Not a… not a cat," he firmly stated.

Pearl pulled back in his arms, her hand sliding from his crotch to his chest. She stared back at him with wide eyes, an expression of uncertainty and skepticism in her eyes. Asim could feel his dragon's panic start to rise up, threatening to choke him.

I bite! She say no. I need bite! His dragon groaned.

No, this has to be her decision, Asim grimly replied.

"A dragon… like Abby and the other women?" Pearl repeated in shock.

"Yes."

"Will it hurt?" Pearl asked, her lips curving up as she fingered the buttons on the front of his shirt.

"It… I've heard it can be very intense… sexually. There… there is a chance… a chance that neither of us will survive," Asim choked.

Pearl raised an eyebrow. "Not survive having too much sex? I can think of worse ways to die," she reflected.

That mean yes! His dragon crowed.

No, it does not! Asim growled in exasperation.

"What happens afterwards? So, if we, by chance, survive driving each other to the edge of sexual immolation and all, what does that mean?" Pearl asked. The way her fingers kept slipping between the openings of the buttons and teasing his heated flesh was quickly dissolving what little control he was fighting to maintain.

"More…." Asim cleared his throat. "We… will be true mates. Together…. Pearl, you are driving me crazy. I'm… My dragon isn't helping, either. He wants his mate as much as I want you," he bit out. His fingers gently kneaded her waist as he resisted the urge to just pick her up and take her.

"I'm old," she warned.

"I'm older and you are perfect to me," he replied.

"I'm not as quick as I used to be," she stated.

"You knocked me in the water before I knew what happened," he reminded her.

"I may be a little rusty," she admitted.

"We will go as slow as you like. I would prefer to savor you like a glass of fine wine – slowly, so I can enjoy each touch and taste," he countered.

You sip, I gulp. You taking too long! His dragon groaned in frustration.

"You have scales running up your neck," Pearl pointed out.

"My dragon wants to gulp the wine instead of sipping it like a gentleman," Asim admitted in a tight voice.

Asim's eyes widened and his lips parted when Pearl gripped the sides of his shirt and pulled with a lot more force than he expected. The buttons holding his shirt closed popped free, scattering across the polished wood of the deck.

"I love a dragon who knows how to handle his liquor," she said before she captured his lips.

This mean yes! His dragon crowed.

Yes, this means yes, Asim groaned, his hands frantically pulling Pearl's blouse free from her trousers. *Bite, you can bite.*

His dragon didn't need to be told twice. Asim was already moving his lips along Pearl's cheek and down to her neck. He felt his teeth elongate, the Dragon's Fire burning through him like a super-heated torch. Opening his mouth, he sank his teeth into her neck and breathed the fire that would change all their lives.

"*Holy Goddess of Love!*" Pearl hissed, her hands tightening around his waist before her legs gave out under her.

Asim held her close, his hands splayed across the smooth skin of her back while her breasts were pressed against his chest.

The fire licked through both of them, scorching them with its fiery touch. His body was humming with tension. Goddess, he wanted to make love to this woman.

≈

The caress of Asim's lips across her cheek down to her neck made Pearl feel young and beautiful again. The fact that, until a few hours ago, she had never met this man before was a minor technicality to her. She had known men for years without really knowing them. She hadn't felt this surge of instant attraction since Joe – even the faint memories of her infatuation for him paled to the physical and chemical reaction she was having to this old Valdier warrior.

Deep down, she knew that she was playing with a different type of fire – but, hell, life was about grabbing it by the balls and holding on, no matter how hot it got sometimes. She had nothing left to worry about now but her own heart. Riley and Tina were safe and happy. Now it was her time to shine and she was going up like the grand finale at a New Year's Eve fireworks show.

"Asim… You better not burn my heart," Pearl warned.

He reluctantly released her neck. It throbbed where he bit her. Instead of being painful, it pulsed along with the feelings of need burning between her legs. It had been years since she was this aroused.

"Never, Pearl. If you burn, we burn together," he swore. "Let the Dragon's Fire begin."

Pearl's eyes widened and a soft moan escaped her as the first wave hit her. Her arms trembled and she was thankful for his strength to hold her upright. Well, until he scooped her into his arms. She turned her head and buried her face against his neck.

"Damn, that is some powerful shit," she said in a strained voice.

Asim chuckled. "It will be a glorious transformation," he promised.

His burning desire for Pearl was nothing compared to his determination that she survive the changes of the Dragon's Fire. He'd seen her strength when she stood up to his symbiot with nothing more than a custard-covered spoon and when she had knocked him into the lake. This was a woman with the heart of a warrior – and a true match for one as well.

He held her close, sensing the fire burning through her veins. He entered the house, striding through the sitting room and past the kitchen that he designed to take advantage of the view. He rounded the corner and climbed the stairs.

The sound of Pearl's soft moan and the shiver of her slender body in his arms told him that another wave of the Dragon's Fire was breaking through her. He drew in a swift breath when he felt her teeth against his neck. The sharp nip excited him.

She has a lot of fire in her, he thought.

Yes. She perfect mate, his dragon stated, very pleased with himself.

"Damn, but whatever you did has me feeling hotter than a marshmallow on fire. I'm burning up and melting at the same time," she breathed.

"It is the Dragon's Fire. Do not fight it. Let it flow through you and embrace the change," Asim encouraged.

"Lordy, but I'm going to be jumping your bones," Pearl moaned, pressing her lips against his neck.

~

Pearl had never felt fire like this before. Menopause been quick and painless, a few hot flashes and she was done. This was like an inferno raging inside her. The only difference was instead of wanting a cold shower and a fan, she wanted a hot man and his cock.

Her clothes were driving her crazy. The touch of them against her skin was like sandpaper against silk. She wanted hot flesh and a hairy chest she could tangle her fingers in.

Turning her head, she ran her lips over Asim's neck, nipping, sucking, and leaving a line of tiny hickeys that were bound to multiply over the course of the night. Her fingers searched and found his chest where she had ripped his shirt open. She tangled her fingers in his chest hair, enjoying the coarse feel against her sensitive fingertips.

When Asim set her on her feet again, she pulled back and was surprised to discover they were in a large bedroom. She briefly glanced around, mostly searching for the bed. She turned her head when Asim placed his hand under her chin and gazed mischievously down into her eyes.

"Are you sure the answer is still 'yes'?" he teased. "I have started the fire, but I will not fan it if you ask me not to."

"Honey, unless you want me to bury a dead body, you better do something about this inferno that you started. The answer isn't yes – it is 'hell yes'. You can add as many exclamation points at the end of that as you want. I plan on working my way down your delicious body while you do that," Pearl retorted, reaching up to unbutton her shirt.

Her lips twitched when more buttons went flying, reminiscent of her actions earlier. Their desire for each other was well and truly a wildfire. Asim growled and finally snapped the front of her bra to free her breasts. Pearl unfastened Asim's pants and buried her hands inside, wrapping them around his cock while her mouth hungrily explored his chest.

She fell backwards, her knees giving way against the bed. Asim took advantage of it and swiftly removed her boots, socks, and pants. Each article of clothing flew in a different direction in their haste.

Asim impatiently kicked his trousers off and wrapped his large hands around her calves. He pulled her to the edge of the bed and stood looking down at her, his cock poised at her moist entrance.

"Are you ready for me?" he asked in a strained voice.

Pearl reached down and felt the moisture between her legs. Hell, she hadn't been this wet without a little help since she could remember. Feeling for his cock, she aligned it with her channel and lifted her hips.

The first touch of his cock entering her coincided with another wave of Dragon's Fire. Asim must have felt the flames overcoming her and the sudden rush of moisture between her legs because he surged forward, impaling her at the same time as the fire peaked. Pearl wrapped her legs around Asim's waist, thanked the goddess of yoga for insisting that she participate, and held on for the ride.

Her sensitive breasts brushed against the coarse hair of his chest, causing her nipples to become taut pebbles. Pearl held onto Asim's shoulders when he bent over her. Her head fell back, exposing her long slender neck. With a smothered oath, he braced his arms on each side of her, sank his teeth into her neck – and breathed.

Silver scales framed by white rippled over Pearl's body and along her arms. Her body felt like it was burning to ash and being reborn. The feel of Asim's stiff cock stroking her channel, his coarse hair teasing her nipples, and the feel and smell of their combined love-making tipped the scales and Pearl came harder than she had ever come in her life. Her orgasm rolled on and on, building, peaking and breaking, only to build again.

Asim didn't stop his driving force. Once she came, he pulled out of her, turned her over until she was kneeling on the bed, and climbed up behind her so he could do it again.

The feel of his cock felt hard and delicious as he stroked her. Her fingers curled in the covers and she bowed her head. Her eyes closed as she felt him grow thicker. She could feel the tension building in his body and knew he was going to come.

His fingers tightened on her hips, holding her as his hips rocked back and forth. He continued to slide in and out of her, faster and harder with each movement. Her head came up when she felt him stiffen and groan as he came. His breath hissed and echoed loudly through the room. He held her still, a shudder shaking his large frame as he pulsed.

Pearl was sure they were through and disappointment hit her hard. Bowing her head, she closed her eyes. A soft gasp escaped her when she felt the fire building inside her again. His cock reacted to the muscles along her vagina squeezing him in response. Opening her eyes, she was stunned to feel him begin to move again – his cock thick and full as if he hadn't just emptied himself deep inside her.

"What…? How the hell?" Pearl asked.

Asim pulled out of her and gently rolled her over. Caging her body with his, he pulled her legs up around his waist and sank as far as he could into her once again. His arms wrapped around her and he held her tight as the Dragon's Fire flowed through both of their bodies.

"It has been a long, long time," Asim murmured, holding her close as he rocked his hips.

Pearl's eyes widened and the smile on her lips grew. Gripping him with her legs and pushing him, she let him know that she wanted him to roll over. Asim rolled to the side, pulling her with him until she was on top of him.

"Hot damn! I've got my own renewable battery pack," Pearl chuckled. She tilted her head and gazed down at him. "Have you ever been ridden, cowboy?"

Asim's eyes widened when Pearl rose before she sank all the way down on him. The smile on his lips grew when Pearl began to ride him. Pearl didn't miss the way her skin changed, fine silver scales dancing across it – or the new voice in her head, encouraging her to ride as far and as long as she wanted. She decided age must have its advantage, because her dragon wasn't taking its sweet time emerging like Abby and the other women had described.

We ready for mate now! I ride my mate next, the voice whispered. *Dragon style.*

8

Asim grudgingly rolled out of bed early the next morning. The insistent someone pounding on his door had refused to leave when he hadn't answered it in the first few minutes. He glanced at Pearl and saw she was watching him with an amused smile.

"I have to answer that," he said, bending over to brush a kiss across her lips.

Pearl chuckled and nodded. "I think I know who it is," she replied, throwing the covers back and sliding out of the bed.

"*Dragon's fire*, but I would be willing to ignore them to keep you in my bed," Asim said.

"Your eyes are flashing again. You'd better answer the door. I have a feeling they aren't going to go away until you do," Pearl chuckled as she grabbed the sheet from the end of the bed, then folded and wrapped it around herself like a sarong.

"Surely they will get the message? I swear if it is Mandra, he can shovel the damn Pactor poop by himself today," Asim snapped in frustration.

He reached over and grabbed his trousers from the floor. He looked around for his shirt, but gave up when the pounding increased.

With a muttered curse, he turned in time to see Pearl step out of their bedroom.

Hurrying after her, he caught up with her half way down the stairs. His gaze ran appreciatively over her sheet-wrapped body and bare shoulders. At least it wouldn't take long to undress her once he told their unexpected company to get lost or he would bite their heads off. He was a dragon on a mission and that was to mate with Pearl in every way he could. He had a lot of years to make up for and so did his dragon.

They reached the bottom of the stairs and turned toward the front door. Striding across the foyer, he stepped in front of Pearl and opened the door. An irritated Vox stood on the other side, his hand raised to bang on the door again. Vox barely caught himself before he rapped his knuckles between Asim's eyes.

"Where is she?" Vox asked in exasperation.

"None of your business," Asim snapped.

"What the… Grandma?" Riley exclaimed.

Asim glanced over Vox's shoulder and saw Vox's mate staring at Pearl behind him. Riley's eyes were opened wide and her mouth was hanging open. He stepped to the side when he felt Pearl run her hand over his right buttock. He might have been alright if she hadn't pinched it. Of course, his body – still burning with the remains of the Dragon's Fire – ignited.

"Hello, Riley. What brings you here this early? I would have thought you'd still be asleep," Pearl commented.

Asim wrapped his arm protectively around Pearl's waist and drew her close to his side when she stepped up beside him. She shot him a questioning glance and shook her head in amusement before turning her attention back to her stunned granddaughter.

"You look like you've been…," Riley started to say.

The scowl on Asim's face darkened when Riley waved her hand at him before turning back to Pearl. The frown quickly turned to a smothered oath. Pearl's left hand was sliding down the back of his pants and she was kneading his taut butt cheek. If he didn't get rid of

Vox and Riley soon, Riley was going to have no doubt as to why her grandmother looked the way she did.

"I have. What have you and Vox been doing? Working on more great-grandbabies for me, I hope. I absolutely adore Roam," Pearl said with an innocent smile.

"I told you she was fine, Riley. Let's go," Vox said, partially turning away.

"Oh, hell no, we are not going! This… this maniac kidnapped my grandmother and you want to just leave her here? She didn't even meet him until yesterday!" Riley stuttered.

"Riley… I really think we should go… now," Vox murmured.

"Would you like some refreshments?" Pearl asked.

"NO!" both men replied at the same time.

"Yes," Riley stubbornly said.

"I really don't think she meant for you to accept her offer, Riley," Vox warned, glancing at Asim's flushed face and the scales rippling up his body.

"Why not?" Riley demanded.

Asim watched Vox bend to whisper in Riley's ear. The younger woman's mouth dropped open again and she blushed. Her gaze darted to him before turning to her grandmother's serene face, then to the front of Asim. Her face turned a bright red.

"Oh!" Riley whispered. "But… She's my grandma!"

Pearl laughed. "I'm also a woman with her hand down the back of a gorgeous man's pants, Riley. I'm old, not dead. I can still appreciate a fine-looking man, a nice bottle of bourbon, and messing up a set of silk sheets," she said with a mischievous grin.

"That's just… too … TMI, Grandma!" Riley exclaimed.

Asim saw Riley's gaze immediately shift back to his waist. Her face wrinkled into a look of dismay. His hips jerked forward when Pearl ran her nails along his skin. His control was shot.

"Alright, she's safe. It's time to go," Vox said with a determined smile. "Sorry to interrupt, Asim."

"Tell the others to stay away," Asim replied in a strained voice.

"I will," Vox promised.

"But… But… Vox!" Riley started to protest.

Asim released the breath he was holding when Vox wrapped his arm securely around Riley and guided her toward their transport that hovered along the narrow road in front of the house. He wrapped his fingers around Pearl's wrist when she pulled her hand out of the back of his pants, turned to face her, and walked her backwards, barely closing the door before he reached for the sheet around her.

"You…," he started to say before he shook his head and released a long, uneven breath. "All I can say is you better be ready for some serious loving, because my dragon and I are fired up again."

Pearl's fingers were already working on the front of his trousers. "I thought we'd never get rid of them," she laughed. "I want to make love to you in the shower. I've always had a fantasy to try it there. We can work our way through the house after that."

"Goddess, I must have been one good warrior to be rewarded with you as my mate," Asim retorted, kicking his pants to the side and pulling Pearl after him.

"When do we get to try it dragon style?" Pearl asked halfway up the stairs.

Asim stumbled on the step, and closed his eyes. His dragon was breathing heavily inside him and pacing back and forth. Pearl had noticed the ripple of scales on her arms last night and heard the whisper of her dragon being born. He had hoped to have a few days alone with her, but something told him that wasn't going to happen.

Give me the shower and I'll show her how to shift, Asim practically begged.

She want dragon style. You get shower after, his dragon demanded.

"*Dragon's balls*! He doesn't want to wait now," Asim groaned.

"What does that mean?" Pearl asked, gazing up at him with a hopeful expression.

"We'd better get to the balcony. He's about to call for his mate," Asim replied in resignation.

"Oh, my. I'm going to get some dirty dragon sex!" Pearl laughed, pushing past him and walking up the stairs. "Last one to the deck is on the bottom."

Asim watched Pearl's delightful ass disappear through his bedroom door. It took a moment for her words to sink in. The thought of him being on the bottom with her on top, riding him….

Go! She getting there first! His dragon complained.

I know, Asim calmly replied with a wicked smile. If she wanted some dirty dragon sex, she was going to get some dirty dragon sex – in both forms. His dragon had stopped pacing, realizing what Asim was planning.

Yes! I like!

"Pokey!" Asim called to his symbiot. "I think it is time for Pearl to see what happens when she teases a dragon warrior."

His symbiot flowed past him up the stairs. Asim followed at a slightly slower pace. He was going to take his time. His mate wanted to try every spot in the house. Well, he knew of a few places they could start with outside. The smile grew on his face when he heard Pearl's startled curse. He climbed the last few steps and paused in the doorway.

Pearl turned to look at him with an expression of growing anticipation. The gold bracelets on her wrists now wound up her arms. Another band wrapped around her neck while two more formed around her ankles.

"I think it is time an old warrior taught you a few new tricks," Asim stated.

"Thank you, Goddess of Love, I'm got a man who likes to play. I am going to be enjoying this," Pearl chuckled.

9

P resent Day:

"Stop right there!"

Asim blinked several times and shook his head. He looked at the two men sitting across from him. Both of them had expressions of disbelief on their faces.

"What?" he asked with a frown.

Brogan, the moodier of the two brothers, raised a hand and ran it down his face, looking more perplexed than on edge. He turned to his brother and gestured – as if encouraging Barrack to ask Asim some questions.

"Don't look at me. I'm still trying to scrub the image of dirty dragon sex between Asim and Pearl out of my brain," Barrack stated.

"Perhaps I shouldn't have told you all the details," Asim thoughtfully replied, rubbing his chin.

"Then I will ask." Bewildered, Brogan turned his attention back to Asim. "You kidnapped her and took her as your mate. Why can't we do that?" he asked, turning to raise an eyebrow to encourage his brother to back him up.

Barrack raised his hands and shook his head. "I still want to know how she knocked his ass into the lake – after I wash the dirty dragon sex out of my head first, of course," he added.

"Forget I told you about that part. The point I'm trying to make is that each one of them is different. Pearl was older and more experienced with life. From what Sara told us, Delilah is young and innocent, but that doesn't mean she can't take care of herself. When you find your mate, she needs to be your partner in every way. If you try to control her, you'll lose her for sure. I've seen each of the Dragon Lords learn their lesson with the princesses," Asim explained.

"So, you do not control your mate?" Brogan asked with a skeptical expression.

"*Curizan fireball*! No, Pearl would roast my balls for dinner and serve them to me on a platter if I tried to tell her what to do. She is my mate, my partner, in every sense of the word," Asim insisted.

"Except in battle," Barrack said.

Asim shook his head. "No, especially in battle," he replied in a quieter voice.

"But – how?" Brogan exclaimed with an incredulous expression. "Females are weak! They are not made for fighting."

Asim leaned forward and plucked the sculpture of the bird out of Brogan's hand. He held it up and rotated it between his fingers. He studied it for a moment before he smiled.

"That leads me to my next story…. This one happened just a few months ago. Pearl and I have been together for a couple of years now, but she continues to amaze me in so many ways. During our time together, I have discovered that love and respect are not finite, but continue to grow. And, despite our time together, I learned that I had never really seen what my mate could do when she was truly riled," Asim explained, his voice beginning to fade as the memories rose.

"You hold that as if it means something. What kind of creature is that?" Barrack asked, nodding at the bird.

"This is called an emu, and it is a part of my story that begins with the dragonlings' unexpected adventure to Earth and one little boy's love for all creatures. Lord Mandra and Lady Ariel's son, Jabir, returned home with some very unusual eggs…. Eggs that made me afraid for him, that attracted danger to the woman I love, and hatched into creatures that would rise up to become the most unlikely army this old Valdier warrior has ever seen. This army was led by none other than a couple of small boys," Asim replied with a chuckle.

"Tell us about this battle," Brogan demanded, leaning forward with his eyes glued to the small, odd-shaped creature made of wood.

"It begins with a story of love…," Asim explained. "This strange creature is part of the story…"

∾

A few months before…

"You need to keep them covered," Pearl said, smoothing the fresh warm grass over the large, green eggs in the barn a short distance from his parents' house.

"Will they be ables to breathe?" Jabir asked worriedly.

"They should be fine, but I don't know what your Grandpa Paul is going to say when he finds out you took some of the eggs from his ranch," Pearl chuckled and bent to pick up the chubby little boy.

"He would tells me I'm a good hunter! Ruby will keeps them warm. She likes my new eggs," Jabir giggled, watching the chicken settle on top of the mound. Tina and Viper had left Ruby at the mountain retreat while they enjoyed their time at the palace. Jabir reached up and wrapped his arms around Pearl's neck. "Ruby promised me that she would take good care of my eggs while I hunts for more."

"Ruby will take very good care of your eggs, I'm sure. Your mom will keep an eye on them as well. We won't be gone long," Pearl promised.

"What happens if Asim finds them?" Jabir asked with a worried frown.

"He'll keep them warm and safe for you. The eggs will be fine. I want to talk to your Grandpa Paul about them before I mention them to Asim. He might be able to help," she chuckled.

"Grandpa Paul knows all about eggs and animals," Jabir replied, happy again.

Pearl watched as Jabir glanced at the small mound of grass in the back stall. Her heart swelled for the little boy who was frantically trying to keep his secret. She and Ariel had discovered a week ago that Jabir had done a little exploring and scavenging when he and the other younglings crossed through a portal to Earth created by Phoenix, one of the twin daughters of Creon and Carmen.

The dragonlings' adventure had started with a simple Valentine's Day story and ended with the younglings traveling across the galaxies to find the lonely woman who could heal a dragon whose heart was turning to stone. The dragon, it turned out, was none other than Jarak Draken, the surly Chief Security Officer aboard the *V'ager,* while the lonely woman was Sandy Morrison, the sister of Paul Grove's childhood friend and attorney, Chad.

The fathers had followed after the younglings. While they were on Earth, the men learned how easy it was to do online shopping and Jabir had discovered the eggs in one of Paul's barns. The return trip had them bringing back a wide range of exciting items – and Jabir's hidden bounty of eggs.

Pearl didn't understand how Phoenix could create a portal that connected the two worlds. There were a lot of things she still didn't understand about this world, even three years later. One thing she did understand was that Phoenix was special – even by alien standards.

She touched by Goddess, her dragon softly murmured.

I already figured that out on my own, Pearl reassured her dragon. *So, how are we going to keep this little secret from Asim? You know we can't lie to him.*

No lie. Just don't tell him, her dragon shrugged. *What he not know, not hurt him. It make Jabir and Ariel happy.*

Pearl chuckled. *I guess we girls do have to stick together.*

Especially if men take Jabir pets away, her dragon snorted.

Yes, well....

Pearl didn't add to that point of view. She and her dragon didn't quite agree that it was time to ship the latest batch of Grombots and Marrats off, but Ariel had grudgingly acknowledged that they were better off on their home world than on Valdier where they were considered a delicacy by the dragons. Of course, tears had flowed down both Ariel and Jabir's cheeks while the men were loading the animals onto the transport.

Mandra and Asim had huffed and puffed, but Pearl noticed that the men secretly kept two pairs of each animal for Ariel and Jabir. The sets included the runts of the group and the ones most unlikely to survive if they were released into the wild. Mandra talked to a local animal doctor who would make sure they couldn't reproduce.

Of course, there were bound to be a collection of more strays from the universe by the time Mandra and Ariel returned from the palace. Pearl came to the conclusion that Mandra must have made a lot of enemies over the years. It seemed like a new creature in need was appearing on the mountain retreat almost weekly.

"Jabir! Time to get ready to go," Ariel called.

"I'm comings," Jabir replied.

Pearl set the little boy down and stood at the door of the barn, watching as he ran across the open area to his mother. She chuckled when he struggled to climb the stairs. He finally gave up, shifted into his dragon form, and used his wings. Her gaze moved to Mandra. The huge Valdier prince had stepped out of the house onto the deck and opened his arms for Jabir.

"When that boy finally has his growing spurt, there are going to be a lot of surprised people," Pearl chuckled, shaking her head in wonder.

She had a lot to do before she and Jabir left to go to the palace in a few minutes. They were leaving a few days early so Jabir could play with his cousins. This would also give her a chance to spend time with Riley, Tina, and her new great-granddaughters, Sacha and Little Pearl, as well as great-grandsons, Roam and Leo.

A smile curved her lips when the small family turned and disappeared inside the house. This world was truly an incredible place compared to Earth and was one that the St. Claire women could call home.

"It is hard to believe I spent most of my life on another world when this one feels more like home," Pearl reflected out loud, gazing around.

Her gaze locked on her mate and she chuckled. Asim was currently arguing with Ariel's newest acquisition, another Pactor. This one had been injured in a mining accident that left it partially blind. It had been abandoned when Ha'ven's brother, Adalard, discovered the poor creature during one of his journeys and shipped it to Mandra as a present.

Pearl had noticed that Mandra and Adalard had a growing competition to outdo each other when it came to gag gifts. Mandra's last gift to Adalard was a pair of Tasiers – a small, round furry creature that could reproduce exponentially if they were not controlled. By the time they arrived at Adalard's home, the two had already multiplied to eight. By the end of the week, Adalard was threatening war against the Valdier again. Of course, the next day the Pactor had arrived to even out the score.

Asim's loud curses floated through the air along with the sound of thuds on the ground coming from behind the animal. The new medicine Asim was giving the Pactor was helping, but it also made it have loose stools. Her heart melted when Asim reached up and stroked the Pactor, murmuring to soothe it, before he walked over to where he had left the shovel and pail.

Turning, she returned to her own little bundle of whatever Jabir had brought home. She wasn't an expert, but she suspected the large, avocado-colored eggs were some kind of bird. Since he had retrieved them from Paul's ranch back on Earth, she wasn't too concerned that they would be dangerous. The eggs reminded her of the ostrich eggs she once saw at the Denver zoo.

"Ostriches aren't too bad. Mandra can always have them shipped back to Paul's ranch, though he may have to fight with Ruby over them first," she decided with a laugh.

Checking on the eggs once more, she was satisfied they would be safe. Ruby was sleeping on top of the pile. She chuckled softly as she shut the door to the stall. She could just imagine all of the men's faces if they were to catch a glimpse of the huge eggs that she, Ruby, and Jabir were fretting over. They would go ape-shit over them.

Pearl never could have imagined that a dragon would go nuts over hard-boiled eggs – especially colored ones! She reckoned it was a combination of their competitive nature and their avarice for pretty things. Personally, she just didn't get it.

Pearl closed the door to the barn and looked around for Pokey. The symbiot was sprawled on the house's deck, soaking up the sun. Pokey rolled to his feet when Mandra came out carrying Jabir. Ariel followed with a small suitcase and a backpack in the shape of a dinosaur.

Pokey shook and jumped to the ground. Pearl watched in fascination as the golden body shimmered and transformed. The living metal creature was stretching and curving until a compact, golden transport hovered slightly off the ground waiting for her. She couldn't keep the smile from curling her lips when she thought of what else that living metal could do.

Yes! Her dragon hissed in delight.

You are a horny bitch, you know that, don't you? Pearl silently chuckled.

You the one that likes on top, her dragon retorted.

Yes, I do, Pearl agreed, smiling.

She walked toward where Asim was working. Leaning against the railing, she silently waited for him to finish what he was doing. Even though she was only going to be gone for a few days, she knew that she was going to miss him. While she had spent most of her life alone, she had quickly adjusted to having Asim's quiet presence in her life and now couldn't imagine having it any other way.

"What are you smiling about?" Asim curiously asked, looking up to catch her expression.

"Sex. On top, on the bottom, dirty dragon style," Pearl quipped, knowing it would start the fire in Asim's eyes.

"Goddess! You mention that to me now when I can't do a thing about it? You are killing me and my dragon, Pearl!" Asim cursed, holding a shovel full of Pactor dung.

Asim dropped the dung into the wagon and walked over to the fence. He propped the shovel up against the rails and pulled his gloves off. Placing them on a post, he leaned forward and brushed a kiss across her lips.

"I'm going to miss you," she said with a sigh.

"I could always fly back and forth each morning and evening," Asim suggested with a smile.

Her eyes glittered with mischief. "With all the kids around...? We'd never have any peace; and you know that I'm talking about the big kids, not the little ones," she chuckled with a shake of her head. "You have enough to do here. It will only be a few days and I'll be spending time with the girls."

"A few days is too long," Asim replied with a mischievous expression. "We could always meet half way."

"Your dragon is stuck on the dirty dragon style, isn't he?" she teased.

"Just a little – so am I," Asim retorted with a wicked grin.

Pearl tilted her head back and laughed. She loved it when they teased each other. It didn't matter what she said, he was able to think of a comeback. Of course, on the few occasions when he couldn't, he used his lips and body instead.

"I'll send you a location for later tonight," she teased, brushing a kiss across his lips with a little suggestive tongue to go along with it.

"Pearl, I ready!" Jabir called out behind her.

"I have to go," she said with a sigh.

"Later tonight," Asim vowed. "Dirty dragon style first."

"You'll have to catch me first," Pearl replied with a wink before she turned and walked away.

10

Asim watched his symbiot rise off the ground. Mandra and Ariel were waving to Jabir who was frantically waving back at them. His gaze was fastened on Pearl. She turned and blew him a kiss before Pokey rotated in the air. A moment later, the symbiot transport was just a faint glimmer in the sky.

He blinked when Hobbler, the Pactor he'd threatened to return to Cree and Calo but never did, nudged him. He reached out a hand to calm the beast. He shook his head, retrieved his gloves and the shovel, and finished his chores.

"I swear that woman loves to drive me insane," he told Hobbler as the creature followed him back to the wagon. "So, what do you think of your new friend? Have you accepted him yet?"

Hobbler stretched out her neck and rubbed her forehead against his hand. Asim was going to take that as a yes. He dumped the last shovel-load of poop into the wagon with a sigh. The more he thought about his conversation with Pearl, the funnier it sounded to him. Before long, his shoulders shook with mirth and he had to stop and lean on the shovel.

"Goddess, but I love that woman," he told Hobbler and the new

Pactor. "I don't know anyone else who could make me want to laugh while shoveling shit."

Humming under his breath, he finished mucking the corral and lay fresh warm grass in the covered stalls. Hobbler had moved closer to the half-blind beast Jabir had named George. Asim nodded in satisfaction when both Pactors stopped at the feed barrels. It would take a few months, but George would fill out like Hobbler had.

He cleaned up the tools and walked to the outer barn. It was empty now that he and Mandra had shipped off the majority of the Grombots and Marrats. Pearl had volunteered to clean it up so it would be ready for any new arrivals that would eventually find their way to the mountain refuge for lost, orphaned, and mistreated beasts.

He pushed the small wagon over to the equipment shed and rinsed it out before doing the same with the bucket and shovel. There was a latch on one of the stalls that wasn't working properly and he wanted to check all of them before he forgot. There was nothing worse than having a new beast loose and wreaking havoc.

He opened the door, leaving it slightly ajar to bring in some natural light. Solar powered light panels along the ceiling turned on as he walked along each stall, testing the doors. He frowned when he reached the last one. He could have sworn it was the one that was broken.

Opening the stall door, he tested it several times before he grunted. It looked like it was working now. Glancing around, he noticed that fresh warm grass was piled in the corner instead of spread out. Perhaps Mandra had forgotten to spread it when he fixed the door.

He walked over to the pile and bent to pick up a handful of warm grass. A movement out of the corner of his eye startled him and he jerked back a step. A dry chuckle escaped him when he saw Ruby flap her wings at him.

"I wondered where you moved to. You don't like me gathering all your eggs, do you? Well, I have to say it is your fault. If they weren't so tasty, we dragons wouldn't want to eat them." He yanked his hand back when Ruby pecked at him. "You are lucky you belong to Pearl's granddaughter or you would be in a pot and then into my stomach," he threatened.

Ruby tilted her head and clucked at him before scratching at some loose warm grass near the small dish of feed that was set out for her. Perhaps this was why Jabir kept sneaking out at night. Mandra said he'd caught the little boy more than once trying to sneak out to the barn when he should have been in bed. The little boy had been pestering his father to replicate the chicken. Jabir really wanted to have a pet chicken like Leo. Of course, neither he nor Mandra were opposed to the idea if it meant they had fresh eggs to go along with the bird.

"Go on with you, I have work that needs to be completed," Asim chuckled.

He bent to spread the warm grass, but stiffened in surprise when his fingers touched something hard under the straw. Pulling his hand back, he studied the pile of warm grass for a moment before he gently brushed it aside. Perhaps Ruby had left some of her delicious eggs for him and Pearl. His eyes widened and a loud curse exploded from his lips when he saw a very large, dark green egg. This was *not* one of Ruby's eggs.

He straightened, staring down at the egg with a frown. He had never seen one like it before. Muttering under his breath, he carefully went through the pile of warm grass, counting the eggs he found.

"Six," he said with a shake of his head. "Where in the galaxy did Jabir find these?"

The little boy must have found them somewhere and snuck them into the barn. His eyes widened again as another thought dawned on him – Pearl. She must know about Jabir's stash! She had been adamant about cleaning the barn on her own shortly after the Dragon Lords and the younglings returned from their adventure on Earth. She even insisted that Pokey could help her with the heavy items if she needed it. There was no way she could have cleaned the barn without knowing about the eggs.

Asim quickly covered the eggs again. He would need to research them to see if he could determine what they were. He turned to leave, but paused when he saw the corner of a sack partially hidden behind the handle of a rake. Pulling the rake aside, he saw now the familiar language of Earth's people. He also recognized the symbol of Paul's ranch on the bag. Lady Ariel had shown him the design once.

"Earth...," Asim murmured before his eyes widened. "Jabir! That boy is going to get himself in trouble one of these days."

Asim wrapped his fingers around the top of the bag and stared out of the barn door. Jabir must have recruited Pearl. That would explain why they had been so secretive lately and kept chasing him out of the barn when he asked if they wanted any help.

His gaze moved back to the pile of eggs. They were larger than any he had ever seen – including the Grombot eggs. He would scan one of the eggs and run it through the database, but he would be surprised if they were even listed.

Perhaps Paul would know what they were; after all, they must have come from his ranch. Satisfied that he would get to the bottom of the mysterious eggs, he started to replace the bag on the hook when he realized there was something still in it. Curious, he glanced inside. A frown creased his brow when he saw it was one of Jabir's books.

Asim was surprised the little boy had left the book in the barn. He loved the storybooks his father purchased for him on Earth. Reaching in, he pulled it out and paled.

On the front cover were creatures Ariel called dinosaurs. Several of the beasts were standing by large nests filled with eggs. Asim's gaze moved back to the pile of fresh warm grass. He remembered that Jabir had a fascination with the beasts and wanted something called a Tyrannosaurus Rex for a pet.

"Dragon's balls!" he whispered, his eyes growing wide. He quickly thumbed through the book until he reached the page that showed a T-Rex, as Ariel and Pearl called the beast. The massive dinosaur was standing over a nest filled with broken shells from at least a half dozen eggs. Under the creature, small miniature versions of herself were snapping at the dead beast hanging from her jaws. "Jabir has found Earth dinosaurs! These T-Rex dinosaurs will eat him!"

Asim looked down at the bag in his hand. He needed to get rid of them, but how? Jabir would be heartbroken and Pearl would kill him for breaking the little boy's heart – not to mention he would also end up upsetting Lady Ariel.

He needed someone who could help him dispose of the eggs quickly and quietly. He could deny any knowledge – no, no, Pearl would know he was lying. He would just say he found them and gave them to one of the princes – but not Mandra.

Who else could he ask? He needed someone who could handle the mission. Someone no one would suspect. Asim glanced down when Ruby strutted over to him and pecked at his boot. A slow smile curved his lips. He knew the perfect accomplice to recruit.

"You want me to do what?" Vox asked, gaping at Asim on the view screen with a confused frown.

"I need you to dispose of something for me," Asim quietly explained.

"You've done it, haven't you? You've finally killed Riley's grand-mother? I don't blame you, but I'm not touching her dead body. The woman would probably come back to life just to haunt me," Vox warned.

Asim heard Riley's voice calling out to Vox in the background. He needed to keep this as quiet as possible. It wasn't easy when he practi-cally had Vox howling with delight at the thought of Pearl meeting a grievous end.

"Vox, Roam wants you to help with the egg coloring. I need to feed Sacha and change Pearl," Riley called in the background.

"I'll be there in a minute," Vox replied before he leaned closer to the vidcom. "I have to say, I expected you to kill Pearl a lot sooner. You two have been mated for what – almost three years now? I was ready to do the job myself on the first day I met her," he said in a hushed tone so Riley couldn't hear him.

"*No*, I have not killed my mate. I love her. This has nothing to do with killing anyone or hiding dead bodies," Asim growled in frustration.

Vox's expression drooped a little before he looked hopeful again. "Please tell me that you at least ate the damn chicken, then! That crazy feathered beast loves to get in the house and lay eggs when Tina and Viper visit. Roam's been hiding them under my pillow for me. I didn't find the last one until it was too late," he said.

"I have not killed Pearl or eaten Ruby! They are both still alive and healthy. In fact, Pearl should be there any minute. I just want you to take something out and leave it in the woods," Asim snapped before he remembered to lower his voice. "Jabir brought back some eggs from Earth. I want you to take them away and leave them in the forest. I'm hoping that they don't hatch; but if they do, I'm hoping a predator will get them before they grow too large."

"Eggs? Just boil them and eat them," Vox replied with a disappointed expression.

"I can't! I told you, they are Jabir's eggs," Asim growled.

Vox shrugged. "We eat Ruby's eggs all the time, so what is the big deal?" he asked.

"This is the big deal!" Asim growled and held up Jabir's picture book of dinosaurs. "If they hatch, all the dragonlings will want one. Do you want this running around your house?" he demanded.

Vox leaned forward and whistled under his breath. "I know Amber and Jade would love one, but I have enough teeth and poop in my house between Roam and the twins, I don't need any more at the moment," he said, shaking his head. "Are you sure they are these creatures?"

"I am pretty sure they are. Each of the eggs are big, green, and heavy just like the ones in this picture," Asim replied, cupping his hands to demonstrate. "I can't take the chance that they will hatch and eat Jabir or harm my mate."

"I can understand that, but why don't you get rid of them? Why do you want me to do it?" Vox asked with a frown.

"Daddy! I's coloring the eggs on my own!" Roam yelled.

"That's nice. I'll be right there. Make sure you save a few for me," Vox called over his shoulder.

"Lady Ariel made me promise years ago that I would not harm any creature that was brought to the retreat. I can't break my word. I also can't ask Mandra because Ariel and Jabir would be upset. If I upset them, then Pearl will get mad. I don't want to make my mate unhappy with me," Asim explained.

"I'm always making Pearl mad. It isn't all that bad," Vox grinned. "Pearl says I have a natural talent for irritating people."

Asim bit back the groan threatening to escape. Pearl was right – Vox did have a natural talent for irritating others. He had three days to set his plan in action. He just hoped none of the eggs hatched before he, Mandra, and Ariel arrived at the palace.

"Pearl and I will babysit the younglings for you and Riley for a week if you'll do this," Asim finally broke down, resorting to bribery.

"A whole week? All three of them?" Vox asked, a grin slowly growing on his face at the thought of having his mate alone for a week. "What do you want me to do?"

~

Present Day:

"Hiding eggs? What does this have to do with the wooden creature and your mate fighting with you in battle?" Brogan asked in disgust, interrupting Asim.

"Perhaps the creatures hatched and attacked the Sarafin king and ate him. The Sarafin waged war and the creatures ate them as well," Barrack suggested.

Brogan nodded. "Possible... but what about Pearl? Where does she fit into the battle?" he asked.

"The creatures did not eat Vox. They did hatch though," Asim interjected with an exasperated sigh.

"You aren't going to go into more dirty dragon sex, are you? I have to tell you that the image of you and Pearl having hot sex together is not one I am enjoying," Barrack admitted.

"I second that," Brogan murmured.

They started to snicker but bit it back when Asim stood up and glared at them. They glanced at each other, trying to hide their amused expressions. Asim shook his head in warning.

"I'm ready to Taser your asses myself," Asim growled.

Barrack raised his hands in surrender. "We apologize, old warrior. Continue on with your grand tale of…"

"Dirty dragon sex," Brogan interjected under his breath.

"Of the great battle your mate won," Barrack continued, trying not to laugh.

Asim groaned and ran his hands down his face. He never should have shared that. Pearl would kill him and the Twin Dragons if she knew.

"She did more than win the battle, she saved my life," Asim grudgingly continued. "I will skip the details of what happened while trying to hide the eggs and continue with what happened *after* they hatched… and the trouble they brought with them."

12

O ne month before:

No, you've already eaten," Asim rebuked the juvenile emu with a shake of his head. "I'll need to build a higher fence if they keep growing."

Pearl chuckled. "Paul said they grow fast and he wasn't lying," she chuckled. "Oh, my, they're in the water again."

"Three and a half months old and they are already a pain in my backside," Asim growled.

"You know you love them," Pearl teased, rubbing the head of one of the emus.

"They love you. They follow you around like that damn chicken of Tina's follows her. I swear there is something wrong with the creatures on your world," Asim grumbled.

"Well, I'm not the only one they bonded with," Pearl chuckled, watching another emu tilt its head to look up at Asim.

"Can we play ball with them?" Roam called out.

"Yes, but make sure Pokey is with you," Pearl replied.

"When will their parents return?" Asim asked.

Pearl turned back and gave her mate a knowing look. "We've still found time," she teased.

"For our dragons, but what about for us?" Asim asked.

"There's nothing to say we can't enjoy a little starlight romance as well," Pearl chuckled.

The sound of giggles told Asim that Roam and Jabir were listening to them – and understanding the innuendoes lacing their grownup conversation. A pained expression crossed his face, pulling more giggles from the boys. He looked at Pearl and raised an eyebrow that spoke volumes.

"My mommy and daddy is always talkings like that," Roam whispered to Jabir.

Jabir glanced back and forth between Asim and Pearl with a frown. "My daddy makes the same faces. He looks like he has gas."

"This is what happens when you volunteer us as babysitters," Asim pointed out.

"Alright, boys, let's go play catch," Pearl laughed, turning away from her mate.

Asim shook his head and watched Pearl round up the boys and the birds. The six emus followed Pearl with almost the same devotion as the two boys. Pokey split in two so that each boy would have protection in case the birds became too rough. He turned and frowned when he felt his dragon stir and stiffen.

What is it? Asim asked, carefully surveying the landscape.

Not sure. I feel something, his dragon warily stated.

A storm, perhaps? Asim asked.

Maybe, his dragon replied.

I'd better make sure everything is secure just in case, he said.

∾

"Hans, what do you see?"

"Credits... and a lot of them," Hans replied. "I'm glad we heard about this place. I've never seen animals like this. We should be able to get a lot for them on the black market."

"When are we going in, Zeb?" a third man asked, kneeling on one knee and staring at the structures below.

"Tonight," Zeb responded, spitting on the ground.

"That's an old warrior. He'll put up a nasty fight," Hans said, lowering the vision magnifier in his hand.

"Crag can handle him," Zeb stated with a shrug.

"It won't be easy. These dragon-shifters are a mean species. They've got that golden thing, too," Hans cautioned.

Zeb turned to look at Crag. A large man called a Drugunulite, he could turn his body to almost solid rock. The dragon might scorch him, but he couldn't turn him to ash. One strike of Crag's fist and the dragon would feel it.

"He's old. I can take him. You kill him; you kill the golden beast. I've seen it happen before," Crag said.

"What about the woman?" Hans asked, lifting the vision magnifier to his eyes again.

"We take her. She seems to know how to handle the feathered creatures and she's different. I heard she don't come from this world. We find out where she comes from and we have a whole new world to collect from," Zeb said, spitting again.

"I heard on Madaris that these warriors would pay huge credits to find a woman who could be their true mate. Even that old dragon found one! We locate the planet, take a bunch of the women, and sell them off to the highest bidder," Crag added, rising to his feet.

"They look weak," Hans commented, focusing on the white-haired female watching the two little boys play. "What about the kids?"

"Leave them. They are worthless. If they survive on their own, more power to them," Zeb replied. "I've been watching them while I was waiting for both of you to arrive. The old dragon has been coming out alone after dark to check on things. Crag, you take him out while Hans grabs the woman. I'll round up the beasts. We'll be in and out in less than an hour. No one will know we were even on the planet," Zeb instructed.

"Stupid beasts can't even figure out how to pick up a ball. This should be easy," Hans reflected, watching the feathered creatures jump and dance around the ball after one of the boys threw it.

~

Pearl looked up when Asim walked into the kitchen. His hair was damp from his shower and his vest was open. She glanced over at the boys playing on the floor with Pokey.

"You know you drive me crazy when you wear your vest like this," she said, walking over to run her hand over his stomach.

Asim wrapped his arm around her and pulled her against him. The smile on her lips grew when she felt his body react to her touch. Even after three years, she loved that she could still turn him on with only a touch.

"I'm not the only one who can get excited," Asim said with a sniff.

"Stop or the boys will know what is going on," Pearl warned, glancing over her shoulder.

Asim shook his head. "They are wrestling now," he chuckled.

Sure enough, the boys had shifted, Roam into his tiger cub and Jabir into his dragon form. They were wrestling with each other and with Pokey. Their parents were supposed to be back late tomorrow morning. He loved being with the boys, but he also enjoyed giving them back – for lascivious reasons, of course.

"I'm going to check on the animals. The Grombots were trying to release the emus earlier. I need to make sure they haven't discovered how to undo the new locks I installed," Asim said, grabbing her hand that was sliding up his chest and pressing her fingers to his lips. "Tonight, after they are in bed?"

"If Pokey doesn't mind babysitting duty," Pearl murmured.

"I'm hungry," Jabir suddenly said from behind them.

"Me, too!" Roam agreed, rubbing a hand across his nose. "I think I got some symbiot up my nose. Wanna see me snort it out?"

"Yew! That's gross. Can I try?" Jabir exclaimed.

"Lovely. I don't remember the girls being like this," Pearl dryly commented.

"It is a boy thing," Asim chuckled. "I will be back shortly."

"That's right, abandon me to the symbiot snorters," Pearl teased.

Asim's eyes darkened and the tiny flames she loved burned in his eyes. He still held her right hand, but she had her left one free. Leaning into him, Pearl slowly met him halfway when he bent to kiss her. She slid her free hand down between them, sliding it across his groin.

Asim pulled back to gaze down at her. Yep, the flames were much brighter now. A small, secretive smile curved her lips and she stroked him again.

"You are playing with fire, Pearl," Asim warned.

"I'll be playing with something else later," she retorted before pulling away when Jabir grumbled that he was hungry again. "I'll have dinner done by the time you get back."

"Let them play. I'm hoping it tires them out so they go to bed early tonight," Asim chuckled.

Pearl released a sigh when he pressed another hot kiss to her lips before smacking her on the ass. She glanced at the boys, but they decided they were more interested in playing with the dozens of toy trucks the symbiot created for them. She would owe Pokey something special for distracting the boys.

Warmth filled her and she could feel the symbiot's amusement. She snorted and shook her head. Just what she needed, help from a living metal sex coach – not!

"I think I can handle that part of my life on my own," she murmured under her breath.

Honestly, she felt younger than she did when she was young. She didn't know if it was because she no longer worried about Riley and Tina, the fact that dragons lived a lot longer, or just being happy, but she wasn't about to ignore the gift she had been given. Hell, if she wanted to think of herself as being sexy, and Asim thought she was too, who was she to argue? She had a few words for anyone who tried to tell her differently.

Humming under her breath, she walked into the kitchen and began preparing their evening meal. She opened the drawer, and pulled out two knives – one for cutting the vegetables and one for cutting the fresh bread. After placing them on the counter, she walked over to the refrigerator. She loved the replicator, but tonight, she wanted to prepare dinner the old-fashioned way. It helped keep her hands busy while her mind enjoyed other things – like removing Asim's clothing.

~

Asim shifted into his dragon, flew over the ranch, and nimbly touched down outside the barn where the emus were – or should have been. A growl of frustration escaped him when he saw the opened door of the barn. In the doorway, he could see one of the Grombots hanging by two of its arms, grinning at him.

"*Curizan spit*! Not again," he sighed. "I swear if it is the last thing I do, I'm going to design a lock that you can't undo!"

The Grombot blinked and tilted its head. Before he reached the opening, it disappeared. While the creatures normally moved so slowly that it was almost agonizing to watch, they were actually capable of moving extremely fast. As much as he hated it, he was going to need Pokey's help to round up all the beasts. Shaking his head, he pulled free the communicator that he wore at his waist.

"Let me guess, they got loose again," Pearl answered.

"Yes. I need Pokey. Both of the Grombots are loose and it looks like they released the emus as well," he said, staring into the empty barn.

"He's on his way," Pearl chuckled. "I'll postpone dinner for a little while."

"No, go ahead and feed the boys. It shouldn't take long. I can warm up something," he said.

"If you need help, let me know. The boys would love to play tag with the emus," she offered.

"If I can't get them, I will call you," he promised.

"We're here if you need us. You know I love you. Good luck," Pearl replied with a sigh.

"I love you, too. I will contact you once I am finished," he replied, hanging up.

Asim decided he'd better try to repair the locking mechanism on the Grombots' cage first. Otherwise, it would be senseless trying to catch any of them now because they would just escape again. Grumbling under his breath, he wondered what else could go wrong tonight.

Danger!

Lost in thought, he didn't hear his dragon's warning until it was too late. When he walked into the barn, someone punched him in the jaw. The blow knocked him several meters backwards. His head snapped back and darkness descended around him. He didn't even feel it when his body hit the ground.

13

"That was easier than I thought," Crag grunted.

"For the dragon-shifter – now we have to capture the feathered creatures that escaped," Zeb snapped.

"What about his symbiot?" Crag asked, turning to look at Zeb.

"It won't attack us if it thinks we will kill him. Contain it in the back room; then tie the old dragon up," Zeb instructed.

"Why don't I just kill him now?" Crag demanded, looking down at Asim's inert body.

Zeb frowned and shook his head. "The creature will attack us before he dies. The only way to get away is to contain it until we are ready to leave. Once we have the woman, it won't come after us or attack us – especially if we kill the warrior."

"Whatever you say," Crag said with a shrug.

Zeb jerked his head toward the building. "Pull him into the barn," he ordered.

Crag reached down and gripped the collar of Asim's vest. He walked into the barn, dragging Asim behind him. Once he was almost to the back, he dropped Asim and turned to wait.

They didn't have long. The symbiot burst through the door. Zeb studied the enraged creature. He had seen how deadly they could be on several of the Spaceports. He pointed his blaster at Asim.

"I wouldn't," Zeb warned. "If you kill me, Crag will snap his neck before you can save him."

The symbiot took a step closer and crouched. The symbiot's body shimmered in a wide variety of colors. The display of colors reflected its feelings of aggression. Zeb gave it a nasty grin.

"Did I mention that my other friend is with the woman and the boys? You can't save them all. What is it going to be?" he demanded. He waited until the symbiot backed down. "You will go into the back room. If you try to come out, I'll have all of them killed."

Zeb knew the symbiot understood him. He could see its eyes narrow. Stepping closer to Asim, he nodded to the room in the back. "Go or they are all dead."

The symbiot hissed and rose back up. It moved with slow, deliberate movements. Zeb stiffened when it paused as it drew even with them before it snarled and continued to the back room. He followed, giving the symbiot a wide berth. Only when it was in the room did he close the distance and locked the door.

"What about this one?" Crag asked.

"Break his leg and lock him in the other barn for now. He won't be able to heal without his symbiot. We don't want him transforming into his dragon or being able to fight. We definitely don't want him and his symbiot near each other. Once we have the woman and feathered beasts, you can come back and finish the job," Zeb instructed.

"I hope we make a lot of credits off the feathered beasts. We are going to need them," Crag grumbled even as he turned and dragged Asim out of the building.

～

"Boys, come here," Pearl said in a sharp tone.

Jabir and Roam looked up from where they were coloring. Both sensed the authority and alarm in her voice. They scrambled to their feet and hurried into the kitchen.

"What's wrong?" Jabir asked.

Pearl's face was tight with worry. She knelt down, and whispered to the symbiot wrapped around her wrists. The thin bands of gold dissolved and divide before wrapping around each boy's arm.

"Something has happened. I don't know for sure what is going on, but Pokey is showing me images. Asim needs my help," Pearl said in a quiet, urgent voice.

"We can helps, can't we, Jabir? We are good at helping," Roam said.

Pearl reached up and touched Roam's blond hair. "I need you to hide. Can you do that for me? Can you hide where no one can find you until Pokey tells you that it is safe to come out?" she asked.

Jabir nodded. "We can goes to my favorite rock. Daddy and I made a fort in it," he said.

"Where is it?" Pearl asked, searching the little boy's face.

"It is in the meadow. It is the one with the tall rocks that sticks up," Jabir explained.

"You have to be very quiet. No one can see you," Pearl said. "Those... They are coming. I need you to go now."

"We'll be just like Grandpa Paul – really, really quiet," Jabir promised.

"I'm always quiet. I'm a cat," Roam stated.

"Hurry and don't get caught," Pearl ordered as she stood up and reached for the knives on the counter. "I've got some trash to take out."

"That means she's going to kick their asses," Roam whispered. "My mommy says that when she gets mad."

"Shush! Let's go," Jabir said, shifting into his dragon.

Pearl watched both boys disappear around the corner. They were going up the stairs to the upper balcony. Realizing that she had to trust in their natural ability and knowing that the small symbiots attached to their arms would help guide them, she turned her focus on the men who harmed her mate.

Rules? Her dragon asked.

Let's start with rule number eleven, Pearl suggested with a grim smile as her fingers curled around one of the knives she was holding.

I like that one, her dragon chuckled.

Hans silently climbed over the railing and landed on the deck. He knelt and glanced around. Through the large section of glass windows, he could see the woman in the food preparation area. He didn't see the kids. He wasn't worried about them since they were too young to be a threat.

He started forward, pausing when his view of the woman was blocked after she activated the window shield. It wouldn't matter nor hinder his mission to capture her. One female was no threat to a cutthroat like him.

He stood and walked across the deck. He had seen the symbiot leave a short while ago and knew that Crag and Zeb were capable of handling it and the old dragon warrior. He almost winced at how easy his job would be in capturing the old woman.

He stepped up to the door and tested it. A humorless smile curved his lips when he found it unlocked. Pulling it open, he silently stepped inside.

This is too easy, he thought as he entered before the smile died and was replaced with a frown.

Hans stared at the woman who gazed at him with a smile on her lips. Unease stirred inside him, but he pushed it away. His gaze ran over her slender form. She looked cool, composed, and – he reluctantly admitted – good in black leather for her age.

"Where I come from it is considered rude to enter someone's home without being invited," the woman said in a cool voice.

Hans frowned. "You are coming with me," he ordered.

"I don't think so. What have you done with my mate?" the woman quietly asked.

Hans gaze narrowed on her face. He could normally tell a lot about his adversary by their eyes. A flicker of fear, a hint of desperation, and panic were normal, but hers were clear and calm. She looked as if she were ready to battle him – and felt confident that she would win.

Once again, an uneasy feeling rose in his stomach. This time it was a little more difficult to push away.

"Do not give me any trouble, female. I'll snap your neck as quickly as Crag is going to snap your mate's. Then, I'll do the same to those two younglings," Hans snarled.

"Listen, asshole, I asked you a question. I'll ask one more time. What have you done with my mate?" the woman demanded.

Hans sneered at the woman's show of defiant bravado. He closed the distance between them. Stopping in front of her, he towered over her. Her face was tight with resolve and determination.

"What species are you?" Hans demanded, his gaze narrowing on her face.

"One you don't want to underestimate," she replied.

"Your mate will be dead soon. If you fight, so will you," Hans threatened. He reached out and wrapped his hand around her upper arm. "Come…."

His breath hissed out when her knee connected with his groin in a swift, hard blow. His eyes widened as pain exploded through him. Dots flashed before his eyes and his fingers loosened on her arm.

A loud groan escaped him as the pain spread. He was defenseless against her next blow. She pulled back her arm and slammed her elbow into his cheekbone. Reaching out, he grabbed at her jacket as he fell backwards, pulling her with him.

The woman's hand rose and she struggled to break free, but his larger frame and gravity were no match for her. Together they fell to the floor. Pain ripped through him and his body jerked in surprise at the source.

He froze and blinked in shock. Following the woman's gaze, he looked down at himself. It took a second for him to realize that he was dead, his mind and body just hadn't recognized it yet. The woman must have had a knife in her hand. When he pulled her down, she instinctively raised her hand to cushion her fall. Unwittingly, the knife between their bodies had pieced his heart.

"How? You are… female," Hans muttered as his body began to tremble.

"Rule number eleven: If you are going to hit someone, make sure they stay down the first time, because you might not get a second chance," she said in a quiet voice, gazing down at him with a mixture of determination and resolve.

"Rules... What rules?" Hans asked in a slightly slurred voice.

"Pearl's Rules for Living," she replied. "Where is my mate?"

"Others... Zeb has him... in... the... barn...," Hans replied before his eyes dimmed and his head fell to the side.

Take out trash, her dragon growled. *No want dead body in house.*

"Amen to that, sister," Pearl replied, stiffening her spine and pushing up off the dead man's body.

With the added boost of her dragon's strength, Pearl awkwardly dragged the man's body out of her house. Once she was done, she shifted into her dragon. She searched the darkness. She was torn between going to Asim first or making sure the boys were alright.

What gut say? Her dragon asked.

The boys – my gut says we need to find the boys, Pearl said.

Then, we find boys, her dragon replied.

Pearl felt the muscles of her dragon contract before she pushed up off the deck. Her wings swept through the air in wide, powerful strokes. She flew low to the ground, following the slight scent trail of Jabir. Her dragon's gaze swept the area, mindful of their other visitors.

Rule number twenty, her dragon whispered.

Yes, Pearl replied.

Rule number twenty was one that had protected her and the girls many times over the years. If you or your family/friends' lives are on the line, ignore all other rules except Rule Number 1. She would use her brain. She was smart, tough, and determined. She might be outnumbered and outpowered, but she had a good head on her shoulders and had enough fights under her belt to know when to fight dirty.

Whoop-ass time, her dragon growled.

Yes, it's time to open a can of whoop-ass, Pearl agreed.

14

A sim awoke to excruciating pain. Nausea churned in his stomach. The pain rocketed through him when he rolled to his side. It was so intense; he feared he would lose consciousness again.

Damage..., he choked out to his dragon.

Left leg broken, jaw fractured, his dragon replied, pacing inside him. *You no can shift to me.*

I know. Symbiot..., he asked, trying to breathe through the pain.

Locked away. They threaten kill mate, his dragon snarled.

Asim clenched his fists against the floor. His head was pounding, making it difficult to think. He had to get to his symbiot. He couldn't shift into his dragon with a broken leg and he couldn't fight. Breathing deeply, he forced himself to roll over. The bits of symbiots around his wrists were moving over his body. The bone in his leg would be too much for the small pieces, but they could heal his jaw.

The symbiot moved upward and slid over his jaw. Some of it slipped beneath his skin. He could feel the tingle of bone being mended. When it finished, it resurfaced through the cut on his lip and healed that as well.

"Thank you, my friend," he murmured.

The small amount of symbiot warmed under his touch. He could feel it moving down his body to his leg. Such a small amount of symbiot would take days to heal him.

"What happened?" he demanded.

Not know, his dragon replied, continuing to pace.

Asim gritted his teeth and forced himself to sit up. Sweat beaded on his forehead and he swallowed back the groan of pain. Holding his broken leg, he waited until he felt like he wasn't going to pass out before he drew in a deep breath again.

"Come to me. I need to connect with Pokey," Asim ordered in a strained voice.

The tiny strands of gold shimmered, but moved onto the palm of his hand. Asim wrapped his fingers around it and closed his eyes. Focusing, he connected with his symbiot. Within seconds, the images and conversation about what had happened while he was unconscious streamed through his mind. Panting, he released the faint connection and opened his fingers. The tiny threads of gold looked pale and listless.

"Pearl," he whispered, bowing his head.

~

"Where is he?" Crag asked.

"He'll be here. We need to find those damn creatures," Zeb said, glancing around the large meadow with the vision magnifier. "There! I see one of them about half way down the meadow."

"Hans should be back by now," Crag said with a frown.

Zeb lowered the vision magnifier and glared at the other man. "He said he would meet us at the barn. It may take a while if he has to carry her. The skimmer," he snapped. "We are running out of time. Let's go."

Both men slid onto a skimmer. The land transport had a long, narrow seat, a handle bar, and foot pedals that operated the speed and brakes. It was simple, but utilitarian. The bikes rose up off the ground. Leaning forward, the men shot out across the ground, cutting a path through the tall purple grass.

Behind them in the barn, two large creatures – each with four arms, two legs, and a knack for locks – climbed down from the rafters. Moving across the bare floor of the barn, the female climbed up on the shoulders of the male and inserted a piece of wire into the lock. It took several tries before the lock clicked and disengaged and the door opened. A slow smile spread over the two Grombots' faces when the enraged Werecat with wings turned to face them.

～

"Jabir… Roam… Are you in here?" Pearl softly called.

She climbed up onto the rocks and peered into the narrow hole in the rock. Fear gripped her when there was no answer. She turned around on top of the large boulder and searched the darkness. She froze when she saw a movement in the tall grass a short distance away.

A soft laugh escaped her when she saw the familiar eyes of an emu staring back at her. A moment later, a second and a third one joined it. Sliding down off the rock, she listened. The smile grew when she heard Roam.

"Why's didn't we do this before?" he was saying.

"Cause we didn't know it was fun," Jabir replied.

"Boys, come here," Pearl ordered.

She blinked when the three more emus appeared near the rocks. Searching, she almost missed Jabir and Roam. Both boys peeked around the neck of an emu.

"You're riding them?" Pearl exclaimed.

"They's just like playing horsey, only better," Jabir said with a smile. "They said they would help us."

"They said…," Pearl started to repeat before she shook her head. "How?"

"They are real good at being soldiers. Jabir says they are a neutral," Roam replied.

"Not neutral – natural. They's smart, Grams," Jabir said.

Pearl turned when her dragon hissed out a warning. In the

distance, she could see two skimmers heading their way. Those would be the men that the dying man had mentioned. If the men were heading in this direction, she couldn't help but wonder what they had done to Asim.

He not dead. I know if he dead, her dragon assured her.

"Boys, we need to keep them away from the barn and Asim. Jabir, can you tell the emus that I need a distraction?" Pearl asked, turning back to the little boy.

"Yes," Jabir replied.

"Whatever happens, don't let those men catch you," Pearl said.

"We won't," Roam replied with a grin. "We needs reins if we are going to goes real fast. It is hard to holds onto their necks."

The symbiots on the boys spread into a thin bridle and reins. Pearl whispered to the boys to be careful once more before she shifted back into her dragon. It was time to show these assholes who they were messing with.

Launching up off the ground, Pearl focused on her plan of attack. She needed to keep the men away from the barn long enough to find Asim and Pokey. Once they were together, there would be no stopping them.

Below her, Pearl could see the dark shapes of the emus moving through the tall grass. She was shocked at how fast they were! She estimated they had to be running at close to fifty miles per hour.

They ran in a V-shaped formation toward the men riding the skimmers. Pearl swooped down behind the men and released a long stream of dragon fire. The tall grass ignited in a flaming wall. She twisted, and rose again, rolling several times when one of the men turned on the skimmer and fired at her.

The man turned back around just in time to swerve when the emus emerged from the tall grass in front of them. The men stopped, shocked to see the birds circling them. Pearl could hear the strong, powerful legs striking the ground. Bits of grass and dirt flew up under their feet. As one, they turned back the other way.

The larger of the two men lifted a blaster and aimed for one of the young birds. In a flash, the emus scattered in all directions. The man who had fired at Pearl turned and yelled for his partner to go after the emu carrying Roam.

Pearl circled around. She couldn't release any dragon fire for fear of hitting one of the emus or the boys. Instead, she swooped down again with her claws extended.

The man – Zeb, she suspected – raised his laser rifle to shoot at Jabir. Pearl's claw snatched the rifle – and the man holding it – right off the skimmer. The added weight was too much for her dragon and she couldn't gain altitude without releasing him.

Pearl's dragon roared in pain when Zeb swung his hand up and the sharp edge of his blade sliced a deep path across her front claw. She opened her claw and released the man. Unfortunately, the move threw her off-balance. Tumbling through the air, she curled her wings protectively around her body and hit the ground on the other side of the wall of flames. Rolling several times, she finally came to a stop. Shaking her head to clear the dizziness, she shifted back into her human form.

Lying on the ground, she stared at the man on the other side. He was searching for her through the flames and smoke. Defenseless, she remained frozen.

Several long seconds passed before he turned away. Trying to push herself up, she drew in a hissing breath when her arm gave out on her. She glanced down and cursed when she saw blood dripping from under the sleeve of her jacket. This was the first time she had been hurt in her dragon form. It would seem it carried over to her human one.

"Son-of-a-bitch!" she muttered.

Standing up, she glanced through the flames before turning to look at the barn. Torn once again, she could only hope the emus were as good as Jabir said they were. She took off at a fast run for the barn.

~

"Where are they?" Zeb growled.

"I don't know," Crag said, glancing around. "One second they were there and the next they were gone."

"Well, find them and kill them. We'll sell them dead," Zeb ordered.

"Where are you going?" Crag asked.

"Dragon hunting," Zeb replied, checking his laser rifle.

"Tell Hans to get the ship ready," Crag grunted before he took off.

Zeb walked over to the skimmer. He released the emergency canister attached to the side and tossed it. He aimed, and fired. The canister, filled with a fire retardant, exploded in midair and created a hole in the wall of flames. Sliding his leg over the seat of the skimmer, he turned the transport around and took off through the hole. In the distance, he could see the shape of someone running. A break in the clouds cast the moonlight down on the white hair of the woman he had seen earlier.

"So, you can shift into a dragon as well," Zeb said under his breath. "Let's see how good you can fight."

15

B racing himself against the wall, Asim glanced up when the door suddenly burst open. His eyes widened and a grim, pain-filled smile curved his lips but never made it to his eyes. He straightened as much as his broken leg would allow and nodded to his symbiot.

"It is good to see you, my friend," he greeted through clenched teeth. "My dragon and I need your healing powers."

His symbiot surged forward. It melted and flowed over his broken leg. Asim closed his eyes, leaned his head back, and relaxed. The warmth of healing energy flooded his body, making him whole once again. The fighting blood of his dragon ignited in his veins. When his eyes opened, the flames of an ancient dragon warrior of Valdier blazed from them.

"Our mates and the younglings are in danger," he snarled, baring his teeth.

The two Grombots that had followed his symbiot into the room turned and quickly vanished. Stepping out of his makeshift cell, Asim shifted into his dragon and took off at a run for the wide, double doors. By the time he hit the doors of the barn, his symbiot had formed armor around his body. He burst through the doors and soared up into the air. Twisting, he scanned the burning field for his mate.

His gaze narrowed on Pearl's white hair. She was running toward the barn. Behind her, a skimmer was approaching at an increasing speed.

Fury poured through him and he plunged forward. He swept over Pearl, placing himself between her and their attacker. He released a series of powerful fireballs at the skimmer. The male jerked the skimmer to the side but was unable to avoid the last fireball completely.

Asim released another burst when the man flew up into the air. The flames engulfed the skimmer. Within seconds, it exploded. The force of the explosion sent shards of the skimmer flying through the air.

Diving for the ground, Asim wrapped his body around Pearl and lowered his head to completely protect her from the flying projectiles. Molten pieces of metal rained down around them, but Pearl and his dragon were protected by the armor of his symbiot. He breathed heavily and trembled when he realized how small and fragile she felt in his claws.

He shifted back to his two-legged form and held her close to him, rubbing his nose against her cheek. The coppery smell of her blood hit him hard and he lifted his head. He didn't need to instruct his symbiot to heal Pearl – it was already moving under the sleeve of her jacket and up her arm.

"I smell blood," he groaned.

"The ass- wipe got in a lucky slice, but not before I jerked his ass off his skimmer," she said, gazing up at him. "The other man said they broke your leg."

"Yes, but my symbiot healed me," Asim said. "Where are the younglings?"

Pearl looked over his shoulder with a worried frown. "Out there on the emus," she said.

Asim glanced over his shoulder and his gaze narrowed in anger. He frantically wanted to make sure she wasn't hurt anywhere else, but he needed to take care of the threat to them first. He released her and stepped back. His body shimmered again. Once more, the gun-metal-gray, battle-scarred dragon stood in front of her. With a nod, Pearl shifted as well – her smaller, silver dragon standing proudly next to her mate. Pokey dissolved, divided into two, and created matching armor for each dragon.

With a loud roar, Pearl pushed up off the ground. Asim quickly followed. His dragon was still very protective of his mate despite her fierce nature. Together, they flew out over the field in search of the younglings.

It took nearly five fly-overs before they spied the small group emerging into the clearing near the tall rock. The emus turned in tight circles, prancing and stomping the ground. On the back of two emus, Roam and Jabir waved to Asim and Pearl.

Asim circled around and landed several meters from the birds. Pearl smoothly landed next to him. The symbiot dissolved and shook before reforming into the large Werecat with wings Jabir loved so much.

"Grams! We ran the bad man off. He rode aways on his skimmer for the mountain and didn't come back," Roam laughed, sliding off of his emu.

"That is wonderful! You were both so brave," Pearl exclaimed, bending down to pick Roam up in her arms. "Your daddy and mommy are going to be so proud of you."

"Are either of you hurt?" Asim asked, looking at Roam before he turned to look at Jabir.

"No, we's okay," Jabir said with a grin.

Asim started to take a step toward Jabir to lift the little boy down when the emu under Jabir jerked to the side and stumbled. Its legs trembled before it slowly sank down to the ground. Less than a second later, a cry escaped Jabir when he was lifted by the back of his neck off the back of the emu.

"Don't move or he dies," Zeb ordered.

Asim took a threatening step toward the man before freezing. The soft sound of Jabir's whimper of pain warned him that the man holding the boy wouldn't hesitate to kill him. His gaze narrowed in helpless rage as Zeb ruthlessly pressed his weapon against Jabir's temple.

"I should have killed you," Zeb growled.

"Release him!" Asim ordered, moving ever so slightly so that he was in front of Pearl and Roam.

"Give me the woman and I'll release the boy," Zeb demanded with a shake of his head.

"Never!" Asim snarled.

Zeb's finger tightened on the blaster in his hand. "The woman – now," he repeated in a cold voice.

"No…," Asim started to say.

"Yes," Pearl quietly interjected.

"Pearl…," Asim hissed, turning slightly in her direction.

"He'll kill Jabir. I can't let him do that," Pearl replied.

Asim watched her lower Roam to the ground and push the boy behind her. She ran her hand along her pants and smiled at him. Stepping closer, she brushed a kiss across his lips and pressed her hand against his.

"Remember rule number eleven," she whispered before stepping away and turning toward Zeb.

"Release him," she said, lifting her chin in defiance.

"Not until you take his place," Zeb countered.

Pearl stepped forward and turned to look back at Asim. A shiver ran through her when she heard Jabir release a cry and the soft thud of him hitting the ground. A second later, Zeb's cold hand gripped her neck. Pearl gave Asim a small nod, her eyes cool and calm.

Releasing a long breath, she swung her clenched fist as hard as she could down between Zeb's legs and twisted sideways at the same time as Asim released the knife she had slipped into his hand. The blade struck Zeb in the upper left shoulder. The force of it knocked him backwards several steps. Pearl followed up with a hard kick to Zeb's stomach, sending him lurching into the tall grass.

The emus followed him. The young birds went on the offensive against their attacker. They surrounded the man and began kicking him with their strong powerful legs. The group disappeared into the tall grass, following Zeb when he tried to crawl away. A shudder ran through Pearl as the sounds of the man's screams and the thuds and clucking of the emus filled the air.

"Make sure he is never a threat to us again," Asim ordered Pokey.

The symbiot shimmered and disappeared into the tall grass. Pearl scooped Jabir up into her arms and shifted into her dragon while Asim did the same with Roam. They both lifted up, carrying the boys away from the last pitiful, choked cries of their attacker.

Later that night, Pearl double checked on both of the boys. They were sprawled out on Jabir's bed, sound asleep with Pokey. It had taken a while to get both of them to calm down. She had fed them, bathed them, and finally read several books before they began yawning and their eyes drooped.

Pearl looked up when Asim opened the door, stepped in, and secured the door behind him. Her gaze softened when she saw the fatigue on his face. She walked over to him, and wrapped her arms around him.

"The boys?" Asim asked.

"Asleep. They were ready to join the hunt for the other man," Pearl chuckled, leaning back to look up at him with a questioning expression.

"I took care of Zeb and the one at our home. The other one escaped. I notified Zoran about what happened. He has dispatched several ships to find the man. I reassured Mandra, Ariel, Vox, and Riley that the boys were fine. They will be here first thing in the morning. I told them it would probably be best as I knew you were getting the boys down for the night," he said with a sigh.

"It helped being here in Mandra and Ariel's house. Jabir had his own toys and bed. Pokey is sleeping with them," she said, stepping back and guiding him to a large chair by the window. "I made you some dinner. Let me get it."

Asim tugged on her arm, pulling her onto his lap and wrapped his arms around her. He held her close, his chin against her hair and closed his eyes. Pearl could feel the heavy beat of his heart. She relaxed against him, understanding that he needed this time.

"I was afraid I was going to lose you," he murmured.

"You weren't the only one," she replied, resting her head against his shoulder and staring out at the dark. "When Hans told me what they had done to you, it pissed me off."

Asim chuckled. "You showed him!" he said, gazing down at her.

Pearl smiled. "He did it to himself, really. Neither my dragon nor I wanted a dead body in the house," she declared.

"I knew the moment that you knocked my ass in the lake that I had met a woman who was a warrior at heart. You proved it tonight," he said with a sigh and his arms tightened around her. "Tomorrow, I'm setting up a security system throughout the valley."

"No, tomorrow you are going to get up and take care of the animals like you do every day. We will not live our lives in fear because of one incident. Besides, we have an army already here! Between the Grombots and the emus, I can't imagine a safer place to live," she said sternly.

"I do believe you are right," he said, bending his head to brush a kiss across her lips.

"You bet your ass I am," Pearl retorted.

She turned and threaded her hands through his hair. Pulling his head down again, she captured his lips in a long kiss that shared the depth of her fear of losing him. Asim deepened the kiss and thanked the Goddess once more for giving him such a perfect mate.

EPILOGUE

Present Day:

"Wait a minute! What happened next?" Brogan demanded, leaning forward with his hands on his knees when Asim stopped talking.

"What do you mean 'What happened next'? We got the kids to safety," Asim said.

Brogan pushed up off the floor and grabbed the wooden sculpture. He shook it in front of Asim's face with a frown. When Asim gave him a puzzled look, Brogan released a growl of frustration and shook the wooden emu again.

"What happened to the other man? What happened to the emu that was shot?" Brogan demanded.

"Oh," Asim replied with a grin.

Barrack stood up and brushed the back of his pants. "Do you want us to hunt down the other man? We are excellent hunters," he said.

"No, no…. Crag was eventually caught for another offense and is serving time on an Antrox prison asteroid," Asim assured Barrack.

"What about the emu?" Brogan asked again.

"You know, emus are amazingly resourceful and hardy creatures. The one that was shot received only a minor wound that was healed quickly with the help of my symbiot," Asim reassured the agitated warrior.

"What about the half-blind Pactor and the Grombots and Roam and Jabir...?" Brogan added, with an intense curiosity that took Asim by surprise.

Asim chuckled and stood up. "Come, I will show you," he said.

The three men walked through the barn. Brogan and Barrack gazed around them in wonder, as if seeing the animals in it for the first time. Grombots – more than a dozen – swung from the rafters. Large nets were strung beneath the beams to catch the little ones still learning. Brogan stumbled when a half dozen Marrats raced out in front of him. Tasiers slept or munched on thick blades of purple grass and watched them from behind the safety of the glass cubicles that separated the boys from the girls.

Asim paused in the door. Out near the corral, Pearl and Ariel laughed as they petted the newest member to their family – Hobbler and George's daughter – Isabel. Adalard and Mandra jumped to the side when half a dozen emus swept past them at a run with Jabir riding the largest one in front.

Jaguin and Sara were standing with two other men and a woman. The small group turned and smiled at Barrack, Brogan, and him. Asim heard the two men next to him draw in a startled breath when they realized the other two men were twin dragons – and they each had an arm wrapped around the small, dark-haired woman between them who was holding a toddler in her arms.

Cree and Calo murmured to Melina before walking in their direction. Asim could see the confusion and suspicion in Barrack and Brogan's eyes as the other twin dragons approached. The expressions on Cree and Calo's faces reflected their own feelings of disbelief and uncertainty.

"Asim...," Calo greeted, not looking at Asim but at Barrack and Brogan.

"What is all of this?" Barrack quietly asked, gazing at the chaotic, yet somehow normal scene before eyeing the two warriors who stopped in front of them.

"Hope. A second chance," Cree said before he clamped his lips together.

"Jaguin thought you might like to know that it is possible to find a mate – and for her to be strong enough," Calo explained, his gaze moving back to where Melina stood holding their young daughter.

Asim turned and looked at the twin warriors. "This is home – a place where family and friends come and share. It is a place where you find love and acceptance for who you are. It doesn't matter if you aren't perfect, that is what makes you special," he explained with a wave of his hand.

"In our village, everyone feared us. Our whole life we were feared and rejected for being who we were – twins," Barrack murmured, staring around him.

"We were treated the same way, but we found Melina. She loves us and fought to save our lives," Calo said, turning to look at the men. "She is our partner. She keeps us grounded."

"I understand now what Pearl and you were trying to tell us," Brogan reluctantly admitted, glancing around him as if seeing their world through different eyes.

"What is that?" Asim asked.

"That there are different rules that can help guide us this time – and help us in making the right choices," Brogan said.

"We grew up with the people of our village believing one thing – that we would never find a true mate. We were fortunate that our parents believed differently. Your mate is out there, but you will need to handle her with care, for she will not understand the ways of the dragon," Cree cautioned.

Calo nodded. "... Or the needs of twin dragons. You will need to be patient," he said.

"And follow Pearl's last rule, no matter what happens," Asim agreed.

"Which rule was that?" Barrack asked.

"Pearl's Unbreakable Rule: Family and Friends come first. Be loyal, be true... and love them like there is no tomorrow," Asim quietly shared, staring across the yard at his mate. Pearl turned to look at him, a small smile curving her lips. "Cree and Calo can explain that one to you."

Asim didn't wait to see if the twins finally understood. His gaze was locked on Pearl. She met him halfway across the yard. He could see the questioning look in her eyes fade to understanding when he gently nodded his head.

"Are they ready?" Pearl asked, lifting her hand to trace the lines near the corner of Asim's right eye.

"They will be. You were smart to ask Jaguin to have Cree, Calo, and Melina come," Asim replied, bending to brush a kiss across her lips. "Perhaps, I can talk them into taking all three Pactors home with them."

Pearl chuckled and shook her head. "You know you'd miss them as much as Ariel and Jabir would," she said.

"Fly with me," Asim suddenly said. "I know this little place in the forest not far from here...."

Pearl reached up and captured his lips. Her hand ran down between them and she brushed her hand across the front of him before pulling back with a grin. She stepped back and turned. Looking over her shoulder, she had a mischievous sparkle dancing in her eyes.

"Last one there is on the bottom," she laughed.

Asim watched his mate transform. The silver dragon flicked her tail, stroking the tip along his chest before she lifted up off the ground. Jabir, riding the emu, swept by him, laughing and waving to Pearl as she flew off.

She going to be top, his dragon snorted, impatiently pacing and wanting to pursue his mate.

I think it is time you tried the bottom, Asim said with a wicked grin.

Oh, yes! His dragon groaned when Asim sent a deliciously wicked idea to his dragon.

Asim shifted into his dragon. In a flash, the battle scarred dragon was in fast pursuit of his mate. Well, fast enough to reach her just a few seconds too late to win. Wrapping his tail around Pearl's silver tail, he locked them together and brought her gently down to the ground where the delicate silver dragon settled on top of the large male who groaned in delight.

Yes! I like, his dragon agreed.

If you enjoyed Pearl's Dragon, there are a lot more stories in the Dragon Lords of Valdier world, including The Great Easter Bunny Hunt - which is included in its entirety in the back of this book! You can also read Abducting Abby: Dragon Lords of Valdier Book 1 for free at all major distributors and in my store at http://sesmithfl.com/store.

Check out the sneak peak of Abducting Abby below!

Abby Tanner is content to live on her mountain creating works of art and enjoying the peace and quiet. All of that changes when a golden space ship crash lands with the King of the Valdier inside, desperately hurt...

Chapter 1

Zoran Reykill pushed the body of the dead guard off him. He paused to draw in a sharp breath as pain sliced through his battered body. He had been in captivity for the past month, and there wasn't a place on his body that didn't hurt from the numerous cuts and bruises from the beatings and torture he had lived through.

He forced himself to roll the guard over and pulled the guard's clothes off his body. His own clothes had been taken not long after he was brought down to the hell they called a cell. This was the first opportunity he had to escape. He had been watching and waiting for his captors to make a mistake, and they finally had, thinking he was too beaten down to fight.

The guard Zoran had killed had come in to *play*, thinking he would relieve the boredom of standing guard over a chained prisoner by beating him some more. Instead, the guard found him hanging lifeless from the wall by his wrists and ankles.

When the guard unlocked his wrists, Zoran had grabbed him, breaking his neck immediately, so he couldn't fight or call out. Zoran knew he would not have survived long in a fight. He was too weak. It took everything in him to push the guard off and find the release on the locking mechanism to release his ankles.

Struggling into the guard's clothes, he pulled the laser pistol and blade from the guard, checking to make sure both were fully charged. He reached down and yanked the security badge from the guard's neck. He knew it was late, and there wouldn't be many guards about at this time of the night. Closing the solid door behind him, he moved down the darkened corridor. The dark did not bother him as he shifted to allow his night vision to take over.

His people were renowned for their ability to adapt to the dark. As a dragon shifter, he felt the beast inside him straining to get out. He hadn't dared shift while in captivity. Without his symbiot to help shield him, he would have been too vulnerable.

He fought to control his inner self as he moved through the prison maze. Even though he had only been half conscious when he was brought to the prison, he knew the way out, having played it over and over in his mind during the last month. Even if he hadn't been conscious, he would have smelled the night air as it called to him.

He was Zoran Reykill, leader of the Valdier. He was the most powerful of his kind, matched only by his brothers.

He had been enjoying time on a remote planet on the outer rim of his own solar system, hunting and enjoying the favors of some of the women brought there for such things. Ordinarily, he would have bypassed pleasure, but he had been gone from his own world for two months on a diplomatic mission.

He spent two days hunting in the thick forests of the planet before heading into the city complex. He did not suspect anything until after the meal, when he started to feel very lethargic. He only had time to send a message to his symbiot that he was in danger.

He woke, chained in a Curizan spaceship. That was a month ago. The Curizans hoped to ransom him back after they obtained information about the symbiotic relationship his people enjoyed with a living metal organism capable of changing shape and harnessing enormous power. The relationship allowed his people to enjoy many attributes, including longevity, the ability to heal at a faster rate, and unbelievable space travel.

Zoran was worried his symbiot would be captured and made sure it remained hidden until he could escape. He knew he would need it when the time came.

The Valdier lived on the outer rim of the Zion cluster of planets. Only in the past three hundred years had they developed a relationship with neighboring star systems. At first, the Valdier were very careful about who was allowed to visit.

They were very protective of the interaction of their species with the symbiot. It was not until other species tried to capture and use the golden metal organism, only to have the symbiot attack and kill whatever species tried to touch it, that the Valdier felt more comfortable interacting with other species.

This presented a problem, since there was not an abundance of females on Valdier, and the symbiot was not very tolerant of females from other species. It forced many males to limit their time with females who were not from their own planet.

Zoran had yet to find a mate, although he had many females who could pleasure him should he desire a companion at the palace. The symbiot could live separate from the host for brief periods. His own symbiot divided so a small part of it could find him in the prison cell, healing his body and giving him enough strength to survive the beatings and torture. The symbiot then returned to the main body to replenish it with his essence. If not for that, both would have perished.

Now, he felt the strength of it calling to him. He rounded a corner near the entrance. Two guards stood talking quietly back and forth in the tongue of the Curizan. Zoran pulled the laser pistol and quickly disposed of both of them. He could only hope there were no other guards outside the entrance.

Holding his ribs against the burning he felt, he swiped the guard's badge over the scanner and stood back as the door slid open. Peering outside, he moved into the shadows heading for the landing area.

His symbiot was waiting for him there in the form of a space fighter. It took on the reflective surface, making it invisible to all around it. It was only their connection that guided Zoran to it. Within moments, he was climbing into the cockpit of the Valdier fighter. With a wave of his hand, gold bands formed up his arms, sliding under his skin until he was one with the golden creature.

"Get us out of here," Zoran murmured softly, trying to hold onto consciousness. He was hurt much worse than he originally thought. He could feel the bones in his ribs rubbing against each other.

The symbiot glowed gold as it began rising out of the compound. Shouts and hisses erupted as the symbiot lost its cloak of invisibility. Moving smoothly, the golden fighter rose and moved out of the compound moving with blinding speed.

Zoran knew he needed to stay conscious until he could find a safe place to land and let his body heal. Warnings sounded in his mind as Curizan fighters scrambled to pursue him. Zoran was not concerned, knowing that as soon as they reached the outer orbit of the planet, his symbiot could move faster than the speed of light.

Focusing on using defensive moves to get away from the pursuing fighters, he commanded the symbiot to plot a course to a quadrant of the galaxy unknown to the Curizan. He would never make it back to his own world in the shape he was in.

He sent a message out to his brothers, hoping they would receive it before he lost consciousness. Zoran gave the final command to leap as soon as they cleared the planet's atmosphere. It was the last thing he remembered.

Chapter 2

Abby Tanner stared at the glass, seeing more in the hot glowing piece than molten liquid. As she began twirling the rod around and around she began forming different layers, bending and shaping them to match the image in her head. She loved how the shapeless glass transformed into a beautiful piece of art. She was also thankful she made a very good living from it. It gave her freedom that not many people could enjoy.

She worked with the piece for the next three hours, blending and blowing until a delicate flower formed. She was almost finished. The piece she was working on had taken her almost six months to finish. She had already sold it for over fifty thousand dollars. For her, though, it was not the money, but the enjoyment of creating something beautiful and enjoyed by others.

Abby looked up when she heard a dog bark. Smiling, she finished cleaning up her workshop. It was a fairly good size wooden barn not far from the cabin she lived in deep in the mountainous region of northern California.

Her grandparents had lived in the cabin before she was born. When her mother took off when she was a baby it became her home. Her mother died of a drug overdose when Abby was two, and she never knew her father. Her grandmother and grandfather had raised her. Her grandmother had passed away five years ago and her grandfather six months ago.

Abby still fought with the depression that overwhelmed her at times. Her grandparents were perfectly happy living in the remote mountain cabin. Abby grew up running through a wooded playground built just for her. She loved the freedom of the mountains and peace it gave her. At twenty-two, she had no desire to live in the nearby town of Shelby or the larger cities. It was bad enough when she left to attend a gallery opening of her work.

Brushing her dark brown hair that had fallen loose from her ponytail back behind her ears, Abby took another quick look around before closing the double doors to her workshop.

Laughing as the big golden retriever came running up to her, Abby bent down and gave Bo a big hug, trying to keep her mouth shut so she didn't get Bo's overeager tongue in it.

"He misses you," Edna Grey said as she walked down the little path following Bo.

Edna had her long, dark gray hair in a braid down her back today instead of up in a bun. She was dressed in a pair of well-worn jeans with a plaid button up shirt tucked in at the waist. Even though she was in her late sixties, she moved like a woman half her age. Abby couldn't help but smile as she saw the twinkle in Edna's light green eyes as she followed Bo.

Abby glanced up at Edna and smiled. She could only hope she looked as good as her friend did when she got older.

Abby knew she looked young even for her age. She gave credit for her appearance to her grandmother's side of the family. She had her grandmother's dark brown hair, dark blue eyes, and heart-shaped face. Her nose was a little on the short side while her lips were a little on the full. Abby often thought the combination made her look like a pouty little girl but her grandfather used to say it made her even more beautiful because he could always see her grandmother in her.

"I missed him too. Yes, you are just a big ole softy, aren't you? Yes, you are," Abby said as she stood up.

Bo jumped back and forth waiting for Abby to pick up the tennis ball he was carrying in his mouth. His long tail swept back and forth as he pranced around in circles barking. Abby picked up the wet tennis ball and threw it toward the cabin. Like a bullet, Bo raced after the slime green prize.

"So, how are you doing?" Edna asked softly, walking back toward the cabin with Abby.

Abby was quiet for a moment before she let out a deep breath. "I'm doing better. It was really hard at first losing Granddad, but each day I seem to be handling it a little better. It helps being busy. That big piece I was working on for the couple from New York is almost done."

Edna put her arm around Abby's waist, hugging her close. "I can't wait to see it. You've never been as secretive about any of your pieces as you have this one."

Abby laughed huskily. "It's one of the most beautiful pieces I've ever done. I can't wait for you to see it. When I was contracted to do the work I was a little hesitant. Normally, I just create based on what I feel is in the glass. This time my client wanted to meet me and asked me to create something based on their home décor. I spent two days as a guest in their house. It was unbelievable. It helped. I was contracted to do it right after Granddad died. Being focused on it has helped me cope with his passing."

"Is there any chance of you meeting a nice young man while you are going back and forth in all your travels?" Edna teased.

"No, absolutely not!" Abby said, horrified. "I like being alone. I've seen enough of men and their behaviors on my trips to make me leery of getting involved with anyone."

"What about Clay? You know he's interested," Edna asked.

Abby wrinkled up her nose in distaste. Clay was the local sheriff for the town of Shelby and had been trying to get Abby to go out with him since she was eighteen. He was a nice guy, but Abby just didn't feel the same way about him as he seemed to feel about her.

Abby made the weekly trip to town to mail the blown glass she sold to her distributors and pick up any items she needed, like groceries or supplies. And every week without fail, Clay would show up at the post office to ask her to go out with him. She would politely turn him down, and he would follow her around town bugging her to have a meal with him.

"Clay's a nice guy and all, but I just don't feel that way about him," Abby said, petting Bo and throwing the ball again.

"One day you'll meet the right man. Thank you again for keeping an eye on Gloria and Bo for me," Edna said as they walked up to the horse trailer attached to the back of her pickup truck.

"No problem. You know I enjoy their company when you take your little trips," Abby said with a laugh, watching as Gloria, Edna's old mule, tried to nudge her head out of the little window. Gloria loved the apples Abby always gave her.

"Well, you are the only one Gloria doesn't try to bite and push around." Edna opened the trailer and backed Gloria out. Bo danced around the old mule's feet trying to play.

"How long are you going to be gone?" Abby asked, pulling an apple out of the smock she wore over her shirt and jeans. "I hear there's a storm coming in tomorrow night that's supposed to be pretty bad." She held out the apple for Gloria, who swept it out of her hand crunching on it as Edna led her over to the small corral near the cabin.

"Yeah, I heard about it. We're supposed to get a couple of inches of rain and possible severe thunderstorms. I plan on heading out as soon as I leave here so I can miss it. I'll be back by the end of the week. Jack and Shelly are having Crystal's birthday party on Thursday. I'll drive back on Friday," Edna said as she let Gloria go with a swat to her flanks.

"Do you have time for a cup of tea or coffee?" Abby asked, watching as Gloria walked into the small barn attached to the corral. Abby had already put down a thick bed of hay for Gloria in one of the stalls and had fresh food and water.

"A cup of coffee would be great," Edna said, following Abby up the steps and into the small cabin.

Abby loved her small home. It had two bedrooms, each with its own bathroom, a small living room, and a combination dining room/kitchen. A huge fireplace dominated the living room, and small pellet stoves occupied each bedroom for the chilly winter months. Luckily, it was getting to be early summer, so except for an occasional cool night she wouldn't need to light either the stoves or the fireplace. The cabin had large windows in the kitchen and living room, which let in an abundance of natural light.

Abby's grandfather owned his own music business in Los Angeles, and her grandmother had been a songwriter. Both had been extremely talented. When Abby's mom fell in with the wrong crowd, they thought moving to the mountains would get her away from it.

Unfortunately, her mother ran away, instead, and at seventeen, she became pregnant with Abby. Abby had only been a month old when her mom dropped her off and disappeared. Two years later, she was found dead from a drug overdose along with her current boyfriend. Abby's grandparents were devastated by the death of their only daughter and did everything they could to make sure Abby was kept out of that type of life.

Abby had her grandmother's gentle personality and love for the arts. Her grandmother used the time in the mountains to write songs and taught herself the art of glass blowing. Soon, her grandfather had taken up the hobby, and it became another business with the help of the Internet. In the past six years, Abby had made a name for herself internationally with her beautiful creations.

Edna and Abby spent the next half hour catching up on Edna's family who lived in Sacramento and Abby's new contracts from several different museums asking to display her work. Bo was content to lie on the rug in front of the hearth watching his tennis ball.

Before long, Abby was watching the tail lights of Edna's pickup truck disappear down the steep driveway of her home. Abby called Bo to come back as he tried to follow Edna's truck, laughing as he looked back and forth, trying to decide who he wanted to stay with. A promise of a treat soon had him running back up the steps of the cabin and into the warm interior.

Chapter 3

Another bolt of lightning flashed, and then thunder rolled across the sky, shaking the cabin walls. The electricity had gone out over an hour ago, and Abby had lit a couple of candles to light the interior, although the way the lightning was flashing, she probably didn't need to.

Bo had taken refuge under the bed in her bedroom. Every once in a while she would hear him whine, and she would call out soft reas-surances to him. Gloria was tucked up in the barn nice and safe. Abby hoped there wouldn't be too much damage, but wasn't too optimistic from the sounds raging outside.

She did what she could to prepare. Rain fell in sheets limiting the view outside to just a few feet. It was going to be a long night. Abby sat at the small table, staring out the kitchen window when another bolt of lightning flashed. It was strange; but, she could have sworn there was something else in the thunder that followed. She caught a glimpse of something in the sky with that last flash.

Bo whined again, this time coming out from under the bed to put his head on Abby's knee. He still had his tennis ball in his mouth. Abby reached down and absently petted Bo's head, scratching behind his ears.

Sighing, Abby leaned over and dropped a soft kiss on the top of Bo's head, "Come on. Let's go to bed. Watching the storm isn't going to make it pass any faster, and I have a feeling there is going to be plenty of cleanup work to do tomorrow. Maybe we can find you a couple of sticks to carry back."

Abby stood up and blew out the candle on the table, then picked up the one in the living room to carry with her into the bedroom. She brushed out her hair and changed into a pair of pajama pants and matching tank top that had little pictures of dogs on it. She climbed into the full-size bed and scooted over, patting next to her for Bo to jump up.

"You can help keep me warm tonight, big guy," Abby whispered as she wrapped an arm around the soft fur snuggled up against her.

~

The next morning was bright, and she saw that the storm had cleared away everything in its path. Abby sipped a cup of coffee as she walked down the front steps of the cabin. There were bits of limbs every-where. A tree had fallen behind the barn, but it hadn't done any damage. Bo ran down the steps and raced around the yard smelling all the branches to see if the storm had brought anything fun to play with. Abby opened the door to the barn and moved to the stall holding Gloria. Gloria leaned her head over the door of the stall looking droopy-eyed at Abby.

"Did the storm keep you up last night, girl?" Abby asked as she ran her hand behind one of Gloria's ears, then down along her jaw. "Come on, let's get you outside to enjoy the beautiful weather."

Abby moved into the stall and opened the sliding door at the back of the stall, which led into the corral. After making sure everything was still secure, she picked up a brush and brushed Gloria before closing the gate.

"Come on Bo. Let's take a walk and see what else needs to be done," Abby called as she moved down the path to her workshop.

She would check it out before heading toward the meadow farther up the mountain, where she had seen the weird light last night. She had dreamed about it. She couldn't really remember much of her dream, just a nagging feeling that she needed to check it out.

Her workshop had survived the storm just fine. She was glad, since she had several thousand dollars' worth of materials inside, not to mention the piece she was almost finished with. Bo pranced around, wagging his tail and marking just about everything. Abby laughed at the male need to mark. It reminded her a little of Clay when he followed her around town glaring at anyone who looked her way.

Bo ran ahead down the path. Abby was a bit slower as she stopped to move some of the bigger branches out of her way. She liked to hike up to the meadow during the summers and just enjoy the scenery. She was lifting a really large branch to the side when she heard Bo barking excitedly.

"Hold on, boy. I'm coming," Abby yelled. She pushed the limb out of the way and jogged up the path.

Abby stopped suddenly, her mouth hanging open, as she stared at the huge golden ship in the middle of the meadow. Bo was walking around it. As he moved closer, the ship seemed to shudder and move away from him. It was almost like it was alive. Abby moved slowly toward the golden ship.

"Bo, come here, boy. I think you're scaring it," Abby said softly.

Bo took one more sniff of the golden ship before taking off on another adventure. Abby walked around the ship, watching as it shivered when she stepped closer to it. It wasn't very big, maybe about the size of a large SUV, but it was absolutely beautiful. She looked at the sleek design. Different colors swirled through the outer coating, making the golden ship almost invisible as it took on the colors around it.

Abby slowly reached out to touch the ship's surface. It shimmered a bright gold, almost as if in warning. It reminded Abby of some of the wildlife she had seen up in the mountains. She and her grandparents sometimes came across frightened or wounded animals over the years and they nursed many back to health before releasing them back to the wild.

"It's okay, baby. I'm not going to hurt you," Abby whispered softly. "It's going to be all right."

The golden ship shuddered again as she brushed her hand gently against its smooth surface. She laughed softly as she felt the smooth, soft metal. She didn't understand what it was or where it had come from, but she didn't get any bad vibes from it.

She let her other hand glide over the surface, as well. She rubbed it lightly while whispering nonsense words. She felt her hands slowly sink into the soft metal, and long strips of the gold reached out, winding themselves around her arms and wrists.

Abby's breath caught in her throat as she watched the gold bands slowly slide up her arms. When she pulled back, two thin, intricately designed gold bands were attached to her wrists like gold wrist cuffs. Abby stared at them, marveling at their beauty, as she ran her fingers over first one, then the other.

Bo's sudden barking turned to a scared yelp as he charged back toward Abby. Abby moved away from the ship looking up startled as Bo raced past her toward the path leading back to her cabin. Turning toward where Bo had come from, Abby wondered what other wonders the storm had brought.

"Well, what got your tennis balls stirred up?" Abby asked bemused.

She was still in a daze at finding something so beautiful on her mountain. A groan from the direction Bo had just run from caused Abby to take a step back.

~

Zoran groaned as he tried to lift his head. He didn't remember much about the landing. He knew he needed to get out; his body was on fire, but he didn't remember much but the fierce weather from the planet. He collapsed, unable to move, as the pain in his body overwhelmed him. He knew he needed to get back to his symbiot but didn't have the energy. He could only hope the message he sent out to his brothers would be received as darkness once again took him.

~

Abby bit her lip as she moved slowly toward the sound of the groan she had just heard. She really hoped this unexpected visit didn't turn out to be one of those horror-film/alien-possession things. She knew the golden ship was not from Earth. It didn't take a NASA scientist to figure that out. She just hoped curiosity didn't end up getting her killed.

Abby saw the figure lying face down on the damp grass. Well, if it was an alien, he sure had the figure of a human—a very big human. Abby wasn't a shrimp at five-foot-eight, but this guy had to be well over six and a half feet if he was an inch.

Moving hesitantly until she stood next to him, she saw he had long black hair and was wearing some type of uniform with black epaulets on the shoulders. She couldn't see what his face looked like because his hair was covering it. She stooped down and gently brushed back his hair, letting her fingers rest for a moment on his neck. She found a weak pulse. What worried her the most, however, was how hot his skin felt.

The gold on one of her wrists moved when she touched the man, turning to a liquid and pouring down her fingers until it wrapped around the man's throat. Abby was afraid at first that it meant to harm him, but then warmth flowed through her and she knew it wouldn't.

"I don't know what you are, but I don't get the feeling you want to hurt him either," Abby murmured under her breath. "Let's see what our man looks like and what we can do to help him out."

Abby ran her hands down the figure looking for any obvious signs of trauma before gently rolling him over onto his back. She drew in a deep breath. He was the most handsome man she had ever seen in her life. He was also the most beat-up man she had ever seen. How someone could hurt another being like this broke Abby's heart.

Blood spotted his uniform on both the front and the back, making it obvious that the uniform had been put on over the injuries since it was not cut up. His facial features were definitely human-like. Abby ran her fingers over his face, gently touching the cuts above his left eye and cheek before moving down to his lips. He had strong, proud features. His nose was a little broader than normal, and he had prominent cheekbones, much like the Native American Indians. His color was similar too with the darker tanned skin. She wondered what color his eyes would be—brown, blue, or almost black—but they were closed, and she did not want to force them open.

Abby checked him over to see if he had any broken bones. She worried about his ribs, since even in his unconscious state, he jerked when she probed them. She realized the only way she was going to be able to get him to the cabin was on a skid. She whistled for Bo to come to her. He had taken off toward the cabin earlier, but she had seen him sniffing around the meadow again a few minutes ago.

Bo wagged his tail as he came toward Abby, keeping his head down and his eyes nervously on the still figure next to her. "Come on, boy. I need you to be a guard dog and protect our visitor until I get back with Gloria," Abby said petting the golden retriever behind the ear.

"Stay," Abby commanded Bo and watched as he lay down next to the man, resting his head on the man's chest. "Good boy. Stay."

Abby took off at a run for her cabin. She would use the old skid she used to haul wood to bring the injured man back to the cabin. She quickly pulled out the harness gear and called Gloria over to her. She hooked up the skid behind Gloria and pulled some thick pads from the storage room of the barn and laid it on top of the skid.

With a click of her tongue, Abby and Gloria moved up the path again to the meadow. Gloria was a pro at this, since Edna would bring her several times a year for Abby to use. It was too cold most of the winter to keep a horse or a mule up this high in the mountains; plus, there was not enough pasture land, so it was a win-win situation for Abby to just borrow Gloria when she needed the extra help.

Abby jumped off the skid once they entered the meadow. The gold ship glimmered as Abby walked by with Gloria. Abby couldn't help but run her hand along the ship's surface again to caress it.

"It's going to be okay. I'm going to help him. Then you can have him back. He just needs some TLC. I won't hurt him," Abby said as her fingers glided from the tip of the ship to the very back. She could almost feel the ship's sigh of relief at her words.

Bo looked up from his place next to the man. After fifteen minutes of grunting and pushing, Abby finally had the man on the padded skid. She was breathing heavily and sweating from the exertion.

"Wow. He's a lot bigger and heavier than I thought," Abby said to no one in particular. She didn't know if the ship, Bo, or Gloria really gave a damn about how big and heavy the man was.

Abby made the short trip back to the cabin at a much slower pace, aware of how the man groaned with every rut she hit. She would have to use the ramp her grandfather had built for her grandmother to get him into the cabin. The skid was narrow enough to fit through the front door of the cabin thanks to the extra wide door her grandfather had installed after her grandmother needed to use a wheelchair to get around. It would be tricky getting him in the room and in the bed, but she felt sure she could do it with a little manipulation.

An hour later, totally exhausted, Abby lay on the bed next to the man. She had pushed, pulled, and tugged until she could barely move, but she had him in the bed. She gave herself a few minutes to regroup before sitting up. First things first, she needed to get his clothes off so she could see the damage. Then she would bathe him and doctor his cuts.

Abby didn't want to cut the man's clothes up, but she found it was going to be the only way to get them off. The cloth was stuck to his skin with dried blood in many places and was stretched across him like a second skin in others. She would go to town later and get him some clothes, once she knew it was safe to leave him. As she cut the shirt off him, Abby noticed the gold on the man's throat had moved down to his chest now. It just lay there curled up as if it was asleep.

Abby couldn't contain the tears that filled her eyes at the number of cuts and bruises on the poor man. She tried not to blush when she got to his pants. He wasn't wearing anything under them and was just as impressive there as he was everywhere else. Abby did her best to keep her touch impersonal and hoped the man wouldn't be offended when he woke up and realized she had taken such liberties.

His legs were covered with bruises as well as small cuts. It was as if he had been tortured. She gasped as she saw the deep cuts around his ankles. Her gaze flew to his wrists and, sure enough, he had deep cuts there as well. Whoever hurt the man had obviously had him shackled so he couldn't defend himself.

Abby threw the clothes into a pile. She would burn them later in the burn barrel behind the cabin. In the bathroom, she filled a bucket with lukewarm water. She needed to get his temperature down. She was afraid to give him any medication for a human, not knowing if it would hurt him. She hoped cleaning the wounds and bringing his temperature down would help.

She rolled him onto his side and laid a vinyl tablecloth down with the plastic face down so she wouldn't soak the mattress. She then laid several towels under him. She bathed his back first, just dampening his hair as best she could. She wouldn't be able to really wash it, but at least it would feel better than it had.

As she bathed him she was careful to make sure she paid close attention to his cuts. It was strange watching the small gold band moving over his body as she moved the man. It seemed to go to the worse cuts and bruises and stay there for a few moments before moving on. Once, it even came to her and wrapped around her wrist while the other gold wrist cuff dissolved and moved to replace it. Abby just shivered when she felt them move over her. It wasn't a bad feeling. In fact, it felt warm and fuzzy.

Abby turned even redder as she washed the man's private area. He was thickly built and long even in his relaxed state. She had never seen or touched a man before, and her hands shook as she gently cleaned him. She was thankful he was unconscious and would never know what she had done.

She tried to think what a nurse would do in such a situation. Hell, she knew even some cosmetologists worked with peoples' private areas. She tried to focus on the gold band moving up and over the man's body from one place to another. She watched in fascination as cuts began to heal right before her eyes wherever the gold band touched. Right now, it was working on his right wrist.

Once Abby was done, she removed the damp tablecloth and towels and covered the man with the thick quilt. She put him in her grandparents' old bedroom. The bed was a king size and seemed to fit him better than her full-size bed. She felt his forehead again, and it felt a little cooler. His complexion looked better as well.

She had enough time to put Gloria in the pen and make some dinner before dark. The electricity was still off, and she didn't want to run the generator any more than she had to. She could measure the man and order him some clothes from the Internet. Luckily, her laptop was fully charged, and she used satellite for her connection since no service ran this far up into the mountains.

An hour later, Abby closed the laptop, satisfied with her order. She had ordered several shirts and pairs of pants, boxers, socks, and after measuring his feet, which she found were ticklish, a pair of boots and a pair of tennis shoes. It wasn't easy finding both in a size eighteen wide. She stood up and stretched.

The gold bands had switched again, and she noticed the one on her left wrist seemed to be stroking her. Abby smiled as she gently rubbed the little gold band. She could tell it seemed to enjoy it when she did that.

She figured she would sleep in the big bed next to the man tonight. There was plenty of room for her skinny butt, and this way, if the gold bands needed to change they could. Plus, she just felt better staying close to him. At least until he woke up.

Chapter 4

Zoran stretched, waiting for the pain to slice through his body. He kept his eyes closed as he sent out his senses to determine what dangers might be close at hand. When he didn't feel the normal wrenching of pain, he froze. He could feel his symbiot moving around his body repairing the damage. Had he found shelter? He frowned; he couldn't remember. Had his brothers found him? He did not detect their presence.

He did a quick internal review. His ribs were healed, though still tender, and the numerous cuts and bruises were also healed. He felt clean, but he did not remember bathing. He also realized he was completely nude beneath a soft thick covering. He didn't recognize any of the scents around him as being from his home.

He let his senses expand to cover the room. He was alone in the room, but not in the structure. There were two other species in it with him. While he did not recognize the scents, they were vaguely familiar. He heard a soft, pleasant sound, a type of soft singing coming from the other room before he heard the sound of footsteps as they approached him.

Abby sang softly under her breath as she prepared a vegetable broth for her guest. She had been forcing the broth down his throat for the past two days, fearful of him becoming dehydrated or malnourished. The electricity had come back on late last night. She was thankful, since she needed to finish the piece she was working on, and it was just safer not using candles.

Pouring the broth into a deep bowl, she set it on the tray. She hoped her guest woke up soon. If he didn't wake up by tomorrow, she was going to have to call for the doctor to come look in on him. She went up to the meadow twice a day as well to pet and talk to the gold ship. She didn't know why, but she had a feeling it was worried about the man. She was rewarded with another gold bracelet, necklace, and earrings. At the rate she was going, she would be so loaded down, she wouldn't be able to walk.

Abby walked quietly into the bedroom. The mid-morning sun shone brightly through the large windows.

"Good morning, sleeping beauty. I've made you some more of that delicious broth you love so much. How about opening those gorgeous eyes and giving me a peek at who's sleeping his life away? Bo would love to have someone to play catch with, and your golden ship seems to be missing you as well." Abby kept up the running monologue she had started yesterday morning, thinking that if he heard someone's voice he might respond faster. The Internet said people in a coma could hear what people said, so maybe this hunk of a man could hear her.

Zoran frowned as the translator imbedded in his brain took a moment to learn and translate the words the creature spoke. He breathed in deeply to catch the creature's scent and was immediately hit by the fragrance of sunlight, woods, and wildflowers. His body jerked in response, his cock filling with need as the beast inside him responded to the female. His fingers clenched under the covers as he fought the overpowering reaction to the female's voice and scent.

He could tell she was not a Valdier. Her scent was wrong, but it was also right. He had never had such a powerful reaction to any of the females on his planet, or any other, for that matter.

He heard her set something on the table next to him before the bed sank down slightly from her weight. He bit back a groan as he felt her soft fingers slide through his hair and down along his face caressing him.

"Come on, fly boy. Don't you want to wake up? It's such a beautiful day outside. I need to go into town today, and I don't like leaving you alone when you are so defenseless." Abby enjoyed running her fingers through his long hair and along his jaw.

Suddenly, strong tan fingers wrapped around her fragile wrist and she was jerked over his body until she was lying on her back under a huge chest. Abby let out a squeal as she was flipped over the long, hard body of the male who moments before had been totally still and unresponsive. She lay still, staring up into dark gold eyes.

Abducting Abby

READ ON FOR MORE SAMPLES!

MAGIC, NEW WORLDS, AND EPIC LOVE...

CHOOSING RILEY

Riley St. Claire has always followed her own rules. When she discovers her current employer is not as law-abiding as she thought, she has to leave town in a hurry or end up buried with the dead guy she discovered. What she doesn't expect is to find herself being picked up by a passing trader from another world.

As the ruling King of Sarafin, Vox d'Rojah was expected to produce a son who would be joined in marriage with the first-born daughter of the King of Valdier. The problem was Vox had no intentions of having any sons, at least not in the near future. He was quite happy with the wide selection of females he had at his disposal. When he is captured by a ruthless Valdier royal and sold to a mining operation, the last thing he expected to find was his bride mate.

Vox isn't sure which would be easier: fighting another war with the Valdier or capturing and holding on to the human female who is unlike anyone he has ever encountered before.

Now, Vox has to escape back to his world while fighting pirates, traders, and Riley!

The King of Sarafin has met his match in Ms. Riley St. Claire from Earth. Now, he just needs to figure out a way to let her know he has chosen her as his Queen—and he has every intention of keeping her by his side forever.

Chapter 1

"Choose," the disembodied voice said.

Choose? Choose what? Riley thought, looking around her in disbelief at the rock walls. *Choose to get the fuck out of this crazy nightmare? Hell, yeah. Choose to kill the bastards who put me in this miserable spot? Oh, hell yeah. Choose...*

Riley jerked when she felt the ice-cold claw poke her in the back for the third time. Looking around, she followed the arm of the creature standing next to her as it pointed down over the edge of a small platform. She really was trying for that nice stage of being totally zoned out, but the damn creatures who kidnapped her twenty days before had an annoying habit of bringing her back to the unfortunate situation she was in.

"Choose," the nearly eight-foot-tall stick figure said again, this time losing some of the disembodied tone.

Riley couldn't help the little smirk that lifted the corner of her mouth. She really couldn't. After the first week of captivity, she had moved from being mind-numbingly terrified to just downright pissed off at life. She figured if she was going to die, she might as well do what she did best: piss everyone off around her. That was what had gotten her into this situation in the first place—her big mouth and smart-ass attitude.

Okay, maybe she shouldn't have pissed off her boss by telling him what he could do with his wandering hands when he grabbed her ass for the third time that day. Better yet, she shouldn't have broken his nose, his hand, and more than likely his nuts since he had been screaming more than an octave or two higher than a soprano. Yeah, that probably wasn't the smartest thing to do. Especially since his daddy happened to be the local sheriff. She was a bail bondsman, for heaven's sake. Any freaking idiot should have known better than to mess with her. Her line of work required she know a certain amount of self-defense.

God, she thought. *I really should have never taken that job.*

When her boss swore she would never leave town alive after she beat the shit out of him, she figured it was time to get the hell out of Righteous, New Mexico. Of course, the fact her boss owned the local bail bond company and had a somewhat lucrative business going with his daddy should have been her first warning that something wasn't right, she'd thought as she grabbed her purse and a large manila folder full of incriminating evidence against both of them. Finding out that daddy and junior were also running illegal weapons and drugs were definitely her second and third warnings.

Of course, the little tidbit of information she had found that morning about the dead guy buried under the storage unit had been the real reason she figured she had made a bad mistake. That information was now safely tucked into the manila folder stuffed in her purse, and it had gone along with her as she left the small town she had been living in for the past six months as fast as her old Ford could drive.

She actually might have had a chance to live a little longer if a series of life's usual little hiccups hadn't been blessed upon her. Again. Of course, if the car had been further than one push to the nearest junkyard it would have helped her great nonexistent getaway plans. It would have been better yet if the damn car hadn't broken down just over the state line on the outskirts of the desert. She knew she should have purchased a new one last month, but she was such a tightwad she wanted to get every last mile out of it. And boy, did she!

Oh, and she couldn't forget her best idea yet—getting in a truck with a guy who had more piercings and tattoos than a model for *Prick Magazine* instead of walking the three miles to the bar she had seen a roadside sign for.

No, I had to get my fat— Riley sighed. *No, my maturely figured ass into the scum-bucket's truck.*

Riley sighed again. *I really, really should have taken those anger management classes like my sainted sister, Tina, said I needed.*

Unable to keep the grin off her face, Riley thought back to the look on the pierced, tattooed guy's face when she shot him the bird as he drove off, leaving her in the middle of that godforsaken hell's beach just as it was getting dark.

Give him a fucking blow job if I wanted a ride out of the desert, Riley thought savagely. *Not bloody likely.*

She showed him! As soon as he pulled over to the side of the road, she had been out of the truck cussing him up one side and down the other. Her Grandma Pearl would have been proud of her. She remembered every cuss word her grandmother ever said and a few her grandma probably didn't even know. Of course, he had left her mature ass in the middle of nowhere.

Riley thought she was a goner until she had seen all those little lights coming toward her. How the hell was she supposed to know the fucking aliens had messed up where Area 51 was and ended up in Nowhere, Arizona? Riley had thought she was about to be rescued by a dwarf biker gang riding dirt bikes, not some alien spaceship out for a Monday night cruise for well-endowed women.

"*Choose!*" the tall creature growled out loudly.

Riley cleared her throat before turning to the stick-figured alien dwarfing her. "Choose what?" she asked, unable to hold back the slightly crazed giggle that had been threatening to escape her.

She giggled again at finally making the creature's blank face break into a frustrated scowl. The creature slowly fisted its clawed hands before its shoulders actually drooped.

"Choose a male," Antrox 785 said wearily.

Riley raised her perfectly arched eyebrows at the creature before turning to look at the selection of men who had been paraded in while she had been reflecting on how her attitude *might* have played a part in her present predicament. She had been watching haphazardly as a different female—at least she thought they were female—had been led to stand where she was now.

She was told—in a rather rude manner if you asked her—that she was being given the last choice because of her being so disagreeable, unpleasant, and downright ugly. She had, of course, taken it all in stride until the last comment and had to be restrained again after she'd punched the stickman guarding her in what she hoped was his balls. Whatever the creatures had under their tunics, it laid the guy out cold.

Now, she was staring at one eight-foot-tall glob of green, oozing snot, something resembling a two-foot, two-headed lizard, and three six-foot-four or more drop-dead gorgeous hunks. Riley's eyes widened. If it wasn't for the fact that she was thirstier than hell, so she didn't even have the capacity to produce enough spit, she would have sworn she was drooling.

She could tell by their build and their eyes and maybe the markings on their arms, chest, and shoulders, oh and did she mention their sharp teeth as they growled at the stick-alien, that they weren't human, but man-oh-man did they look yummy! Riley thought dreamily for a moment before perking up again.

"What happens to the males that aren't chosen?" Riley asked curiously, never taking her eyes off the three males.

"They will be used as food," Antrox said with a frown. "Choose! All mated males will be kept to work in the mines. Mated males are easier to control as they are protective of their female. Now choose your male!"

"What if I don't want to choose a male?" Riley asked sarcastically as she turned to face the tall creature next to her. "What if I don't *feel* like choosing a male? What if I don't even *like* males?" Riley added.

Right at that moment, she honestly believed she might not ever like any male ever again! After all, it was men who had started this whole hateful series of events starting with her no-good, dim-witted boss. Now, this overgrown toothpick expected her to just pick one of the bastards and mate with him?

That is so seriously not going to happen. Restraints or not, I will beat the shit out of any guy who tries to mate with me, she thought fiercely.

She wasn't going to mate with any alien, no matter how cute they looked. She had watched enough science fiction movies to cure her of ever wanting any alien booty! What if those things decided to do some body snatching or exploding out of her? A shudder went through Riley at the thought.

Antrox 785 looked back and forth between Riley and the men on the platform below him with a confused expression on his face. "Why would you not want to choose a male? You are female! All of our data points to you being the weaker of your species and in need of a male for protection." Antrox looked from the males back to Riley again. "Why would you not like males?"

Riley let loose a slightly hysterical laugh. Okay, maybe she was still just a little terrified. "Why don't I like males? Now, that is the sixty-four-thousand-dollar question, isn't it? How about we go get a bottle or two of your strongest booze, get good and drunk, and I'll tell you why I don't like males anymore!" Riley's voice was growing louder with each word. "Let's start with you!"

Vox looked up in surprise as he heard a husky feminine voice shouting. He growled low as he caught his first sight of the buxom female who had turned toward the Antrox male. He wanted her. He didn't understand why, but he wanted her—right now. His body instantly responded to her voice. He felt the primitive need to mate. To possess.

When he saw the face and body that went with the voice, it took everything in him not to struggle against the restraints holding him captive. She was curvy, with large breasts, a small waist, and hips that made his mouth water at the thought of holding on to them. Her hair was the color of their sun and flowed in thick waves down her back almost to her lush, rounded ass.

She is built for loving, he thought in awe as he watched her.

She was wearing a light pink top that molded to her lush curves. He couldn't see what she looked like below her waist, but he could imagine it. He wanted to see her eyes. He knew they would be flashing with fire, and he wanted that fire turned on him. He snarled as another guard joined in using the stunning rods to force him back away from the edge of the platform.

He jerked in surprise, and his eyes widened as the female, who was tiny compared to the larger male, started jabbing the Antrox male in his chest and yelling at him. Vox snarled again when one of the guards pushed him back harder with one of the long rods. He ignored the sting from the shock and focused on the female's hands, which were shackled in front of her.

Why would the Antrox shackle a female? Females were weak and to be protected. Vox had never heard of an Antrox male using shackles on one before. He listened in disbelief as the normally impassive species roared out in a loud, aggravated voice at the female.

～

"CHOOSE! Now, female, or I will choose for you!" Antrox 785 roared out.

He didn't know what else to do. He was in charge of the mining facility. It was not his job to question who was brought to the mines. His job was to match a female with a male to ensure the males would be more docile. He had never encountered a hostile female before and did not know how to handle a female like the one poking her sharp nails into his chest.

Riley looked at the stickman standing in front of her and let out a sniff of indignation. "Well! There is no reason for you to get so uptight!" she said, turning her back to him and tossing her heavy mane of blond hair over her shoulder. "I choose all of them," she said with an exaggerated sigh.

"What?" Antrox 785 practically shouted.

Riley turned to look at him and rolled her big, baby blue eyes. "I said, I will take all of them," she repeated slowly with a slight shake of her head showing she thought he was a dumbass.

"But...but..." Antrox 785 stuttered in confusion. He looked down at the five men looking up at him and then back at the female. "No, you must choose one."

"No, I don't have to choose just one. I choose all five," Riley said stubbornly. "Five or nothing!" she added with another determined shake to her heavy mane of hair.

"How can you have five males?" Antrox 785 asked in frustration. "All other females choose just one."

"Well, I am not all other females. I am Riley St. Claire from Denver, Colorado, and I choose five," Riley said with a stubborn tilt to her chin. "If you have a problem with that, you can just get over it. I've made up my mind, so there," she added with a raised eyebrow, daring him to tell her no.

She would have crossed her arms to show she meant business if they hadn't been tied together. Since she couldn't do that, she put her nose as high as it would go in the air and gave her best "that's my final answer" look. She even thrust one hip out to show she could not be intimidated into changing her mind. If she learned one thing while being a bail bondsman, it was that body language could be a very effective weapon.

Antrox 785 ground his gums together in frustration. Throwing up a hand to the guards below him, he signaled for them to take all the men to the cavern assigned to the female. With a jerk of his head, he motioned for the two guards standing back behind Riley to come forward.

"Take her to her living quarters where her mates are and bring me the trader who brought the female here," Antrox 785 said harshly.

One of the guards looked cautiously from Riley to Antrox 785 before replying. "The trader has already left, 785," Antrox 921 said.

Antrox 785 looked down at Riley, who was baring her teeth at him and snapping them together. He took a step away, curling his clawed fingers into the palm of his green hands. With a nod of his head, he watched as the two guards escorted Riley out of the choosing room. Antrox 785 had already decided if it had not been for the law preventing an Antrox from harming a female—any female—he would have gleefully fed the female to the pactors, the large creatures they used to pull the ore out of the mines, as food. Antrox 785 made a note to himself that the next time the trader came to the mines, he would not be leaving.

Chapter 2

Vox jerked at the collar around his neck and received another burning zap from it. He growled at the other males who watched him. He knew two out of the four.

Tor was his chief of engineering, and Lodar was his medical officer. They had both been with him when he left his warship, the *Shifter*, to purchase crystals at the Valdier spaceport. All three of them had been enjoying some refreshments when a Valdier warrior approached them and said one of the members of the royal house of Valdier wished to speak with them.

Vox vaguely wondered at the time if it was in reference to the tentative peace agreement they had established almost a hundred years before. As the ruling King of Sarafin, Vox d'Rojah, was expected to produce a son who would be joined in marriage with the first-born daughter of the King of Valdier. The problem was Vox had no intentions of having any sons, at least not in the near future. He was quite happy with the wide selection of females he had at his disposal.

They had sat down to drink with an older Valdier warrior named Raffvin. He said he had news for Vox that concerned the peace agreement between the two former warring species. He had already made up his mind to ignore whatever the old warrior was going to say.

The male had been pestering some of his councilmen to meet with him. He was annoyed the Valdier had not taken the hint he wasn't interested in meeting with him. As far as he was concerned, if he wasn't their leader, Zoran Reykill, or Zoran's brother Creon, he really didn't give a damn what the man had to say.

He had met Zoran Reykill off and on during their many years of war and respected the man for being a strong and fair warrior who fought with integrity and cared about his people. It was his friendship with the youngest royal, Creon, that had sealed the end of the war and produced a long and lasting alliance. Creon had saved his life during an assassination attempt by some of his own warriors aimed at igniting fury at the Valdier during the Great Wars.

The resulting friendship had led to a collaborative effort to discover who was behind the war. A small group from the elite royal houses of Valdier, Sarafin, and Curizan were discovered to be working together to bring down the current ruling class of each star system so they could gain power.

Vox was determined to cleanse his star system of those who would betray their own people. He had gone after them without mercy, whether they were male or female; to him, a traitor was a traitor. He knew it had affected Creon badly when he found out the female he was in love with, a Curizan princess, was one of those responsible for instigating the war.

They had discovered it almost too late to save their friend. Ha'ven, the ruling Curizan prince, had been kidnapped in a plot to implicate the Sarafin and Valdier and to gain important information about the location of the Curizan warships. Vox had discovered one of his warriors returning late one night after sneaking off. He and two of his brothers had confronted the man. They discovered he had met with Aria, Creon's lover. The warrior had been passing Sarafin information on to her. Vox had tortured every last piece of information from the man before he killed him and left his body on display in front of the palace for any others who thought to betray his trust.

He had approached Creon with the information he had discovered. At first, Creon had not believed him, but eventually he could not deny the evidence building up against Aria. They decided to set a trap for her. It had worked too well.

Only he, Creon, and Aria knew of their reported secret mission to transport a captured prisoner. When the mercenaries Aria hired showed up at the trap, they had killed all but the leader of the group. Creon had extracted the information from him. The man's dying words were of Aria's betrayal.

Later that night, Creon had the location of Ha'ven's prison, and Aria was dead. Vox never asked his friend how he got the information out of her; he knew what he would have done. They had found Ha'ven three days later in a mining asteroid not unlike the one he and his men were currently imprisoned in. Ha'ven had been tortured and was more dead than alive. It was a miracle he had survived as long as he had, considering what Aria's men had done to him.

Vox jerked back to the present when the door to the rooms he and the other men had been escorted to suddenly opened. He watched as three Antrox males entered. Two had long stunning rods, and the other had a strange-looking rectangular pink object on wheels. They were followed by the female he had seen earlier. She was talking to a fourth Antrox male who was following several steps behind her.

"Oh dear," she was saying as she looked around the room. "This place screams classic caveman! Fred and Wilma really outdid themselves this time. I'll have to be sure and send a thank you note for the lovely rock walls. Really, would it have hurt to have updated the décor by a few million years? I really am going to have to mark you down on Trip Advisor. This is simply too blasé considering today's fashions and travelers' expectations."

The Antrox male behind her was grinding his gums together as she continued to ramble on about the furniture, floors, ceiling, and everything else in the room. Vox's eyes followed the female as she tapped a slender finger on her chin when she stopped in the center of the room to look around once more. Heat filled him as her eyes swept by him. He wasn't sure at first if the heat was from irritation that her eyes kept moving by him as if he didn't even exist or his reaction to having her closer to him. One thing he did know, she was his and he wanted her now!

"Darling, can you put my luggage next to the bed? I hope you changed the sheets. I absolutely refuse to sleep on someone else's dirty linens. Oh, Sticky-pooh, be a sweetheart and take off these adorable bracelets. As much as I like them, they really do clash with my outfit and totally say 'prison inmate' all over them," the female said, walking up to the Antrox who was standing next to the one placing her suitcase next to the bed.

She smiled up at him and innocently fluttered her eyelashes. Instead of making the tall Antrox feel better, he actually took a hesitant step backward, looking at the male behind her for guidance. The one who had carried the strange large pink box looked relieved that she was focusing on someone other than him.

Vox's blood heated to boiling when he saw her beautiful face glow in amusement as she watched the way the Antrox moved nervously around her. Her plump pink lips parted to show off smooth, even white teeth, and a small indent appeared on her cheek. He had never thought smooth-edged teeth were sexy before, but he decided right then and there he loved the way they looked on her.

The Antrox behind her nodded once to the other male and stepped back another step. The Antrox lowered his stunning rod and held out the key to the locking device. He motioned for the female to extend her hands in front of her. She did with a wide-eyed look and a nibble to her lower lip. Vox's eyes followed the movement, and he almost groaned out loud as his cock swelled to a level of pain he had never encountered before.

The female gently rubbed her wrists and wiggled her little nose. "I hope you aren't expecting a tip," she said with a dismissive wave of her hand. "Because I have to say, I am not sure of the hospitality yet, much less the rest of the accommodations," she added as she put her hands on her hips and tapped her booted foot.

"We must leave," Antrox 264 said from behind her. "You will keep your mates calm and satisfied. They will be working the first shift so you may be near them."

"Whatever," the female said with a casual shrug. "I want clean towels brought in daily, and I'll need a line of rope and several blankets delivered immediately."

Antrox 264 nodded at the other guards to move toward the entrance to the cell. "Why do you need these items? They are not budgeted for workers."

The female turned and glared at 264 through narrowed eyes, causing him to jerk backward another step. "Darling, put it in your budget unless you want me upset. You won't like me when I am upset, do you understand? I am *not* a nice person when I am upset," she said, taking a menacing step toward him with her eyes glittering with fury and determination. "Now go get me what I requested! Chop, chop!" she growled out with a snap of her fingers, causing all four guards to jump and hurry out.

Riley drew in a deep, calming breath to steady her nerves in preparation to meet her five new 'mates'. She was shaking like a leaf on the inside, but she had learned a long, long time ago not to let it show. She put her hands back on her hips, drew in another deep, steady breath, and tossed her heavy mane of blond hair over her shoulder before turning around to face the five males again.

At five feet ten inches tall, she was a big woman. When you added in the fact that she was a solid size sixteen on a good day with double-D cup breasts, she was Xena on steroids. She had learned to live with her big-boned stature a long time ago.

She didn't have much choice since she practically towered over everyone she'd ever met between the ages of four and eighteen while she was growing up. She had reached puberty early and had to live through all the Amazon and she-giant jokes that any sensitive young girl would have had to endure. Only, other sensitive young girls didn't have Grandma Pearl raising them.

Grandma Pearl showed Riley how to punch anyone who made fun of her in the nose. When the fourth school's social worker threatened Pearl that Children's Services would take Riley and Tina away from her, Pearl showed Riley how to use her mouth as the weapon of choice after that. Riley had excelled at that much better than she had the physical forms of retaliation. Over the years she had plenty of opportunity to perfect her talent, as her grandma called it.

Releasing the breath she had been holding, Riley smiled brilliantly at the five alien males staring at her. "Well, boys, it looks like Auntie Riley is going to have to set some ground rules while we are together," she said, looking at each one of the males carefully to assess how she was going to handle them.

Alien number one was about three and a half feet tall, had two heads, and looked like a combination of a lizard and ET. He was cute in his own special way. Each head had large, black eyes that moved nervously back and forth between her and the other four men. He was a dark green with areas of tan, black, and red on him running in long lines down his body. He was wearing a small leather vest and cloth, plaid-colored pants with child-size boots to match. He must have decided she posed less of a threat than the other males because he emitted a weak squeak and scurried for a corner of the room. She also decided he looked like a "Fred."

Her eyes moved to the next alien creature. He—she was assuming it was a he, since the Stickman called him one—was almost eight feet tall. He towered over all of them, including the other three males standing next to him, but he just wasn't all that scary.

He reminded Riley of the big tub of Jell-O in the movie *Monsters vs. Aliens*. He was green instead of blue, but he had "Bob" written all over his wiggling body. He even left a light liquid that she hoped wasn't radioactive or anything behind him.

He appeared to be wearing some type of robe over most of his body. She didn't even want to think what might be under it. It was his eyes that gave her the feeling he wouldn't hurt her. They were big, round, and the color of peach gumdrops with tiny black pupils in the center.

He was emitting a low humming noise that struck her as if he was terrified. She wasn't sure what he was so scared of. So far, she felt like everything was going pretty damn good considering she had been kidnapped by aliens. At least Daddy and Dudley Dip-shit back in New Mexico couldn't find her here.

Her eyes finally moved over the last three males. She felt like she needed an old fashioned fan like the women in the movies used to fan themselves to keep cool, because she could definitely feel the heat increase when she looked at them. The first one was hot!

He had his long hair pulled back at the nape of his neck. It was a long, golden blond with different shades coursing through it. He had patterns on his chest and left arm that looked like spots and was wearing a black vest, black pants, and black boots. Against his lighter color they really stood out. His dark golden brown eyes remained focused on her as she assessed him. He looked more curious about her than "interested." Riley was thankful for that because she had a feeling that her mouth and her one physical ability to bop someone on the nose wouldn't stop him for long if he decided to sink those sharp teeth of his into her.

Alien number four was the same height as the first one. She figured based on her own height they were probably about six feet four inches or so. It should have been nice to finally meet some guys she actually had to look up to except for the fact they were aliens!

Alien number four was looking at her with the same curiosity as number three had. He had more of a reddish-brown-colored hair and a darker tan. His hair was short and had stripes of darker reds and browns running through it. His eyes were a light greenish-tan color with specks of dark green in them.

He was dressed in the same type of clothing as the other guy. Riley assumed it must be a uniform of some sort. It was kind of like a biker outfit that the guys back home dressed up in on Sundays when they put their three-piece suits up for the weekend. Only she got the feeling these guys dressed like this all the time, and this wasn't a costume to just look bad for a day. She got the impression from all the muscles on the guys that they were bad all the time.

Her impression proved correct when she finally looked at alien number five. She had avoided looking at him in the hope he was somehow less intense than the first time she saw him standing on the platform in the "Choosing" room. If she thought he was hot from a distance, he was scorching up close!

It took everything inside Riley not to reach out and touch him just to see if he burnt her fingers. Thankfully, Grandma Pearl's wonderful teachings saved her from that impulsive behavior. Pearl drilled into both her and Tina not to play with fire. Ever! Pearl explained that fire came in many different forms and most of them had two legs, one head that hung between them, and no brains to speak of. Riley thought her grandmother was like that because she and her daughter, Riley and Tina's mom, had been left to fend on their own after the loves of their lives got them pregnant and left town.

It didn't take long for her to realize it happened to others, as well. Pearl pointed out to Riley and Tina just how often when their friends or just girls that lived in their neighborhood would ignore the signs. One by one, Riley saw the girls in her neighborhood fall for the "bad" boy only to be left at the first sign of another pretty face in the neighborhood, more often than not, with a baby to raise on their own.

Riley decided at twelve that she was not going to be one of those girls. Of course, that was also the same time that the dirty old man who ran the grocery store on the corner propositioned her. No, she was going to have a ring on her finger before she said yes to anything. She wasn't going to get stuck raising a kid on her own like her grandma had or her mom would have if she would have stuck around. As far as Riley was concerned, the guy could put up or shut up.

It's funny, in a way, Riley thought. *That's about the only thing Tina and I ever agreed on without ending up in a major yelling match first.*

Riley looked back at the huge male glaring at her. *Alien number five is not just screaming bad-to-the-bone, but he has an international market on it,* Riley thought before a giggle escaped her. *Make that an intergalactic market,* she corrected silently as she saw his face darken at her laugh.

He was the same height as the other two, but seemed taller for some reason. Either way, he still towered over her by almost six inches. His black hair was cut short, almost military style. His upper chest was visible through the same black vest the other two were wearing.

He had darker spots across his chest that looked almost like a leopard's, not that she had ever seen a real leopard before. Riley let her eyes roam down the eye candy, appreciating the tight fit of his... Her eyes widened when she saw the very distinctive bulge in the front of his pants. Her eyes flew up to his in surprise, and she fought to draw in a breath.

Somebody is horny, she thought in dismay, staring into the intense, burning tawny eyes.

"Okay," Riley said, rubbing her hands together. "First rule. That is your side of the cave and this is mine. You stay on your side, and you remain in one piece. You come on my side, and I cut your dicks off and feed them to you for breakfast," she said with a small smile and raised eyebrows. "I claim dibs on the bathroom for exactly thirty minutes every morning, and one hour every night, alone," she added as she turned and walked over to where her suitcase had been dropped next to the bed.

She bent over to unzip one of the side pockets. A low, rumbling growl behind her had her reaching in quickly to grab the item she had been hoping to retrieve since she had first been taken. Her hand wrapped around the small, leather-covered device with a relieved sigh. She turned just as the huge male took a step toward where she was bent over. She looked up into the glittering eyes and swore silently. It looked like she was going to have to prove she would follow through on her instructions.

"Get back on your side of the room. *Now!*" Riley growled out, clutching the small device in her hand. "You stay! Bad alien. You are not to come on this side of the room!" she said fiercely, pointing her finger to the side where the other males stood.

"You are mine!" The huge male growled out as he took another menacing step toward her. "I claim you."

Riley's temper flared at his outrageous claim. "Last warning. Get your ass back on your side of the room, or I'll do it for you," she snarled back, straightening to her full height.

Vox grinned, showing off his pearly white sharp teeth. "I'd like to see you try," he smirked, taking another step toward her until he was within arm's reach of the female he knew was his mate.

Choosing Riley

THE DRAGON'S TREASURE

Choose your treasure carefully, thief...

Drago, King of the Isle of Dragons, is the last of the magnificent dragons of the Seven Kingdoms. Bitter and alone, he abandons the emptiness of his realm and retreats to the caverns beneath the palace. In the form of his dragon, he remains hidden from the world, protecting the Dragon's Heart, the last legacy of his people – until he is disturbed by a most unlikely thief.

Carly Tate's trip to Yachats State Park takes an unexpected turn when she is caught in a sudden storm. Seeking shelter, she stumbles through a magical doorway into a cavern filled with treasure! Yet, as incredible as the piles of glittering gold and jewels are, her gaze is transfixed by the slumbering form of a magnificent dragon.

Carly's appearance begins a series of events that will not only change Drago's life, but will affect all of the Seven Kingdoms. Can a centuries-old dragon protect his most valuable treasure, or will the evil that destroyed his race take Carly from him as well?

In the Beginning...

Long, long ago, peace reigned over the Isles of the Seven Kingdoms. Each kingdom: the Isles of the Dragon, Sea Serpent, Magic, Giants, Elements, Pirates, and Monsters were ruled by seven powerful leaders who watched over their realms. Each ruler was given a gift by the Goddess who created their world; a gift that promised harmony among the kingdoms as long as these gifts were kept safe and not used against each other. The rulers were fair and just, and understood their kingdoms needed each other to flourish.

Alas, the peace was not to last. One night a strange and brilliant light fell from the sky and landed in the ocean. Those who saw the meteor streak through the dark skies made lighthearted wishes. One young sea witch saw the falling star and swam out to sea to catch it. She was unaware that something dark and evil lived within its core – a darkness that would slowly overpower her and threaten the very fabric of the Seven Kingdoms.

Prologue: The End of the Great Battle

"Return to the isle, I will join you soon," Drago ordered.

"Drago, do you think it safe?" Theron asked, glancing across the waves at the man who had emerged from the inky blackness.

Drago released a growl of warning. His second-in-command tilted his wings and fell back, increasing the distance between them. Five dragons, all members of his elite guard, hovered close by. The three males and two females kept a wary eye on the water below them. Even with a dragon's eyesight, they could see nothing within the growing darkness of the storm clouds around them or through the turbulence of the waves.

"Return now," Drago ordered.

"Yes, my king," Theron reluctantly agreed, rising higher and issuing a sharp order to the other guards.

Drago kept his gaze locked on Orion. The Sea King gazed back at him with the same intense expression on his face. The large sea dragon that Orion rode shook its head, feeling the tension between the two men.

"Orion," Drago growled.

"I come asking for a truce, dragon. You are the last of the kingdoms. The others agreed to peace," Orion stated.

Drago snorted, small puffs of smoke swirled from his nostrils and blew away in the gathering wind, floating toward Orion. The sea dragon jerked in alarm. A smile of satisfaction curved Drago's lips when he saw Orion fight for control of the huge sea dragon. The sharp, angry glare Orion shot him told Drago that the Sea King was well aware that he had frightened the sea dragon on purpose.

"What brings on this sudden desire for peace?" Drago asked in a mocking tone.

Orion's mouth tightened in irritation. "It was all lies," he replied.

"What were lies?" Drago demanded.

"I had no desire for your treasure nor to steal the Dragon's Heart, Drago. The Isle of the Sea Serpent has its own treasures. We do not need the enchanted gold and jewels of the dragons and I know better than to try to steal the gift of the Goddess," Orion said.

Drago snapped his teeth. "You claim that, yet I've captured your men who swear just the opposite. You also blamed the dragons for scorching your fields above the sea. None of my people attacked your kingdom and still they lie at the bottom of the ocean while their mates and children cry in sorrow," he retorted.

"I know, but I swear on the Trident that those who you captured are under a curse of dark magic, forced to do deeds they would never have done otherwise. I also swear that it was not my people who struck the dragons from the sky. They... Drago, they lay as statues, turned to stone by a spell I have never seen before," Orion replied, his voice barely audible above the sound of the wind and waves.

"You swear? Then who did such dark magic? The only ones with such power are those from the Isle of Magic," Drago demanded.

Orion hesitated and looked out over the sea before returning his gaze to Drago. Drago could see the regret in the other king's eyes. He could also see the sincerity.

"Nay, it was not the Isle of Magic, it was my cousin Magna," Orion finally said.

"The Sea Witch?" Drago asked.

"Yes, something has happened to her. I have banished her, but I fear that is not enough. Her magic grows more powerful and must be stopped once and for all. It was her lies and treachery that started the wars between the kingdoms. She cast a spell – there is a darkness within her unlike anything I have ever seen before, Drago. It is unnatural. The more we fight each other, the stronger it grows. The only way to defeat the spell is to work together," Orion said.

"I sensed the darkness in her when she came to me for asylum. I should have killed her then, but instead gave my word to protect her from you when she said you had gone mad. Know this, Orion, if I find her first, all the water in the ocean and her black magic will not save her from the fire of my dragon," Drago swore.

"I hope it will not come to that. Do you accept the truce, Drago? I pledge to do everything I can to bring justice for the hideous deeds Magna has done," Orion said in a solemn tone.

"Yes, Sea King, I have no desire to continue the battle – especially one that fuels the dark magic of the Sea Witch. There has been enough death and destruction. I accept your truce, Sea King, but be warned – the Sea Witch will pay for her treachery if our paths ever cross," Drago said, tilting his wings so the winds could lift him higher.

"I understand. Go in peace, Dragon King," Orion replied.

Drago watched Orion pull on the reins of his sea dragon. The beast eagerly turned and dipped its head. Within seconds, all that was visible was the turbulent sea. Lightning flashed, cutting across the sky, followed by the rolling sound of thunder.

Turning, Drago thought about what Orion had said – a truce, the end of the Great Battle. Peace had finally come to the Seven Kingdoms again, but not before there had been great suffering caused by one woman's greed for power. Rage burned deep inside Drago. He had meant what he'd said to Orion – he would show no mercy to the Sea Witch.

As king of the Isle of the Dragon and ruler over all dragons, it was his duty to keep his people safe. When the Sea Witch had washed up on the shores of the Isle of the Dragon, he had believed her lies. Her body had been shrunken and pale. She had sworn to him that her cousin had gone mad. Her claims that Orion wanted to steal the dragon's hoard of treasure to finance his bid to take over the Isle of the Dragons had sounded foolish until raiders from the sea were captured. They had all said the same thing.

Next, had come the attacks against the dragons flying to other kingdoms. Many had disappeared, having fallen to their deaths into the deep abyss beneath the ocean that separated each kingdom, including his own parents. The Sea Witch, Magna, had whispered into Drago's ear that it wouldn't have happened if only he had the stones of the Trident. If he did, then not only would he control those beneath the waves, he would also have a treasure of unimaginable power.

Drago understood the dangers of controlling an artifact that was not from his realm – to do so could tear the delicate threads of magic holding the Seven Kingdoms together. There was a reason why dragons could not control the trident, just as there was a reason that the people of the sea could not steal the Dragon's Heart. The sacred stones controlled the very essence of each species – water and fire. Each kingdom had an ancient artifact.

His father had groomed him to always take into consideration the far-reaching consequences of his decisions. What good was it to have such a powerful treasure if the world no longer existed? Magna's quiet whispers finally became too much and he had threatened to drop her back into the sea and let Orion deal with her if she did not stop. She had disappeared the next day.

With a loud sigh, Drago soared along the water as fast as his wings could carry him. His body rose and fell with the building waves. Storm clouds swirled high above, and the rumble of thunder and the static feel of the electricity building in the atmosphere warned of the severe gale about to strike.

Drago and his guards had been conducting one last patrol of the waters surrounding the island before the storm hit when he had seen Orion. A quick scan of the sky warned him that the squall was likely to turn into a full-fledged cyclone. As if to confirm his thoughts, icy spears of driving rain began to fall in thick, blinding sheets.

Drago was several kilometers away when he heard the first cry for help from his people. Confusion swept through him when more and more cries of terror rang out. Fighting against the savage winds, an uncharacteristic fear drove him onward, pushing him at a reckless pace to reach his home. The fear wasn't for himself, but for his people.

The anguished cries of his people resonated inside his head. His confusion grew when the sounds of their piercing screams suddenly began to fade.

Drago's blood boiled inside him. He snapped his tail like a whip, shattering the sound barrier with its speed, and the crack echoed through the air like lightning. He had been betrayed – but, not by Orion. Something else was attacking his people – something alien to their world.

The cries of the other dragons pierced his soul, making his struggle to reach them seem painfully ineffective. As each voice grew silent, a sense of panic began to wash over him. When there was nothing but a black void where his connection to the other dragons had once been, the panic engulfed him completely.

"No!" Drago roared out, spying the Isle of the Dragon through the rain.

In the distance, he could see a figure on the rocky cliff turning to look at him in triumph – the Sea Witch! Her black hair swirled around her pale form. Dark threads of sorcery radiated outward from her fingers. Drago saw Theron and two other members of his elite guard flying toward her. The dark threads pierced them. Drago watched in disbelief as their bodies stiffened, turning to stone. As if in slow motion, each dragon fell from the sky. Two of the dragons tumbled into the sea and disappeared beneath the waves. Theron's form crashed to the ground, tumbling over before coming to a stand-still – the fire from his dragon frozen for eternity just centimeters from the Sea Witch.

"They are gone, Drago. You are all alone. Give me the Dragon's

Heart and I will give you back your weak, pathetic people," the Sea Witch whispered, her words carried to him on the wind by magic.

"Never! Die, Witch!" Drago roared.

"I will have it when you are gone. A dragon cannot survive alone for long. Not even your precious treasure will keep you alive," she retorted with a mocking smile.

Infuriated, Drago released a powerful ball of white dragon fire. The Sea Witch's mad laughter rose above the sound of the storm as she dove from the cliff into the waves below, disappearing into the dark depths surrounding the island. The dragon fire exploded against the cliff, sending an avalanche of super-heated rock into the sea below and scorching Theron's frozen form.

Drago scanned the edges of the cliffs. The still figures of his people stared back at him. Their faces forever etched in expressions of horror. All Drago could see was his failure to protect them.

He glided over the edge of the cliff. His powerful wings folded and he dropped down next to Theron and shifted to his two-legged form. He raised a trembling hand to touch his friend and comrade. Grief unlike anything he had ever known surged through him, encasing his heart as if in the same stone that had transformed his people. Tilting his head back, Drago released a roar of rage that spread across the Seven Kingdoms. Each ruler sensed the void and knew that while the Great Battle between them was over, a far deadlier war was about to begin. Fear reached out, wrapping its greedy hands around the hearts and souls of the other inhabitants, then the world stilled when the sound of Drago's roar faded to a deafening silence.

Several days later, Drago stepped back to survey his work. He had all of his people that he could find inside their homes to protect them from the elements. Those that lived and worked in the castle, he had moved to inside the great hall.

He turned his gaze to the figure nearest him. Theron stared back at him. He raised his hand and ran it over the black streak along the side of the dragon's neck in remorse.

He paused and closed his eyes as the familiar, agonizing shaft of pain ripped through him again. For a moment, he wished it was powerful enough to strike him dead. The pain, emptiness, and feelings of helplessness and remorse were almost more than he could endure.

All of his attempts to locate the Sea Witch through magic had been fruitless. It was as if she no longer existed. Without knowing how she was able to transform his people to stone, there was no way of reversing it. There was nothing else that could be done. Not even the Dragon's Heart had the power to break such a spell – he knew because he had tried to use it. Drawing in a deep breath, he opened his eyes and stiffened his shoulders in determination. One day, the Sea Witch would resurface and when she did, he would be ready. Until then, he would protect those that could not protect themselves.

Drago turned and walked through the doorway of the great hall, shutting the massive doors behind him. He uttered a spell to lock the doors of the room before striding through the double doors leading outside. With a whisper, he cast a spell to enchant the castle. He would do the same for the entire Isle of the Dragon. No one would be able to set foot on the island – not even those of the magical realm. It was a spell no others knew. Those unlucky enough to make their way to the shores would perish, trapped between the high cliffs and the water.

Shifting, he launched himself up into the air. He circled the isle five times, re-enforcing the spell until the mists grew thick and heavy. Only when he was satisfied did he return to the castle. Landing on the top tower, he scanned the isle one last time. This would be the last time he would see it.

Drago blinked and turned his gaze to the ground. Pushing off of the turret, he swept downward. A moment before he impacted with the hard surface of the courtyard, the ground opened and he disappeared inside. The chasm was nearly thirty meters deep and as he shot through, the opening sealed behind him. He curved his body, swooping down the elaborate stone staircases and through the arched doorways to the massive cavern below. In the deepest chamber, he swept over the sea of treasure until he landed on a mountain of gold coins and jewels. His body slid down the avalanche of treasure to where a large platform towered.

Drago stepped up the stairs to the top. With a swipe of his tail, he brushed off the coins and jewels that had fallen onto the stone platform before turning in a circle and lying down. His gaze swept over the immense wealth of the dragons. In the distance, he could see the replicas of his father and mother. They had been the first to disappear, shortly before the Great Battle had begun. They had traveled to the Isle of the Monsters to see Nali. Their loss had hit him and the other dragons hard.

"I let you down, Father, but I will not give up," Drago vowed, gazing at the statue of his sire. "I have nothing left to protect but the Dragon's Heart that you hold. I will guard it until the very end."

Drago lowered his head, closed his eyes in grief, and as the silence grew, began the task of guarding the treasure of his people. Soon, hours passed into days, and days passed into weeks. The weeks blended into years, and the years faded into the chasm of emptiness that grew inside Drago. He eventually grew tired, sleeping more as his loneliness and the magic he needed to use to keep his body strong began to take its toll on him. He briefly woke when a slight disturbance shook the isle. The ground trembled beneath him, but he did not sense another's presence and he soon fell back to sleep.

The Dragon's Heart glowed brightly, shimmering as if the Goddess was aware that the last of the dragons was in danger of perishing. Drago was unaware of the huge blood-red diamond rising from its resting place between the claws of his father's statue. Lost in the realm of his dreams, he slept as a nearby passage slowly opened to another world.

Chapter 1

Carly Tate hummed to the music playing on the radio as she slowed to a stop at the front entrance to Yachats State Park. Today was the day! She was taking control of her life. In reality, today was actually the third day of 'Today was the Day'. She was going to start exercising, lose some weight, focus on getting a better job, and perhaps even think about moving out of Yachats, Oregon. Heck, she might even consider moving to Portland or Seattle.

"One baby step at a time," she said out loud, repeating her new mantra.

She just needed to concentrate on staying focused, which was not something that she was especially good at. Luckily, her roommate and best friend, since forever, loved her just the way she was – most of the time. Poor Jenny had the best shoulders to cry on, and only went a little nuts when Carly went to pieces after she chose to date the wrong kind of guys – like Ross Galloway.

"How many?" the ranger asked in a slightly bored tone.

"Just me," Carly replied, handing him her state park pass.

"Be careful along the trails; it looks like we have a storm coming. Park closes at sunset. Please park in designated areas only and don't feed any wildlife," the ranger said, handing back her pass, along with a map, and the parking pass for her car dash.

"Thank you," Carly responded.

She decided it was probably best not to tell the ranger that they had had this same conversation the last three days in a row. This would make her fourth trip in as many days. She now had a nice stack of maps littering her passenger seat.

Accelerating, she followed the winding road. The same old feelings started to choke her the farther she drove. She reached over and turned up the music just as she had done for the last three days, hoping it would kick her adrenaline into gear and not her imagination.

Tall redwoods and other evergreens lined the narrow, winding road. Green moss grew on the rocks, making them slippery, and lush ferns rose up past her hips. Carly knew exactly how slippery the moss was and how high the ferns were because yesterday when she'd reached the top of the path, she had stepped up on a rock for a "Rocky movie moment" and had promptly – and very inelegantly – landed on her ass in the middle of some ferns.

Carly was not a graceful athlete. In fact, just using the word athlete and her name in the same sentence was enough to qualify to go on the Comedy Central Standup Comedian circuit. She had decided the day before that she had a better chance of becoming a mega-star comedian than she did losing the weight she wanted and hiking the full length of the trail without killing herself in the process. Still, she had sworn to Jenny – her very athletic best friend – that she was going to do this even if it killed her.

"Unfortunately, it just might," Carly muttered when she shifted in the driver's seat of her dark red Ford Focus and felt the bruises and protesting muscles from her fall the day before.

She was still muttering under her breath when she pulled into the parking spot near the entrance to a hiking trail and turned off the ignition. She hadn't tried this trail yet. Picking up one of the maps from the pile, she glanced at it and wrinkled her nose before releasing a low groan.

"Four miles," she moaned, leaning her forehead against the steering wheel. "You can do this, Carly. It's only four miles. It will be a walk in the park." A snort escaped her at the pun. "Okay, you do this and you can treat yourself to a small ice cream at the Dairy Queen on the way home, how's that for a reward?"

Leaning back in the seat, she bent over and picked up the small backpack from the floorboard and shoved the map inside. Opening the door, she slid out with another loud groan before glancing around to make sure no one else could see or hear her. She turned, slammed the door shut, and pocketed her car keys.

"Ice cream. Remember the ice cream," she mumbled under her breath as she forced her aching muscles into motion.

She stepped onto the trail and pulled the denim and leather backpack onto her shoulders. Gripping the straps, she started down the uneven path. "Ice cream..." she muttered with each of the first two hundred and seventy-one steps before she started focusing on other more important things – like hungry bears, mountain lions, and Big Foot.

~

Nearly two and a half miles later and barely half way into her hike, Carly was in a foul temper. She had fallen – again – when the large iced coffee she'd drunk earlier flooded her bladder and made stopping for a pit stop an urgent priority. Since there were no restrooms along the trail, she had been forced to find a bush to water.

Of course, there was no flat ground to be found. The only options available were a rock wall to climb up or a steep slope to climb down. Her protesting muscles and lack of coordination, plus the fact there was nothing to hide behind if she climbed up, meant she was left with no alternative but to navigate the steep drop off. She had made it but not without a few slips and slides. The seat of her jeans and her knees were covered in damp, cold mud which added to the misery of her aching body.

Fortunately, she had discovered a small stream of water coming out of the rocks a little further up the trail to clean up a little. The icy water had given her an opportunity to wash the dirt off of her hands and refresh herself. Of course, now her fingers were frozen.

Think positive, Carly. At least you're not still completely filthy, she thought ruefully as she continued to trudge up the trail.

Carly couldn't help but think that if all of her earlier misadventures hadn't been enough to convince her that she should have just gone to the gym, the unpredictable Oregon weather should have been the final decision maker. The dropping temperature and the rolling, thick clouds told her that she was an idiot for being a miser and letting her embarrassment get the best of her. Those two concerns had kept her from going to the local gym – money and Ross – and not necessarily in that order.

She had been reluctant to purchase the annual membership until she knew she was going to stick with her exercise plan. She had bought the membership once a couple of years ago – and never went. Of course, she was older and more mature now which should have meant she was more disciplined – only Carly knew herself well enough when it came to exercise to know that she wasn't. If she had thought more about it, she should have just purchased the monthly contract, but it would have cost her five dollars more each month, which in a year would have been a whopping sixty dollars more than the yearly membership.

The real reason she didn't go to the gym, though, was because of her reluctance to run into Ross Galloway. Ross put the bad in 'bad boy'. Jenny had warned her, but Carly had been all goo-goo eyed when Ross had shown up in his faded jeans, ratty t-shirt, black leather jacket, and his devil-may-care attitude down at the local bar near the waterfront. She really knew better than to date a guy she met at the bar. She had known better than to date Ross Galloway – hell, he had been bad in high school! Still, she had been feeling pretty mellow after her first beer when he had asked her out – not something that happened all that often. He also went to the gym – the only one in town.

By the fourth date, Carly had realized her mistake and called Jenny to come pick her up. Granted, it hadn't all been Ross's fault. She hadn't meant to release the fishing net on his boat. It had been an accident. Also, he had been the one who had wanted a smoke! It wasn't like she had dropped the match on purpose. You'd think if the guy owned a boat, he'd know if there were flammable items on board.

Carly looked up when a fat raindrop landed on her cheek. Almost in tears, she focused on the trail in front of her when another drop hit her on the end of her nose. Lightning flashed across the sky, followed by an earth-shaking roll of thunder.

"Really? You think I'm enjoying this so much you wanted to add to the fun? You could have waited, you know. I'm almost half way back. Just another hour… or two," Carly argued with the sky. She was rewarded with three more large drops and a heavy mist approaching at a rapid clip. "Great! Thank you so very much… not! I hope you are having fun because I have to tell you that this really sucks big time. I HATE EXERCISING!"

Of course, arguing with the sky wasn't something most sane people did, but it made Carly feel a little bit better. She cringed when a bolt of lightning struck close enough that she thought her hair was standing on end. Okay, maybe the sky gods were listening and they were not entertained by her yelling at them.

Picking up speed, Carly tried to half walk, half jog along the uneven trail. She smothered a cry when another bolt of lightning struck. Didn't the weather know that it was just supposed to rain, not have a full-fledged electrical storm? She should have checked the weather forecast before she got out of her car.

"Shouldn't the ranger have insisted that no one go hiking? He frigging knew there was a storm coming. Isn't it his duty to help protect idiots like me from themselves?" Carly cursed under her breath.

She jolted to a stop when a small group of rocks tumbled onto the trail ahead of her. Then the rain started coming down in thicker sheets, drenching her. She pulled the hood of her jacket up over her head, cursing again when it caught on her backpack. She needed to find a safe place to weather the storm. A loud cracking sound made her look up. Her eyes widened in horror when she saw a leaning tree sway dangerously toward her. Small rocks rained down around her, hitting her shoulders.

Carly jumped closer to the rock face and was surprised when she noticed a dark crevice running vertically from the ground to almost a half meter over her head that appeared to be a very narrow entrance to a cave. Perhaps her luck was changing. It might not be the local hotel, but it was better than getting struck by lightning or crushed by falling trees and rocks.

Carly squeezed into the narrow crack in the rock face and released a frustrated groan. Why couldn't the stupid opening be just a few centimeters wider? It wasn't until she was halfway in the crevice that the sudden image of horrible, scary bugs flared in her mind. She really hoped there weren't any spiders, snakes, or other creepy crawly things in the dark recesses.

A flash of lightning and the crackle in the air had her frantically sucking in her stomach so she could slip inside. Of course, she became stuck. Wiggling back and forth, she added a few loud curses to go with the new bruises she was adding to her collection before she popped through the opening into inky blackness.

She turned and grabbed a branch just outside the opening; then wildly waved the damp branch around, hoping against hope that it was enough to chase off any of the nasty gremlins and their sticky webs that might be lurking near the entrance. The rain picked up even more, pouring down the side of the mountain until the entrance looked more like the back of a waterfall. Carly hiccupped in the dark.

"This is why I hate to exercise," she groaned with a shiver.

Turning away from the wall of water, she absently waved the branch with her left hand while she reached for her cell phone with her right. She tried sliding it to unlock the screen and cursed loudly when it didn't work. She slid the thin branch between her dirty, jean-clad knees and used her right index finger to open the flashlight option on her cell phone. Slowly shining the light along the walls and floor, she looked around the narrow cave.

"I told Jenny this would be the death of me. Archaeologists are going to find my mummified body a thousand years from now and say 'Yep, this is a perfect example of Darwin in action'," she muttered in her best 'learned scientist' voice. She stared at the walls with growing dread, certain that she could see them moving with all kinds of deadly bugs determined to suck her dry. "Forget being mummified. I'm going to be picked clean to the bone!" She took a breath, then her lips quirked up. "I guess that is one way to lose some weight."

Jenny Ackerly, her best friend and roommate, had laughed earlier this morning when Carly had dramatically foretold her own death by exercise. Well, Jenny wouldn't be laughing when Carly went missing.

Carly vowed she would come back from the dead just to point out to Jenny that hiking was not for everyone. Of course, she would also have to admit that Jenny was right. After all, Jenny had been the one to point out that Carly sucked at exercising and would be better off – and much safer – to just buy the gym membership.

"Okay, it wasn't really a hike, so much as a stroll, but it still counts," Carly told the dark walls in defiance. "The state should have put up better signs and they need to hire rangers who tell you that you're stupid if you ignore them when they say a storm is coming."

Carly tilted her head when she thought she caught a glimpse of light coming from the back of the cave. Her mind swept through all the possibilities. What if there was a serial killer waiting for her, or a vampire, or a... she slammed the door shut on her wild, out of control imagination when the sudden vision of the walking dead appeared in her mind. Drawing in a shaky breath, she swore she would never attend Horror Night at the local college ever again.

"Or horror movies," Carly whispered, her hand beginning to shake. "No more Saturday night horror movie marathons. God! Why did I have to go on an alien binge this last weekend?"

Swallowing, Carly felt herself drawn to the warmth and light coming from the back of the cave like a bug to a bug zapper. Unable to resist, she stepped closer on trembling legs. The walls and floor of the cave were smoothing out the farther she walked.

Turning the corner, she stopped in surprise when she saw the light was coming from a glowing torch in a sconce attached to the wall. Further down the passage, she saw an arched doorway. It reminded her of old castles, like the one out of the Dracula movie she had watched the night before.

"Carly, you really, really need to get a better taste in movies!" she growled to herself in annoyance. "Romantic comedies are good. Animated cartoons are even better."

She released a long breath and glanced down at the phone in her hand. She didn't need the flashlight anymore. Swiping her finger across the screen, she turned it off. There was no sense in wasting the power on her phone now that she had the light of the torch. Plus, she needed to conserve the power so she could call the ranger and admit that she needed help – a lot of it.

Fascinated by the beauty of the elaborately carved stone that formed the walls and floor, she soon became lost in the twists and turns as she followed the passageway. A magnificently carved entrance held her spellbound. The pillars were carved into the shape of dragons.

"Oh, oh, oh! I love dragons!" Carly breathed, hurrying forward to run her hands over the beautiful sculptures.

Her mind swirled in awe. If there had been any way she could slip the huge dragons into her backpack, she would have done it in a heartbeat. Her bedroom was covered in dragon figurines and medieval castles. Carly lovingly ran her hands over the rough stone belly of one of the dragons.

"Wow! This is just... Wow! Who would have thought to put something like this here? I've never seen this part of the park before, that's for sure!" she breathed out in excitement.

Turning her head, she gazed through the entrance, expecting an amusement ride attendant to be greeting her. Since when did the state parks get into the theme park business? Hell, how could they have built this without her knowing anything about it? She worked at the bank, for crying out loud. If anything happened in town, the first place to learn about it was at Barb's Hair-n-Care; the second place was at the walk-in clinic; and the third was at Bank of the West where she worked. All gossip went through those three venues.

Carly's hand flew to her mouth to hide her gasp when she stepped through a curved archway into the massive chamber. Rivers and mountains of gold and jewels glimmered in the faint light. She didn't know if they were real or not. They looked like it, but she wasn't an expert.

Despite the beauty of the glittering treasure, the gold wasn't what caught and held her attention. No, her attention was caught by the truly magnificent form half buried at the bottom of the mountain of gold and jewels.

The statue of a brilliant, midnight black dragon lay curled up in sleep. The unbelievable detail of the creature held her mesmerized. If there was one major thing Carly had a weakness for, it was dragons. She absolutely adored the mythical creatures. She had collected them, painted them, and dreamed of them ever since she could remember. She was so bad about it that Jenny liked to tease her. Jenny often said that the only way she would ever find a man she could love was if he was part dragon. Carly completely agreed.

She swallowed and slowly descended the steps. Her feet slid and she wobbled, trying to keep her balance when the pile of gold shifted. In the back of her mind, she wondered if she was dreaming or had died and gone to her own version of heaven. If so, she was ready to move in.

"It sure beats the hell out of being mummified or gnawed on by bugs like a starving dog at a barbecue," she observed.

Halfway down, she fell. The pile of coins shifted under her and she was pulled down to the bottom of the mountain. Her eyes widened and she leaned back a little to try to keep from tumbling over. Digging in her heels, she braced them against the base of the half buried platform, stopping her descent. Carly lay stunned for a moment, staring up at the dragon curled in peaceful slumber.

He's so beautiful, she thought in awe.

Her eyes glowed with delight as she ran her gaze over the silky scales covering his head. His brow was high, with two large ridges curving around his eyes. Thick, long lashes lay against the smooth, black scales like twin crescent moons. A series of ridges ran down his face to the narrow tip that made up his nose.

He looked… real. She knew it was impossible, but he looked like he was warm and soft. Standing up, she bent forward and climbed up onto the steps. She had to use her hands to help steady herself against the loose debris scattered across the steps. Once she was at the top of the platform, she stood for a second, just staring at the creature in fascination.

Carly rubbed her right hand along her damp jeans before lifting it to run her fingers gently along one of the ridges of his brow. She gasped softly when she felt the warmth of the dragon's scales beneath her touch. Shock coursed through her when the dragon's eyelashes rose to reveal dark, sapphire blue eyes with a glitter of gold sparkling in them. She swayed when she felt more than heard a strangely accented voice whisper.

"Choose your treasure carefully, thief," the soft, honey-rich voice stated.

Her hand fell to her side and she stumbled back a step in shock when the dragon's mouth moved as he spoke. Carly decided she must have died in the storm after all. Her trembling legs refused to support her. She sank down onto the pile of coins. Her lips parted, her gaze lifting to maintain eye contact when the dragon raised his massive head.

Carly fell back when the dragon stretched his neck in her direction. She could feel his warm breath sweep over her. A soft moan escaped her, echoing in the large cavern. The warm air of his breath surrounded her, melting the bone-chilling cold that had encased her body from her rain-dampened clothing.

Carly raised her hand as the dark head drew nearer. She tenderly ran her fingers along one nostril, tracing the outline in gentle exploration. She didn't notice his long, sharp teeth. Her gaze was focused on where her fingers followed the vivid contours of a scale. The warmth of his breath heated her blood with strength and hope instead of fear.

Licking her suddenly dry lips, Carly slowly rose to her feet again. She lifted her head to gaze into the brilliant eyes of the dragon watching her with an intense expression. She didn't think, she just whispered the first words that came to her mind.

"Can I choose you?" she asked in a barely audible voice.

The Dragon's Treasure

MERRICK'S MAIDEN

Merrick Ta'Duran is the powerful leader of the Eastern Mountain Clan on the Prime world of Baade, and he feels the weight of responsibility as the males within his clan become desperate to find mates among the few remaining females. When word comes that a new species has been discovered, he knows he must do what is right for his people - even if it means traveling to a strange, alien realm to do it.

While on Earth, he is injured and captured by a ruthless group of humans. Drugged and held against his will, he is the subject of experiments and testing as the humans try to discover where he came from and duplicate his strength and ability to heal quickly. After months of captivity, he fears his life will end on the strange world – until one chance encounter gives him hope.

Addie Banks' world has been one of silence since a devastating illness when she was sixteen. Determined to stand on her own two feet, she goes to school during the day and works at night to put herself through college. It's during her shift at Keiser Research that she stumbles across something she wasn't supposed to see. Now, she hears a voice in her head - and it is driving her crazy. Her only hope for peace is to help the creature talking to her escape from the men holding him.

~

Merrick jerked awake and rolled. He barely made it to the toilet before the contents of his stomach emptied. He didn't know what they had pumped into him this time, but he could feel his body rejecting it. Heaving, he gripped the bars until the nausea passed.

Several minutes later, he slowly straightened. With a softly muttered curse, he released the bars and stepped over to the sink. He twisted the knob for the cold water. Bending, he washed his mouth out before washing his face. It took several minutes before he felt slightly better.

Standing back straight, he rolled his shoulders. The chains around his wrists rattled as he pushed his hair back from his face. The faint memories of hands on his body sent a ripple of distaste and rage through him. His stomach churned again, but this time for a different reason. He turned back to the bed and stripped the thin cover off of the mattress. Tearing a strip from it, he dampened it and quickly wiped his body down to get rid of the feel of Dr. Rockman's hands on it.

He closed his eyes as his hands slipped under the waistband of the thin, cotton pants he wore. He cleaned himself as thoroughly as he could before tossing the cloth against the bars in fury. Throwing his head back, he bit back the loud roar that threatened to escape him. He would not give the guards the satisfaction of knowing how violated he felt.

His eyes moved to the door when he heard the sound of footsteps outside it. The lights were off in the room, but the darkness did not bother his vision. Moving to the side of the cage so the thick corner sections of it partially concealed him, he waited as the sound of the lock disengaging echoed in the cold room. Perhaps he would get the chance to kill another one of the guards.

A cold smile curved his lips as the door opened and the light came on. His eyes narrowed when the door opened wider and he saw a slender figure backing into it. Long blonde hair, piled into a messy ponytail, hung down the back of what had to be a female. He couldn't see her face, yet. She appeared to be trying to pull a large cart into the room.

Amusement and curiosity reluctantly tugged at his lips when a low, muttered curse escaped her when the cart became stuck in the opening. He watched as the figure straightened and groaned as her gloved hands moved to her lower back. She rubbed it as if she was in pain.

A tired sigh escaped her this time and she leaned forward to grab something off the cart. He stiffened until he realized that she had turned to the counter. His eyes followed her as she sprayed foam on the countertop before wiping it down. She did the same to the cabinets and sink.

A soft growl escaped him when she bent over and opened the trash can to pull the bag out. The movement pulled the black cloth trousers she was wearing tight over her ass. Merrick frowned in annoyance. First, because he didn't understand why his body was reacting to the female with such an unexpected intensity. The second reason was because he knew she must have heard the sound that escaped him, but she continued to clean the room as if he wasn't there.

He watched as she pulled a long stick out of a yellow bucket. She pressed the strings until most of the water was removed before she started cleaning the floor. A frown creased his brow when he noticed she still hadn't turned around to look at the cage. The need to see what her face looked like was beginning to grow to an irritating, but persistent ache.

The frown darkened as she tiredly brushed her cheek against her shoulder. It was obvious from her demeanor that she either had no idea he was there, or she was pretending. He rattled the chain on his arm against the metal bar to draw her attention. His brow furrowed suspiciously when she still didn't turn around.

It must be another test, he thought as the murderous rage he had felt earlier swept through him.

Dr. Rockman had tried to 'research' his mating habits once before. She had a drugged-up woman brought in two months ago at the previous place they kept him. The foul smelling female had taken one look at him, licked her lips, and run her eyes over him as if she had been given something sweet to eat.

The look of desire on her face hadn't lasted long once he proved he wasn't interested. Her screams and wretched cries for help had echoed once she came close enough for him to wrap his hands around her neck. He would never mate with such a female, no matter how desperate he might become.

He continued to follow the movements of the woman as she ran the mop from side to side. He tugged on the chains holding him. Frustration burned through him when he realized that he couldn't reach through the bars far enough to grab her. She would have to actually be against them before he would be able to touch her.

All thoughts flew from his mind when she suddenly turned until she was facing him. A soft squeak escaped her and her eyes widened in shock when she saw that she wasn't alone. Dark green eyes stared back at him in surprise before it was replaced with confusion as she noted the bars and the shackles around his wrists.

A low, menacing snarl escaped him when her eyes returned to his. His own glittering gaze captured and held hers for several long seconds as they both assessed the other. It took him half that time to realize that the feeling of rage had been replaced with another emotion. An emotion that he wasn't quite sure how to describe.

He impatiently waited for her to speak. The frown marring his brow deepened when the silence dragged on as they continued to stare at each other. He finally released a frustrated grunt when she blinked in slow motion, as if she wasn't sure if he was real or not.

Merrick watched the female's face as a multitude of emotions swept over it. Surprise, confusion, uncertainty, and finally, curiosity glittered in the expressive green depths. Another jolt of unease ran through him as he felt himself being pulled into their brilliant depths. He tightly clenched the bars in aggravation knowing that he would never be able to reach the woman from this distance. His lip curled in warning as a figure suddenly appeared in the hallway behind her.

"Hey! What are you doing in here?" A voice demanded angrily behind her.

Merrick's eyes flickered from her to the guard called Crawford before moving back to her. He watched as she turned to look at the man in confusion. Her eyes flickered back and forth between him and the guard. A low growl of warning escaped him when Crawford pulled the cart out of the doorway and caught the door before it could close.

The female stumbled backwards away from the guard when he pushed the door hard enough that it banged against the wall. Her foot caught in the tangled strands of the mop and she lost her balance, falling against the bars of his cage.

Triumph filled him as he wound his fingers into her hair, pulling her close enough for him to wrap the fingers of his other hand around her neck. The triumph quickly changed to surprise when an electrical shock flashed through his fingers the moment he touched her skin. It was so unexpected that he jerked back, releasing her.

"Damn it," Crawford snapped, reaching out and grabbing the female by her forearm and jerking her away from the bars. "Get the fuck out of here!"

Merrick slammed into the bars at the woman's cry of pain when the guard roughly pulled her away. He hit his fists against the bars again and flashed his teeth, which had elongated, at the guard when he continued to push her toward the door. An overwhelming need to capture and protect the female swept through him.

"Holy shit!" Crawford whispered, stumbling backwards after the woman who was staring at Merrick with a combination of horror, confusion, and fear. "They didn't say nothing about you being a Vampire."

Merrick's eyes glowed with silver flames and he knew his face was distorted into a mask of rage as he stared at the woman who was holding her left hand protectively against her chest. Her eyes widened even more when she saw his eyes glowing with a fierce possessiveness at her before the contact between them was broken. Crawford jerked open the door and pushed the female through it before pulling it closed behind him.

Merrick struck the metal bars again. Stepping back, he stared at the door in disbelief and confusion. His eyes slowly lowered to his clenched fist while his mind swirled with a barrage of unexpected thoughts. Uncurling his fingers, he stared down at the delicate pattern forming in the center of his palm. The intricate patterns seemed to mock his earlier thoughts.

I have to escape, he thought with a growing determination as he clenched his fist and raised it to his chest. His eyes moved to the door. *I have a mate.*

~

Addie stared at the guard with a combination of fear and confusion. She absently rubbed at her arm where he had grabbed her. She knew she would have bruises from his fingers.

She didn't understand what had just happened or why there was a guy locked up in the exam room she was cleaning. Her eyes flickered to the door, then back to the guard. She stumbled backwards when he turned furiously on her and shook his head.

"You don't go in there!" he ordered, pointing to the door in aggravation before he looked back at her. "You didn't see anything, do you understand? Nothing! They will kill you if they knew you saw him."

Addie's eyes widened when he pointed his fingers at his eyes and shook his head vehemently at her. She slowly nodded her head. Raising a trembling finger to the corner of her eye, then down to her lips, she slowly shook her head.

~

Crawford released the breath he had been holding. He had caught a glimpse of the cart in the hallway video monitor and rushed downstairs. Fortunately, Josh had changed places with Ted for a scheduled break. Josh would have reported the incident immediately and shit would've hit the fan, or worse.

I would've been dealing with another dead body, he thought in growing aggravation.

Ted didn't know what was going on. He just nodded when Bradley told him to stay put at the upstairs desk until he got back. Now, Bradley turned back to glare at the frightened green eyes staring at him. In the back of his mind, he knew he should report what he had seen, but he wouldn't. Reporting that the new girl assigned to housekeeping had seen whatever in the hell the creature was in the other room would've opened a shitload of other questions.

This wasn't what he had signed on for when he accepted the fucking job as a security guard. Drawing in a deep breath, he released it. Pulling a pen and a piece of paper out of his front shirt pocket, he quickly scribbled down a note for Addie.

He waited as she tentatively reached for it. Her eyes stayed locked with his for several long seconds before she dropped it to the paper in her hand. She frowned and bit her lip as she read the brief line.

Say nothing and you won't get hurt. Understand?!

He nodded his head at the cart when she raised her head and looked at him again. A frown darkened his features when she jerked back against the wall as he reached out and snatched the paper out of her hand. He crumpled it up, scowling in frustration when she slid along the wall before hurrying to push the cart back down toward the elevators.

"I fucking *hate* this job," he muttered as he followed her.

Addie breathed a sigh of relief as she pushed the door to the building open and exited it. She glanced over her shoulder where the guard from earlier stood watching her. He had followed her as she returned the cleaning cart to the janitorial closet before escorting her to the exit.

Focusing on her car, she hurried over to where it was parked. Her fingers were trembling so badly it took her three tries before she could press the unlock button on the remote. It was only when she was safely locked inside that she stopped to think about what she had seen.

It had been almost two-thirty in the morning when she went into the exam room. That had been the last level of the night that she needed to clean before she could go home. She had been so tired that she was running on autopilot. It had taken everything in her to just lift the mop. Since every other room had been empty, she had assumed that one would be as well.

Sighing again, she shook her head and started the engine. She didn't understand what was going on. After the first moment of surprise, she had thought it was someone participating in a test group. She had just finished a class where several of the students had signed up to be in one study group or another to earn extra money. It might have made sense if Crawford hadn't written that note. *Say nothing and you won't get hurt.*

Why would anyone want to hurt her for what she had seen? The guy had been chained, as well as, caged. Why? Had she just imagined that his teeth had grown longer, like a Vampire? What was going on with his eyes, too? They had been a strange color and glowed?

This is not what I need right now in my life, Addie groaned to herself even as she waved her hand to Ted as he raised the gate for her. *I just want to finish my degrees and open my own business.*

Addie glanced back and forth before turning onto the deserted street. Biting her lip, she couldn't help remembering the furious expression in the man's eyes as he stared back at her. A shiver escaped her when she remembered the shock she had felt when he first touched her. Rubbing the palm of her left hand on the steering wheel cover, another shiver wracked her body at how sensitive it felt.

I hope life doesn't get any crazier than this, she thought as she turned onto the freeway.

∾

Forty minutes later, Addie pushed opened the door to her small, one bedroom apartment and tossed her car keys onto the narrow entrance table. Turning, she quickly locked the four deadbolts. Whoever had lived here before had been extremely paranoid. It was either that, or they had a lock fetish. Either way, she decided it wouldn't hurt to use them since they were available.

Ted had re-keyed all the locks for her the day she moved in. That was the good thing about having a Locksmith-slash-security guard as your next door neighbor, she decided. Addie kicked off her tennis shoes by the table and walked into the narrow sitting room.

She didn't bother turning on a light. She always left the one over the stove on. Since the apartment was so small, that one light practically lit the entire thing. Opening the refrigerator, she rubbed her left palm along her pant leg as it itched again. She was thirsty, but didn't want the water, orange juice, or milk on the shelf.

With a grunt, she reached into the door and grabbed the wine cooler that Pam had left last weekend. Tonight was a good night to have something with a little kick to it. Shutting the door, she turned and leaned against it while she used her shirt to twist off the metal cap.

The cold glass felt good against her itching palm. Raising it to her lips, she drank almost a quarter of the Strawberry Daiquiri flavored liquor. Lowering the bottle, she leaned her head back and closed her eyes for a moment.

"Why? Why do they have him chained? Who is he?" Addie whispered out loud.

Even though she couldn't hear the words in her ears, knowing that she could still speak helped ward off the feeling of not being whole sometimes. One of her teachers at the School for the Deaf had shown her how to measure the volume by the force of air she expended in her diaphragm.

According to her teachers, the fact that she lost her hearing at sixteen helped with her understanding of speech patterns and enunciations, making it easier for her to speak in a clear voice. The fact that she didn't speak often was because people tended to think she could hear them. Often times, they would turn away from her when they replied and she hated having to ask them to repeat themselves.

Opening her eyes, she pushed herself away from the refrigerator door and walked into the sitting room. She turned, and half fell-half lowered, herself onto the flowered sofa. Her eyes flickered to the street lights outside. The light looked as if it was dancing because of the wind and trees that lined the front of the apartment building. The nice thing about being on the third floor was that she didn't have to close the blinds most of the time.

"Why?" she asked again, switching the wine cooler to her right hand so she could rub her palm against her leg again.

Addie growled in frustration when the itching got worse. Turning her palm up, she glanced down at it in irritation when the slight sensation of burning and itching continued. Her eyes widened in surprise when she noticed something in the middle of it. Setting the wine cooler on the coffee table, she leaned to the side and turned on the table lamp next to the couch.

Holding her palm under the light, she frowned when she saw a circular design in the center of it. Pushing herself up off the couch, she walked back into the kitchen and opened the drawer where she threw everything that she didn't know what to do with. She pushed aside the manuals to the coffee maker, the scissors that she had been looking for the day before, and a variety of other items before she wrapped her fingers around the small magnifying glass in the back of it.

Closing the drawer, she returned to the couch and balanced her palm on the edge of the armrest. Using the magnify glass, she peered at the mark. Her lips parted in amazement when she saw that inside the circle were what looked like symbols of some sort.

"What the...?" she breathed, blinking to make sure she wasn't seeing things.

Frowning, she stood up again. This time, she headed for the tiny bathroom. Flicking on the light, she walked over to the pedestal sink and turned the water on. Grabbing the bar of soap and her fingernail brush, she began scrubbing at the mark on her hand.

The growl she emitted turned to a startled yelp and the soap and fingernail brush dropped with a rattle to the bottom of the sink when a voice suddenly resounded in her head. A voice that was definitely not hers! Staring up at the mirror in shock, Addie stared at her reflection. Dark green eyes, pale pink lips, a small nose covered with a light dusting of freckles, and a slightly dimpled chin framed by a mass of long, blonde hair gazed back at her.

What... What is a bond mate? She thought back to the voice.

You are my bond mate. It means you belong to me! Tell me your name, the distinctly male voice demanded.

Addie felt a sudden, strange light-headedness cloud her mind. The dizziness threatened to send her to her shaking knees. Gripping the edge of the sink, she sank down onto the toilet, thankful that the lid was down for once. Breathing deeply to keep from fainting, she forced her swirling mind to go blank.

Merrick leaned back on the bed in his narrow cell. The fatigue and anger that had consumed him for the past months still burned inside him, but so did another emotion. He stared at the palm of his hand with a sense of amazement and wonder. He had found his mate.

His eyes flickered to the door when it opened. The corner of his lip pulled up into a sneer. Crawford glanced at him and blanched. The man was nervous as he stepped into the room.

Merrick kept his eyes on the male as he closed the door. He didn't get up off the bed. Instead, he waited to see what the male wanted. A low oath escaped Crawford and he stunk with fear.

"Listen...," Crawford began before he stopped to clear his throat. "I know... I think... Hell, can you understand me?"

Merrick watched the nervous twitch at the corner of Crawford's right eye. The smell of the man and his body's reaction were not something the human could fake. He debated whether he should respond. This was the first time that this human had approached him alone and he was curious as to what he wanted. Merrick finally inclined his head in acknowledgement of the question.

"What happened tonight...," Crawford paused and drew in a deep breath again. "Listen, you can't tell anyone about the girl coming in here. The docs... I don't know what the others might do to her. It is bad enough as it is. I don't want to be responsible for any more deaths. Hell, I just want to get out of this mess in one piece! I didn't know that they... who these people were... I just needed a job after I got out of the Army. My girl is pregnant and I needed to earn some money to support us. Shit, this is all a fucking mess."

Merrick watched as the man cursed under his breath again and ran his hand over the back of his neck. Crawford shot him another look of frustration and worry before he turned on his heel and walked back to the door. Merrick knew he was taking a chance, but it might be the only one he got.

"Release me," Merrick ordered in a low voice.

Merrick watched as Crawford's hand froze on the doorknob and he slowly turned around to face him. The human's face paled when he slowly rose from the bed and walked to the door of his cell. He stared back at the wide, dark brown eyes gaping back at him in shock.

"You speak... you understand...," Crawford stuttered.

"I learned your language... some," Merrick replied with a sharp nod. "Release me."

"I can't," Crawford whispered hoarsely. "Hell, I'm going to be lucky to get out of this alive as it is. If I release you, I'm dead. If Weston Wright doesn't kill me, Markham will. They even threatened my family if I said anything or tried to leave."

"Then help me," Merrick demanded.

"Didn't you just hear what I said?" Crawford asked in frustration. "If I so much as lift a finger to help you get away, not only am I dead, but so is my girl. That was made very clear the first night you were brought in."

"Call a number for me, then," Merrick insisted in a low voice. "The human can protect your family. He can send you and your female to a place where neither of these men can harm you."

Crawford gave a bitter laugh and shook his head. "Are you fucking kidding me? I did my research on these guys after they threatened me! Unless you can send me and Becky to another planet, there isn't a fucking rock on Earth where they won't hunt us down," he retorted.

"You would not be on your world," Merrick murmured in a low voice. "You would be on mine."

Crawford swallowed and paled. Merrick knew he had taken the human by surprise with his comment. It was a risk, but it was one he had to take if he was to get free.

"You... you aren't shitting me, are you?" Crawford whispered. "You really are a fucking alien."

"Yes," Merrick answered, staring intently into Crawford's eyes. "I know that they intend to kill you. Weston has joked about it when they do their tests on me. They do not realize I can understand them."

Merrick didn't think it was possible for the human to get any paler than he had been, but he did. He actually swayed for a moment before a flash of anger ignited in the depths of his dark eyes. He knew the moment the human made the decision to help him. His eyes followed Crawford's hand as he reached into his pocket and pulled out a small piece of paper and a pen.

"You said that there was a human that could protect Becky and me? Do you really think that? Do you think he could send us somewhere that we would be safe?" Crawford demanded in a harsh voice.

"Yes," Merrick replied calmly.

"Who is he?"

A smile curved Merrick's lips as he returned Crawford's intense stare. His fingers curled around the cold, steel bars. Finally... finally, the Goddess had heard his plea and answered him.

"Cosmos Raines," Merrick said. "You can reach him at this number."

～

Merrick sat back a few minutes later on the bed. A sense of expectancy filled him as he watched the door quietly close behind

Crawford. Pulling one leg up, he uncurled his left hand again so he could touch the intricate pattern in the center. He closed his eyes and he concentrated on the face of the female. Opening his mind, he waited for the connection born of their bond to connect him with her.

A satisfied smile curved his lips when he felt the link between them connect. He could feel the confusion, fear, and worry coursing through her. He wished that he could hold her and reassure her that she needn't feel that way. Suddenly, her thoughts cleared and he could 'hear' the question resonating through her mind as if she was standing in front of him.

What the...? A clear picture of the same pattern that graced his palm formed in his mind.

The marking shows you have found your bond mate, he answered in a soft, whispered thought.

What... What is a bond mate? She hesitantly thought back.

Merrick could feel the trembling of fear in her thoughts. Frustration gnawed at him. He hated that he could not be there with her. Resentment tempered his response to her.

You are my bond mate. It means you belong to me! Tell me your name, he ordered.

He sent the demand more forcefully than he intended. A sense of regret filled him when he felt her instinctively flinch at the harsh projection of his thoughts. He had forgotten to ask Crawford for her name before he left. Now, he desperately needed it. It was almost as if he knew her name, it would give him the lifeline he needed to remain sane until Cosmos could send a team to free him.

Merrick leaned forward and clenched his fists to keep from howling in rage when nothing but silence met his demand. He tried pushing his thoughts into her head again, but it was as if she was no longer there. Pausing, he drew in a deep breath and released it. It took several minutes before he felt her tentatively reach out to him again. When he met her halfway, she hesitated, but didn't withdraw.

Merrick's Maiden

THE GREAT EASTER BUNNY HUNT

THE FULL NOVELLA!

Alien eggs can only mean one thing – an adventure!

A pile of unusual eggs leads to an exciting Easter egg hunt for the kids and the adults alike in this delightful holiday tale. The children must work together to recover Jabir's coveted eggs after the Great Easter Bunny is caught taking them away. Can the Dragonlings and their besties save the day?

Chapter 1

"No. It's not happening, Vox. You can leave me out of any of your crazy missions," Trelon stubbornly said, shaking his head.

"Don't be such a wuss, Trelon. It will be fun!" Vox chuckled and slapped Trelon on his shoulder.

"Wuss? What is a wuss?" Trelon asked with a confused expression on his face.

"Scaredy-cat, wimp, coward – you know, wuss. Riley taught me that one," Vox replied, still grinning.

"I'm not a scaredy-cat – I'm a dragon. This is going to end badly, you do know that, don't you?" Trelon groaned.

He sank down into the chair in his living room and laid his head back to stare up at the ceiling. If Trelon had known it was Vox banging on his door, he never would have opened it. He had been enjoying a few hours of peace and quiet. Amber and Jade were playing with Spring and Phoenix, Cara was shopping with his mom, and he was finishing up the nursery. Cara was due any day and he wanted everything perfect for their son.

Vox gently kicked Trelon's boot to get his attention and sat down across from him. "Asim says it's essential that we get rid of those damn eggs Jabir brought back from Earth. Have you seen the size of those things? He doesn't have a clue what's inside them, but he isn't taking any chances," he explained, leaning forward and resting his elbows on his knees.

Trelon lifted his head and glared at Vox. "Then let Asim deal with it! This is not my problem. I've had enough adventures to last a lifetime and the girls aren't even teenagers yet! Do you have any idea of how crazy life is at the moment? Cara is due any day with our son. Amber and Jade are on high alert. They have decided it is going to be their duty in life to make sure he is protected. They have been creating a fortress in his room! It has been a full time job just trying to keep them out of mischief and you want me to help you get rid of a pile of eggs? Just bury them!" Trelon growled.

"We can't! Pearl has threatened that if Asim harms one egg, she'll pickle his tail and serve it at the next family meal. Under no circumstances can he be involved with getting rid of the eggs. If that isn't bad enough, Tina's chicken, Ruby, thinks the eggs are hers and has been lying on top of them. Viper told me that he and Tina visited last week and now Leo wants to bring home whatever hatches out of them. If we don't do something, I'll end up with one of the creatures! Have you seen the size of the eggs? They are huge!" Vox said in exasperation, holding his hands out almost half a meter.

"Again – let Asim deal with it! You know if we get involved, something bad is bound to happen," Trelon dryly remarked.

"Come on, Trelon. Did I happen to mention that Roam heard Jabir say that Amber and Jade want one of the eggs – each? That means two of whatever hatches," Vox informed Trelon with a smirk.

"What?! Oh, dragon's balls! That's all I need!" Trelon groaned and ran his hands over his face before dropping them to his lap to gaze back at Vox with a look of resignation. "Alright, I'll help you. I have enough creatures running around the house with just those damn demented symbiots. I swear the girls are still making them. They keep popping up every once in a while."

"You've got nothing to worry about; I've got the perfect plan," Vox stated with confidence, sitting back in his seat with a smug grin.

Trelon shook his head. "Why does that sound suspiciously like we are screwed? That, by the way, means trouble – big, big trouble," he muttered under his breath.

Chapter 2

"Decorated eggs! Has it been a year already?" Zoran exclaimed with a wide grin.

Abby nodded her head and tapped Zoran on his knuckles when he reached for one of the brightly dyed eggs. "Those are for the Easter Egg Hunt," she admonished.

"Yeah, Daddy, those is for us to hunts," Zohar stated.

"Then why is your tongue blue?" Zoran pointedly asked with a raised eyebrow.

Zohar glanced at his mom and grinned. Sure enough, his lips, tongue, and teeth were all blue. Abby released a sigh when she saw the remains of the egg shells on the floor under Zohar's chair. Between father and son, she'd be lucky to have any eggs left for the Easter Egg hunt planned for the next day.

"I has to taste test them," Zohar said with a firm nod. "I'm tastings just like Mommy does when she cooks them."

"One... I said one, Zohar," Abby replied, leaning over and pressing a quick kiss to the tip of Zohar's nose.

"Yew!" Zohar grumbled.

"Do I get a kiss if I eat an egg?" Zoran asked with a mischievous smile. "I promise not to say 'yew' if you do."

Abby chuckled. "You can get a kiss any time you want," she promised, leaning up to brush a kiss across Zoran's lips. "I think you taste perfect the color they are."

A soft, rumbling growl escaped Zoran before he could smother it. Abby shot him an amused glance before turning away. He gently wrapped an arm around her waist and pulled her back against him. Abby smiled when his hand moved lower to protectively cover her abdomen.

"How is he?" he murmured.

Abby chuckled. "You know very well how he is doing. You've been connected with me since our dragons shared I that was pregnant again," she teased.

"What's preg-ant mean?" Zohar asked, staring back and forth at his parents with wide eyes.

"Uh-oh," Abby murmured.

Zoran pressed a kiss to Abby's neck and straightened. "You're going to be a big brother," he explained.

Zohar tilted his head and frowned for a moment. "Okay," he said with a shrug. "Can I colors more eggs?"

"Yes, you can color more eggs," Abby said with a raised eyebrow at Zoran. "He took that better than I expected."

"He's a born leader," Zoran chuckled, rubbing a hand along Abby's side before he pulled away. "Can I help him color more eggs?"

Abby laughed. "As long as you don't taste test them all," she teased.

"Leo, no!!! Viper, help!" Tina called in exasperation.

"What...? What in the cat's....?!" Viper exclaimed, walking into the living quarters he and Tina were sharing with Riley, Vox, Roam, and their twin daughters, Sacha and Pearl. "He's purple."

"I can see that he is purple," Tina growled, holding up their young son under his arms. "Can you see if you can wash any of it off while I clean up this mess?"

Leo hissed at his father and tried to swat a tiny paw at him. Viper shook his head and grabbed the small kitten by the back of his neck. Leo immediately went limp, hanging from his father's hand with a glum expression.

"Aw, Aunt Tina. We were trying to makes Leo look like an Easter Egg. He was going to hide so we could all try to finds him," Roam complained.

"I told Roam it wasn't such a good idea," Bálint said.

"I thought it was cool. They were going to do me next," Jabir replied with a grin.

Tina's lips twitched at Jabir's innocent admission. The sight of her son, shifted into his cat-form and sitting in a large mixing bowl of purple dye with Roam, Bálint, and Jabir holding cups and pouring the dyed water over Leo's head rose into her mind. At least Leo had been getting a bath – of sorts. Maybe she should have added dye to Leo's bath water. Lately, he had started hissing and growling at her and Viper until one of them dumped a pile of toys in with him. Of course, having Roam there had also made it easier. The two boys could spend hours playing in the tub if there were enough bubbles and toys.

"I think we'll have enough Easter Eggs," Tina promised, grabbing a damp cloth and bending to wipe the floor.

"How can you be sure? My daddy keeps eating the ones Mommy and I makes," Jabir asked.

Tina glanced at the three boys. "Well, the Great Easter Bunny will bring some more," she said.

"The Great Easter Bunny?" Roam repeated with a slight awed sound in his voice. "Mommy and Daddy didn't tell me about the Great Easter Bunny."

"Mine neither," Bálint said, sitting down next to Jabir on the floor.

"Mines didn't either. What's the Great Easter Bunny?" Jabir asked.

"Well, he's big – really, really big. He has to be to carry all the Easter Eggs. He has a big, fluffy tail and long ears. His ears help him listen for the sound of children's laughter. He has to make sure he leaves the Easter Eggs where they can be found," Tina explained as she stood to rinse the washcloth and dump the colored water down the drain.

"How bigs is he?" Jabir asked.

"Well, at least this tall," Tina said, lifting her hand up until it was about as tall as Viper.

"Is there just one Great Easter Bunny?" Bálint asked, gazing up at Tina.

Tina shook her head. "Oh, no. There are quite a few of them. It takes a lot of Easter Bunnies to deliver all those eggs – especially the really special ones," she added in a dramatic whisper.

"The special ones? What special ones? What do they looks like?" Roam demanded.

Tina glanced around, as if to make sure that no one else could hear her before she bent down in front of the boys. Her eyes twinkled with mischief. She knew that Abby and Morian had been making a Mr. and Mrs. Easter Bunny costume to surprise the kids. Ariel and Trisha had made some large Easter Egg Piñatas, and Riley, Cara, and she were making up games.

"Well, they are about this big, a really pretty color, and they are filled with all kinds of wonderful to eat treats," Tina said, holding her hands up to show how big the Piñatas were.

"Wow!" Jabir whispered, his eyes glowing with excitement.

"Okay, he's clean. He's still purple, but he's clean," Viper said, standing in the doorway with a very fluffy, riled, purple kitten.

Leo shifted back into his two-legged form when Viper set him down on the floor, giggled, and headed for Roam. Roam twisted onto his hands and knees and waited for Leo to crawl up onto his back.

"Horsey!" Leo called out.

Tina glanced back at Viper, and realized that he was soaked. An amused, tender smile danced on her lips. Leo didn't like to get a bath – until he was in it; then, everyone got one. Viper gazed down at Leo with so much pride and love, it made her heart ache. Standing up, she walked over to her mate, wrapped her arms around his waist, and laid her head against his chest.

"Thank you," she murmured.

Viper's arms wrapped around her and he hugged her close. "For what?"

Tina tilted her head back and smiled. "For being such an amazing dad and mate," she said.

Chapter 3

"Whatever you do, don't get caught," Asim warned, standing outside of Trelon's living quarters. He handed a bag to Trelon before he handed another one to Vox. "Be careful. I've got them packed in warm grass to keep them from breaking."

"What is in this thing?" Trelon asked with a frown as he lifted the bag with one hand.

"Eggs – big, alien eggs that Jabir hid among the things you and the others brought back from Earth," Asim stated with a shake of his head. "I guess Mandra didn't know Jabir had snuck them in."

Trelon glanced back and forth between Asim and Vox. "And why did you two get me involved in this? Why isn't Mandra taking care of it?" Trelon asked in exasperation.

Asim shook his head. "Mandra doesn't even know about them. Even if he did, he couldn't be involved; Ariel would know. Jabir has been sneaking out every few hours to the barn. That isn't so unusual, but when Tina and Viper came to visit a few days ago, they brought that damn bird with them. It has been laying eggs all over the place. I was collecting them and heard it in the barn area. It was sitting on top of an enormous green egg unlike anything I had ever seen before. When I picked it up, I saw more buried in a bed of warm grass that I use when one of the other creatures we have are nesting," he explained.

"Okay, that explains Mandra and Ariel, but it doesn't explain why you are in such a hurry to get rid of the eggs. What is the problem? You have all kinds of creatures up on the mountain, what are a few more?" Trelon asked in exasperation.

Asim smothered a growl and glanced around. He had flown here early this morning with the cache of eggs hidden under the seat of the transport he had traveled in with Lord Mandra and Lady Ariel. Jabir had come several days earlier with Pearl and his symbiot so he could play with his cousins and see Leo and Roam. As it was, he was running out of time. He had promised to meet Pearl in just a few minutes. Fortunately, she didn't know about the eggs either – or at least as far as he knew.

Asim ran a hand down over his face and sighed. "Little Jabir and Lady Ariel have brought home an abundance of animals, but they are all ones I'm familiar with. I've never seen eggs like this. What happens if they can't survive on our world? I don't want Jabir to be heart-broken if they don't make it and don't get me started on Lady Ariel! She tries to hide it when one of the newborn creatures dies, but I know she still cries. Then I worry about how dangerous they could be to the tiny lord and his mother. I'd never forgive myself if something happened to one of them. I swore to your father, Lord Trelon, that I would protect the royal family. It is my responsibility; I should have taken care of them. I'll take the bags," he murmured, and held his hands back out.

"No, Asim. You've done enough. I don't want Ariel and Jabir upset with you. You are there every day. Vox and I will take care of them," Trelon promised when a wave of guilt swept through him.

"You need not worry, Asim. I have a plan," Vox replied with a grin.

Asim looked critically at the smile on Vox's face. Trelon bit back the groan that almost escaped. He wasn't so sure that Vox's plan was going to work. Vox had only given him a brief overview and it sounded simple enough – take the eggs with them out to the meadow and hide them – deep into the forests where there was no chance of them surviving the predators that lived there. They would be honest about what they were doing – they were hiding eggs.

"If you are sure," Asim replied with a slightly skeptical expression.

Vox slapped Asim on the shoulder and nodded. "I'm sure. It will be easy," he promised.

Trelon watched Asim nod before the other man turned away. He waited until Asim had disappeared around the corner before he shifted the bag of eggs in his hand. Opening the bag, he blinked in surprise when he saw how large they were.

Taste good? his dragon asked.

You can't eat them! If we ate these, forget about what Mandra would do to us; think of what Ariel and Cara would do! Trelon growled.

I eat Ruby eggs, his dragon pouted.

Those are different. I don't know how, but they are, Trelon retorted.

These no look as tasty, his dragon agreed with a grumble.

True. Who would ever want to eat green eggs? Trelon replied.

"Trelon, come on. We've got to go talk to Ha'ven," Vox said.

"Ha'ven! What does he have to do with all of this?" Trelon asked, dread filling him.

"I've got a new idea," Vox said.

"Why does that not sound good?" Trelon muttered, closing the bag of eggs.

Chapter 4

"You want me to do *what?*" Ha'ven asked in an incredulous tone before he shook his head.

"Do that thing that Emma did at Halloween when she made those costumes for the women. You know, like when she made Riley into that sexy ghost," Vox replied with a grin.

"I'm blaming Pearl for this," Ha'ven muttered under his breath. "I think she shot you one too many times."

"That was in his ass, not his head. I think his brains were scrambled when Riley used that device she had for shocking him," Trelon replied with a chuckle.

Vox scowled at the other two men. "Riley hasn't used the Taser on me in years. I took the battery out of it and told her it was broken," he stated, rubbing his chest at the memory.

"You really want me to create a costume – for the both of you – so you can do what?" Ha'ven asked again.

"I have a picture of it. I had Adalard send me a picture of one for the kids. He sent me this thing called a movie that is supposed to be good. It has a large bunny that throws this thing called a boomerang and talks with a funny accent," Vox said, pulling a small vidcom from his pocket.

The three men watched a large creature with long ears hop across the screen. Behind the creature, tiny decorated eggs walked. It was obvious that the characters were not real, but there was something enchanting about the images that kept the men's eyes glued to the screen. It wasn't until almost the end that Vox muttered a curse under his breath and shook his head. He scrolled through the list before he found what he was looking for, a drawing of two Easter Bunny costumes from Earth.

"This is what we need," Vox said, holding up the vidcom in front of Ha'ven.

Ha'ven stared back at Vox for a long time before he turned a pained expression to Trelon. "Are you serious?" Ha'ven asked, staring at the two rabbits holding hands on the screen.

Trelon returned Ha'ven's gaze and nodded. "Amber and Jade want to keep one of the creatures in the eggs – each. With my luck, whatever is in the eggs has to have long rows of teeth and poops a lot," he replied.

"That's called a baby dragonling," Ha'ven chuckled. "When do you want the costumes?" he asked with a shake of his head.

"First thing tomorrow morning," Vox said, glancing at Trelon. "We'll volunteer to hide the eggs. All you have to do is meet us just inside the edge of the woods. You can create the costumes and be back before anyone knows you are gone."

"That's all?" Ha'ven asked in a dry tone. "Trelon, please tell me you can see how many things can go wrong with this plan."

Trelon raised his hands up in the air. "I just don't want any more demented creatures crawling around my house. I have enough with Amber and Jade, and Cara is due any day. I'm in survival mode," he said.

"I'll warn you now. I will deny all knowledge of this," Ha'ven vowed.

Vox chuckled and slung his arm around Ha'ven's shoulders. "You don't have to worry about a thing. What could go wrong?" he asked with confidence.

"I know nothing," Ha'ven repeated, shaking his head.

"I'm pleading insanity," Trelon only half joked.

Chapter 5

Early the next morning, Paul chuckled and set Morah down on the ground. The little girl shifted and bounced over to where the other children were playing. Morian walked up behind him, carrying a platter of fresh fruit. He leaned over and picked a red piece of fruit that reminded him of a plum and popped it into his mouth.

"She is growing so fast," Morian said with a smile, watching her tiny daughter stop to touch Leo's purple hair in awe.

"Too fast," Paul agreed.

"Mommy, can I have purple hair, too?" Alice asked in excitement.

Emma sighed even as Viper and Tina laughed. Alice had already changed her yellow dress to purple with dozens of small colorful eggs on it. Leo was eating up all the attention his new color had drawn from the girls.

"Thank goodness she hasn't learned how to change her hair color yet. Is Melina going to make it with Hope?" Emma asked as the small group walked up to Paul and Morian.

"No, they are doing a special Easter Egg Hunt with Christoff and Edna back at the village. I wish they could have made it, but I guess the tradition is spreading," Abby replied, placing several of the baskets for the kids on the table.

"It is amazing how much fun it is. I don't remember Easter being this cool when we were growing up," Riley said, picking up a cookie and eating it.

"It helps having a meadow like this to hide them in, though you have to admit all the bikers did a bang up job for you girls," Pearl agreed, holding her granddaughter on her hip.

Riley leaned over and tickled one her tiny daughter's toes. "Hiding money in liquor bottles decorated with paper isn't quite the same," she drawled.

"It worked and I didn't hear you complaining about the cash inside," Pearl commented.

"You mean the cash that you made us put into our savings account?" Tina quipped.

"You had more in your savings accounts than most of those high society misses, and you married princes. I'd say you did pretty well," Pearl retorted, pressing a kiss to baby Pearl's temple. "Isn't that right, my little princess? I taught your mommy how to kick some ass too."

"Butt, Pearl. I don't want the girls' first words to be 'ass'," Riley teased. "No, we don't, do we?"

Pearl chuckled when little Pearl's lips parted on a giggle. She glanced around with a frown. Her expression relaxed when she saw Asim talking with Paul. She quickly glanced away when he turned his head toward her. There was no sense in letting the grouchy old dragon think she missed him or anything.

"Where are Vox and Trelon?" Riley asked.

"They volunteered to hide the Easter Eggs this year," Cara replied with a slight groan.

"Are you okay?" Trisha asked, walking up to help Cara when she dropped a ribbon on the ground.

"Yes. I just had a slight twinge. I think this baby is ready to see some daylight," she admitted with another wince.

"Why don't you sit down? We can take care of the rest of this. You've been doing too much for the last few days," Trisha gently scolded.

"I feel like a bloated whale about ready to pop," Cara said, sinking down into a chair.

"You look like...," Kelan started to say before he winced when Trisha elbowed him. "You look – big."

"Thanks, Kelan. I'll remember that on your birthday," Cara promised.

"Goddess, I didn't mean it as an insult, Cara," Kelan replied with a shudder. "The last gift you gave had those bizarre creatures from Halloween in it."

"That was a mistake," Cara said with a wave of her hand. "I meant to send that to Dulce. He's helping me figure out why the symbiots turn out that way when the girls put them in the replicator."

"Your girls should not be allowed near anything mechanical, Cara. At least not until they are about a thousand years old," Zoran interjected.

Cara leaned her head back and smiled sweetly up at Zoran. "Try and stop them," she said.

The sound of laughter echoed through the group when Zoran muttered he never got any respect anymore. In the background, Ha'ven casually glanced around before he stepped behind a tree and disappeared.

Chapter 6

"Really, Ha'ven? You just couldn't resist, could you?" Trelon asked with a disgusted voice.

"You look fine, Trelon," Vox said.

"You aren't the one wearing a dress and pink toe nails," Trelon retorted.

Trelon awkwardly turned and rested his paw covered hands on his hips. His vision was partially blocked by the cover of the mask he was wearing. This had to be the absolute stupidest stunt he had ever been involved in before.

Ha'ven's lips twitched. "I have to get back before Emma and Alice miss me. You asked – I created. Now I'm denying any knowledge. But before I go, I have to say, you make a striking couple," he added.

"Ha-ha," Trelon muttered in a muffled voice and tried to lift the middle finger of his paw.

"I think it is great! He even put springs in the feet so we can bounce," Vox said.

Trelon turned toward Vox to add another biting comment, but instead he paused and fully took in what Vox looked like. Vox looked

– ridiculous. Ha'ven had created a perfect costume from the image. Of course, Vox would have preferred the one from the movie vidcom to the one from the picture.

Vox was decked out with long, white ears that stood straight up. He had large, dark brown eyes with long eyebrows above each eye, a short pink nose, and a wide mouth with two long teeth hanging down. Trelon chuckled when he saw the large yellow bow and shiny purple jacket. His gaze moved down over Vox. His body was covered in a soft fur material that looked so real, Trelon actually wanted to touch it. His gaze moved down to Vox's feet. If he thought Vox had big feet before, it was nothing compared to the mammoth bunny feet he now wore.

"Turn around," Trelon ordered.

"Why? You know, you make a pretty bunny. I like the floppy ears, less likely to get caught on a tree branch," Vox commented before he turned and glanced over his shoulder. "I've got one fluffy tail."

"It wiggles," Trelon laughed.

"Let me see if you have one," Vox ordered, twisting back around.

Trelon turned around. "This dress makes me look bigger," he complained.

"No, it doesn't," Vox assured him. "Amber and Jade would love to see you dressed like this. I can just see Cara crashing the communications system again if she were to broadcast you in that outfit."

Trelon shot Vox a glare. Of course, it was pointless as Vox couldn't see his expression. Still, it made him feel better.

"It better not happen, because if it does, I know who to hunt down," Trelon warned.

"We'd better hide the big eggs first so they can be eaten first," Vox said, glancing through the trees.

"That sounds...," Trelon's voice faded when he heard a soft gasp.

He turned and tilted his head to get a better view. He glanced around, trying to see, but his vision was limited. Twisting back to look at Vox, he saw the other man searching as well.

"Do you see anything?" Trelon asked.

Vox's large bunny head shook back and forth. "No, but we'd better get these eggs hidden fast if we want to get rid of the others. Maybe this wasn't such a good idea after all," he said, turning and almost tripping over his feet.

"You think?" Trelon muttered behind him.

Neither man saw the three heads peering up from the hole in the ground. Three sets of large, rounded eyes watched in awe and excitement as the two large rabbits haphazardly bounced down a wide trail in the forest. Another soft gasp escaped the little blue dragon that was staring at one of the eggs peeking out from a knapsack – a large, very familiar green egg.

"It's the Great Easter Bunny that you told us about Jabir," Spring whispered.

"There's even a girl bunny!" Phoenix exclaimed, turning bright shiny eyes to her sister.

"But… the bunnies got my eggs. I don't want our daddies to eats my new eggs. Phoenix, I can hears the babies chirping. We got to saves them," Jabir pleaded.

Phoenix looked at her sister with concern. "We'll need help. They are hiding the eggs," she said.

"Let's get the others," Spring replied, turning in the hole she had dug.

Chapter 7

"Those sound an awful lot like Emu eggs, Asim," Paul was saying. "I know Chad was talking about raising some. Their meat is supposed to be good. Where did you see them?"

Asim swallowed and raised a hand to rub along the back of his neck. He'd been having second thoughts about what he'd done. The more he'd thought about it, the more he wanted to just talk to Mandra and Lady Ariel about his concern. He didn't know why he hadn't thought of Paul Grove. If anyone would know whether or not the eggs were dangerous, it would be the human mate of Lady Morian.

"Jabir hid them among the items that Mandra brought back. I noticed he was going out to the barn a little more frequently than normal. Then, Lady Tina and Lord Viper came to visit and she brought Ruby. The chicken was laying eggs everywhere. When I was searching for them to gather for the Easter egg event, I found her on top of one of the large green eggs," he admitted.

"Well, I don't think you'll have to worry too much about them. They can have a powerful kick and have a claw, but you've handled bigger and more dangerous things than that. I would make sure that you explain to Jabir that he needs to be careful. If you raise them from hatchlings, they should be fine with the other large animals. If you have any problems, I'd be happy to come out and help," Paul recommended.

"Thank you, Paul. It would appear I should have talked to you sooner," Asim replied, looking out at the woods.

"Any time," Paul said, turning when he heard Morian call his name.

Asim nodded. "I hope I can find them before it is too late," he murmured.

"Too late for what?" an amused voice asked from behind him.

Asim grimaced. With a loud sigh, he turned to face Pearl. He rubbed his hands together and tried to think of a way to tell her what had happened – without really telling her what had happened.

"I need to go find Trelon and Vox," he said.

"And...," Pearl asked with a raised eyebrow.

"I may have given them something I shouldn't have," Asim admitted.

Pearl chuckled and stepped forward. Asim's eyelids lowered when she raised her hand and stroked his cheek. Goddess, but this woman never ceased to amaze him.

"Good luck. I think you are going to need it," she murmured.

Asim nodded, and turned his head to press a kiss against her palm before moving with quiet sure strides toward the edge of the forest. He would cut around the meadow so he wasn't seen.

Chapter 8

"Zohar! Zohar!" Spring and Phoenix called out.

The two girls darted through the crowd of adults. They both skidded to a stop when their mom and dad stepped in front of them and knelt down. Phoenix shifted first, falling into her dad's arms with a breathless gasp.

"Daddy, you have to help us," Phoenix cried.

"What's wrong?" Carmen asked, hugging Spring.

"The Great Easter Bunnies have Jabir's eggs," Spring said.

"The Great Easter...," Creon started to say before stopped and looked at Carmen with a confused frown.

"It's true, Daddy. We saw them. They was in the woods. They have Jabir's eggs," Phoenix anxiously said, reaching up to cup Creon's cheeks between her tiny hands. "Please, you have to help us. Jabir says he heard them chirping."

"He heard what chirping? The bunnies?" Carmen asked.

Spring shook her head. "No, the eggs. They took his big eggs, not the little ones like what we made. These are really big," she said, holding her hands out wide.

"He is afraid that they will gets eaten," Phoenix explained, turning dark, golden eyes to her father. "You'll help us, won't you, Daddy? You'll save Jabir's eggs."

"Where is Jabir?" Carmen asked, glancing around.

"He's in the woods. He says he's going to stop the Great Easter Bunnies from giving his eggs away," Spring replied.

"Creon...," Carmen murmured, turning to gaze at her mate.

"I'll get the other men together and we'll find him," Creon promised, setting Phoenix on the ground.

"I knew you would," Phoenix exclaimed in relief.

"I'll let the women know what is going on," Carmen said. "These creatures that took the eggs...."

Creon glanced at Carmen. "We'll find them," he promised.

"Yay!" Spring said, pulling away from Carmen.

Both girls watched as Creon motioned to Kelan, Mandra, Zoran, Viper, and Paul. They turned and hurried over to where the other kids were playing. They still needed to tell Zohar, Alice, and Roam what was going on. While the daddies hunted for the Great Easter Bunnies, they would find Jabir. No dragonlings would ever be left behind or alone.

"What's wrong?" Zohar asked.

"Jabir's in trouble," Spring announced.

Bálint turned with a low snarl. The sound was so unexpected that even Morah and Leo stopped to stare at him. Alice stepped closer to Bálint and slid her hand into his.

"What happened?" Alice asked with a worried expression.

"It's the Great Easter Bunnies. They took his eggs. He is chasing them in the woods," Phoenix explained.

"Yeah, our daddies is going to go catch them," Spring added.

"But we still gots to go help Jabir get his eggs back," Phoenix insisted.

"You're right. Spring, can you gets us to the woods?" Zohar asked.

"I already gots a tunnel," she said.

"We'll needs weapons," Roam suggested.

"I can make those," Alice said, waving her hand. A small bow appeared.

"Bálint, can you tracks the Great Easter Bunnies?" Zohar asked.

"Yes," Bálint nodded.

"I wants to goes," Leo said, rubbing his nose. "I's good at finding stuffs too."

Roam started to protest before he looked at his cousin's wide eyes. No dragonling – or cub – gets left behind or forgotten. He turned to gaze at Bálint. The other boy understood his silent plea and nodded.

"Come on, Leo, you can help me," Bálint instructed. "You gots to be quiet and listens."

"I can listens really good. I'm a panther," Leo stated, shifting into his panther form.

"What about me? Daddy teaches me how to hunts," Morah said, her lip trembling.

"You can help us girls. We can makes lots of traps," Amber and Jade said with a grin.

Morah's eyes lit up with delight. "I can make good traps!" she promised.

"The daddies are going," Zohar said, watching the men taking off across the meadow.

"Let's go. Bálint and Leo are already in the tunnel," Roam said.

"I's going on my first adventure," Morah excitedly whispered. "Mommy and Daddy is goings to loves this!"

Chapter 9

"Hold up, I think I dropped another egg," Trelon complained.

"You're supposed to drop them," Vox said before he cursed. "One of my ears is stuck again." He dropped his basket and knapsack onto the ground by his feet so he could try to free his ear from where it was caught on a low branch.

"You should have gotten the floppy ones. I'm not having any trouble with them," Trelon chuckled, brushing a pink paw down over one of his floppy ears.

Vox tried to turn, but he couldn't. "Would you mind helping me? I don't want to rip the ear off," he said with a loud sigh.

"I swear, I can't take you anywhere anymore," Trelon joked, setting down his basket and shrugging off the knapsack filled with green eggs. "I only have four eggs. I did drop one."

"We'll go back and look for it. I think we are far enough in to leave them. We need to get back and start hiding the others," Vox said.

"That sounds good to me. This thing is getting hot," Trelon complained. "Your ear is free."

"Thanks," Vox said.

Trelon turned to hop back over to where he had left the basket and knapsack. "I have to admit, this is a good workout," he said before he stopped to glance around him with a frown.

"What's wrong?" Vox asked.

"My knapsack is missing," Trelon replied, turning in a slow circle.

Trelon muttered under his breath. His paw moved toward the ground, re-enacting his movements from just a moment ago. He lifted a paw and absently scratched his cheek. It took a moment for him to realize that he couldn't reach the real itch.

"You've lost all your eggs?" Vox asked in disbelief.

Trelon shook his head. "No, just the knapsack – the basket of eggs is still here," he said.

Vox hopped stepped closer and gazed around. "You just put it down," he said.

Trelon glared at Vox. "I know I just put it down. Now it is gone," he stated.

"Well, that takes care of that," Vox replied.

Trelon shook his head. "How can you... Something has your knapsack!" he exclaimed, pointing a paw at where Vox's knapsack was moving through the ferns.

Vox awkwardly turned to see what Trelon was pointing at. He stumbled forward, his large foot catching on the other. His arms circled as he tried to keep his balance, but it was a futile gesture. He fell face-first into the high ferns lining the path. Reaching out, he grabbed the bottom of the knapsack, trying to hold onto it.

"What is it?" Trelon asked, trying to maneuver around Vox's prone form.

"I can't see," Vox growled, pulling on the bag as best he could with the thick, furry paws around his hands.

Trelon awkwardly lowered himself down next to Vox, trying to see into the shadows of the bush. A low snarl escaped the animal pulling on the bag. With a tug, it slipped from Vox's paws.

"Oh no, you don't," Trelon snapped.

He reached into the brush to pull the bag back out before he emitted a muffled curse and withdrew his paw. He lifted it, wincing when the sharp teeth pinched the skin of his hand. Hanging from his paw was a small, chubby, blue dragonling with flashing gold eyes.

"Jabir?!" Trelon exclaimed in surprise.

Jabir released Trelon's hand and dropped down to the ground. With a threatening snarl, he backed into the bush and disappeared. It took a moment for the surprise to evaporate and the knowledge that they had been caught to sink in.

"Vox, get up," Trelon ordered, struggling to stand up.

"I'm trying! It isn't easy moving around in this thing," Vox snapped. "How did Jabir find us? Do you think the others are here?"

Trelon smoothed his dress and turned. He wanted to rip the head off his costume, but was afraid of scaring the dragonlings if he did. He glanced back toward the bush.

"Jabir, come out. We aren't going to hurt you," Trelon said. "Jabir? Jabir?"

Vox knelt in the ferns and bent to peer down into the bush. The boy and the eggs were gone. He pushed up off the ground until he could stand.

"He's gone," Vox said, looking around. "There! The ferns are moving."

"We've got to get him," Trelon said, snatching up the basket of colorful eggs as he half-hopped, half-stumbled by it.

~

Jabir's heart raced. He had stowed the two bags he had taken inside a hollow tree. He knew from watching the animals on the farm that the parents often would hide their young and lead the predators away from them.

He raced through the ferns as fast as he could, trying to make as much noise as he went. Glancing over his shoulder, he saw the two huge rabbits chasing him. A soft cry escaped him when his back leg caught in a vine and he tripped and rolled. He struggled to kick it off, but it was tangled.

"I've got you," Bálint said, slicing through the vine with a sharp rock.

Leo hissed at the two approaching creatures.

"This way," Bálint instructed. "Leo, takes them to the others."

The tiny purple and black cub sneezed and turned. Jabir glanced at Bálint once more, but the little boy had already shifted into his dragon form. He watched Bálint lift up off the ground with a single bounce. Turning, he raced after Leo.

~

Bálint knew he needed to slow the two bunnies down. The others weren't far behind them. When he was racing toward Jabir, he had noticed a Whisper Fly nest. The creatures wouldn't hurt the bunnies, but they would swarm them if their nest was disturbed.

Flying up to the branch, he waited until the two rabbits were almost directly under him before he turned and kicked the nest. Bouncing up onto the limb, he pushed off, going higher so they wouldn't see him. He made it to the fork in the tree and pulled a section of leaves in front of him to shield him.

A dark swarm emerged from the bottom of the hive. The small winged insects paused before narrowing in on the two large rabbits under their nest. The swarm started forward again, swirling down in a spiral until it covered the heads of the fluffy bunnies.

Satisfied that they would be delayed for several minutes, Bálint pushed away from the tree and soared back down to the forest floor in the direction that Leo and Jabir had gone. It wouldn't take him long to catch up with them. He stayed low, only glancing back once to make sure that the bunnies couldn't see him.

~

"Ouch!" Trelon groaned, falling backwards.

"Sorry, Trelon, I was aiming for the swarm," Vox said, tossing the branch he had been swinging to the side.

"Have I told you that this is a very bad plan?" Trelon growled as he rocked back and forth, trying to get up. Why did he let Asim and Vox talk him into this? When was he going to learn that Earth holidays were a dangerous time for him? He should be with his mate, not running through the woods in a costume from the bowels of a Super Nova.

"Here," Vox said, reaching a paw down.

"What are we going to do now? We can't leave Jabir alone in the woods," Trelon said, brushing the leaves off of his dress before he bent to pick up the eggs he had scattered when he dropped his basket. "Where's your basket of eggs?"

"Cat's tail! I forgot it back on the trail," Vox muttered.

"Go get it. I'll see if I can find Jabir," Trelon said.

"It's not far," Vox replied, turning to go back to where they had been just a few minutes before.

Trelon shook his head. He dropped the last egg into the basket, wincing when he heard a crack. Of course, that was the moment his dragon decided to perk up.

Eggs? his dragon murmured.

"Not yet, I'll wake you when it's time," Trelon promised.

I likes colorful eggs, his dragon murmured in approval.

"I know you do, my friend. I just wish it didn't come with a holiday," Trelon chuckled with a shake of his head. "When will I ever learn?"

Chapter 10

Paul paused, blinked, and shook his head.

This is going to be another one of those adventures, he couldn't help but think to himself.

He silently watched the two Easter Bunnies bounce in separate directions.

We watch? his dragon asked.

Oh, yes. We are just going to sit back and enjoy this show, Paul said.

In his solid gold dragon form, no one could see him. Creon was very close to being invisible as well. The biggest difference was Paul could reflect his surrounds while Creon needed to stay in the shadows.

Paul had moved out into the front, tracking the large prints that looked oddly familiar, yet strange. He had arrived just in time to see the swarm of Whisper Flies surround the two men. A moment later, Bálint had appeared. Pride washed through him at his grandson's resourcefulness. He had also been amused to see Leo had joined with the other kids. He was just thankful Morah wasn't old enough yet.

Focusing, he reached out for his mate. Almost immediately, he could feel her warmth surround him. He was about to pull away when he felt her amusement and exasperation.

What is it? he asked.

Have you seen the younglings? They are missing, Morian asked.

Paul's silent chuckle was answer enough. He felt her sigh. Curious, he waited.

Morah is missing, Morian said.

Morah.... Her symbiot? Paul asked, his gaze sweeping the thick ferns.

She is with Alice. They are making traps to catch the Great Easter Bunnies, Morian replied.

Paul turned his gaze to the two large rabbits. *I think I know why Ha'ven said he would stay and protect the women,* he replied in a dry tone.

Morian's laughter washed through him. *I think the only ones missing are Asim, Vox, and Trelon. If I had to guess....*

From the curses, Vox and Trelon, Paul responded, landing on a large limb.

The women are going to love this. Are you going to tell the other men? Morian asked.

Not in a million years, Paul chuckled.

Find Morah, but let her have fun, Morian whispered, pulling away.

I will, Paul replied.

This way, his dragon murmured, turning his head back toward a thick bed of ferns in a small opening in the forest.

Paul knew his dragon was connected to Morah's symbiot. The small bracelets and earrings had become a constant companion after witnessing what the other dragonlings, Alice, and Roam had been up to. It was only to be expected that Morah would follow in their footsteps. She was, after all, just like her older sister and mother – strong, beautiful, and full of curiosity.

Paul lifted off the branch and glided through the large trees. He would observe, but not interfere unless he was needed. He had taught Bálint and the others just like he had taught Trisha. They were younger, but had a natural instinct bred into them from their dragons. He also knew that each had a small part of their symbiots with them.

Landing in another tree, he turned his head. In the distance, he could hear the men moving through the forest. He had played tag enough times to recognize the slight difference in the sounds. If he had to choose who to be more concerned about – the kids or the men – his bet would be on the men. They had no idea that the kids were planning on a little hunting of their own.

You got bad sense of humor, his dragon snorted.

I don't see you making any noise to warn the men, Paul retorted dryly.

I part of you. I have bad sense of humor, too, his dragon replied, folding his wings in and settling down on the branch. *This be fun to watch.*

"They are *what?!*" the group of women all said at the same time, staring at Morian in disbelief.

Morian couldn't control her laughter. "I don't know why any of us are surprised anymore. Whose idea was the Easter Bunny costumes? They are obviously not the ones we made, Abby. These look much more detailed," she said.

The women all looked at each other with a puzzled expression. It wasn't until Emma laughed out loud that they turned to her. She was staring at a very uncomfortable looking Ha'ven.

"You didn't," Emma murmured, stepping up to rest her hands on his chest.

"I deny everything," Ha'ven replied with a glitter of amusement in his eyes.

"You are so bad," Emma giggled.

"What? Oh man, the only ones missing are Trelon and Vox. Those two are worse than the kids!" Cara chuckled before she released a moan and rubbed her belly.

"We have got to see this," Riley said. "Cara, I'm totally taking a vidcom of it so you can blast it out to the universe. I just hope they don't take the costumes off before I get a chance."

"You're on! Just let me have this baby first," Cara chuckled.

"Oh, you'll have plenty of time, Riley. I didn't put any fasteners on the costumes when I created them. I just crafted the outfits around them in one piece. They'll either have to be cut out or be very nice to me," Ha'ven grinned.

"Oh, that is good," Ariel and Trisha said at the same time.

"Yes, it is," Ha'ven chuckled.

Chapter 11

Zoran held his hand up and the others with him froze. He waited, hearing the muffled sound of what sounded suspiciously like curses. He glanced over when Kelan stepped closer to him.

"I saw – something," Kelan murmured, his voice low and uncertain.

"White?" Zoran asked.

Kelan nodded. "With pink in it," he added.

"I saw it as well," Creon said. "I don't know where Paul went, but I'm going in closer."

"Be quiet," Zoran cautioned.

"I will," Creon responded just before he shifted.

Mandra started toward them before he released a stifled curse and disappeared. Zoran and Kelan turned at the same time with a frown. Threading their way through the undergrowth, they stared down at where Mandra was sitting in a deep hole.

Both men knelt down. "What happened?" Zoran demanded.

"It's a trap. It was covered over with leaves and twigs," Mandra said, standing up and brushing the dirt and leaves off the seat of his pants.

"Where's Viper?" Kelan asked, glancing around.

"He shifted and moved up into the trees," Mandra said.

Zoran and Kelan reached down and grabbed Mandra's hands. They pulled him out of the pit. Zoran stood gazing down at the hole with a frown. It wasn't very deep.

"Tunnels," Kelan murmured, nodding to several small holes.

"Maybe the rain caused the tunnels to cave into these holes at the natural weak spots," Zoran said, glancing back around. "We've lost track of the ears. Come on."

~

Viper moved along the branch of a tree, pausing when the two creatures below him stopped. His cat's mouth had started watering the moment he saw them. All he could think about was how good they would taste and how much fun he would have playing with those fluffy tails. He might even take one home for Leo.

Stop thinking like that, Viper hissed. *You know Tina would have a fit if you brought home a fluffy tail.*

Soft, his cat purred.

Viper would have rolled his eyes if he was capable of it. Instead, he moved forward. He was almost directly over them when his left front paw sunk into something soft on the branch. He tried to pull it free, but he couldn't. Placing his other paw next to it, he immediately realized his mistake – now both were stuck. He extended his back claws, burying them into the bark and jerked backwards, breaking free – but losing his balance at the same time.

A loud hiss escaped him as he twisted around. In the back of his mind, he processed that someone had wrapped part of the branch with the threads of the Sticky Worms. There was only one person he knew who loved the stuff – Spring Reykill.

"What the...! Viper?" a voice below him called up.

Viper waited for the impact with the ground, but it never came. Instead, he found himself hanging in midair – face down – staring at the long eared creature that his cat had been fantasizing about.

It took a moment for him to realize two things: First, that the creature's voice sounded an awful lot like his older brother; and second, that he was hanging from a netting of Sticky Worm silk that looked like it had been placed to capture the two men below him when they walked under it. His jerking on the branch had triggered the trap that he was now hanging from.

"Vox?" Viper asked, staring down at the pink nose, long whiskers, and stiff, smiling face.

"What are you doing up there?" Vox demanded, staring up at his younger brother.

"Hunting," Viper said with a sigh.

"What are you hunting?" the other rabbit that sounded suspiciously like Trelon asked in a cautious tone.

"You," Viper admitted.

Both rabbits looked at each other before they glanced around them. They finally looked back up at him. Viper released a sigh...

No bunny tail tonight, his cat glumly exclaimed.

There's always Tina's tail, he murmured.

Oh, yes... much better! his cat purred, happy once again.

"Can you two help me get down, because I have to tell you – I'd love to know what you two are up to," he asked, gazing back and forth between the two men staring up at him.

Creon moved silently through the shadows. He paused, watching and listening. His ears twitched when a sound, almost inaudible, teased his senses.

This way, his dragon murmured.

Creon followed his dragon's urging, trusting him to know which way to go. He was almost to a small opening when he saw a tiny white head pop up out of the ferns before disappearing again. His lips twitched in amusement. A moment later, it popped up again.

He watched Spring glance around before she disappeared again. Curious, he moved closer. Shifting, he stepped behind one of the large, thick trees and watched.

"I's can do it," a voice insisted.

Creon's lips parted in a low hiss. He started forward, jerking to a stop when he felt a hand on his shoulder. Turning his head, he saw Paul standing behind him. Paul shook his head and lifted a finger to his lips.

"Be careful," Alice whispered.

"I will," Morah promised.

Paul and Creon watched as the tiny gold and white dragon crept out of the tall ferns. Their eyes widened when Morah shook her body. The white scales shimmered and turned a warm gold. Within the blink of an eye, Morah vanished.

"Incredible," Creon murmured.

"She hasn't shown us that trick yet," Paul quietly chuckled. "I'll follow her while you keep an eye on the others."

"How will you know where she is?" Creon asked.

"My dragon will," Paul assured his son-in-law.

Shifting again, Paul disappeared as quickly as his daughter did. Creon shook his head. These younglings were much more powerful than any of them had realized. That thought brought both comfort and stress. He turned his head, jerking back in surprise when he realized that he was no longer alone.

He blinked, staring mesmerized into the glowing worlds reflected in his youngest daughter's eyes. She was floating in front of him. Her wings were raised, but not moving. He couldn't help but wonder if she had known where he was the entire time. The question was answered when she nodded her head.

Creon's throat tightened and he opened his arms. Phoenix moved into them, shifting back into her two-legged form and wrapping her arms around his neck. He held her close, savoring every second he had with her.

"We came to find Jabir," Phoenix whispered.

"Did you find him?" Creon asked, pulling back so he could see her face.

"Yes," Phoenix replied.

She waved her hand at where the others were in the small clearing. As if a large mirror appeared, Creon could see Jabir, Leo, and Spring around a pile of large, dark green eggs. The scene shimmered and changed. Next, he saw Roam and Zohar. They were sneaking up behind the two large bunnies. It took a minute to realize that they were after the two baskets filled with colorful eggs.

"Where did Morah and Alice go?" Creon asked in a voice thick with emotion.

"To capture the Great Easter Bunny and his mate. Amber and Jade are there, too," Phoenix replied, waving her hand again.

Creon's lips parted – half in warning and the other half in amusement. He watched the scene unveil in slow motion. Both girls reappeared within a few meters of the two large rabbits. They both raised a long straw to their mouth and blew. Tiny, round pellets exploded from the ends. Both bunnies jumped in surprise when the pellets exploded around them, releasing a red and yellow dust. Before they had a chance to react, both girls had disappeared again.

"Sleeping pollen," Creon murmured.

"Bálint knew where some was," Phoenix replied.

They watched both bunnies sink to the ground underneath where Viper was hanging from the web. A moment later, Amber and Jade crawled out from under the bushes. They had their faces covered with a mask of leaves and were pulling long cords of vines behind them. In a matter of minutes, they had the two bunnies tied up and were giving each other hand slaps.

"Remind me to have a long talk with your Grandpa Paul," Creon said with a shake of his head.

"Okay," Phoenix giggled. "Can we hunt for eggs now?"

Epilogue

"I think they'll live," Riley said.

"Not... not so loud," Vox groaned, laying an arm over his eyes. "Ow! What was that for?"

Viper glared down at his older brother. "The Great Easter Bunny?" he asked with a raised eyebrow.

"I thought it was a good plan," Vox mumbled, turning to cover his eyes again. "What hit me? It feels like it was large and very hard."

"Morah and Alice," Riley chuckled. "Those two girls are after my own heart. I hope Sacha and Pearl are as creative as those two."

"Goddess help the world if they are," Vox replied with a shudder.

"We's sorry, Uncle Vox. If we had known it was you and Daddy, we wouldn't have knocked you out and tied you up," Amber said.

"Yeah, we thoughts you were just going to steals Jabir's eggs and eats them," Jade added. "That's why we had to stops you."

"Viper wanted our fluffy tails," Trelon chuckled before he groaned. "Paul, we need to have a serious talk about what you are teaching the younglings."

Paul laughed, holding Morah in his arms. "Alice and your little sister were pretty good at tagging you. I think we'll need to do some remedial training," he suggested.

The women burst out laughing when the men all released a loud groan. The group suddenly turned when Trelon sat up and froze. A shudder went through his body when he turned to look at Cara, his eyes wide.

Her lips were parted and she nodded. "It's time," she whispered.

"Oh, Goddess, I felt that!" Trelon muttered in a strained voice.

"Felt what?" Mandra asked, stepping forward and placing a hand on Trelon's shoulder when another shudder went through him.

"Is that what it feels like?" Trelon panted, glancing over at Cara with stunned eyes.

"What is going on?" Kelan asked.

"I think you'd better disconnect from her symbiot, Trelon. She is going to need you in one piece," Morian gently instructed.

Trelon nodded and drew in a deep breath. "Never again," he swore, standing up on shaky feet before he shook his head to clear it. "Call for the healer."

"Trelon," Cara started to say when he bent to pick her up.

"I'm so sorry," he murmured.

Cara winced and nodded. "You can pay me back later," she said before turning to look at Paul and Morian. "Can the girls stay with you for a bit?"

"Of course," Morian said.

"What's wrongs with Aunt Cara?" Zohar asked.

"She's having our baby brother," Amber and Jade said with a grin. "We's building a fort to protect him."

"Do I need to do that for my baby brother, too?" Zohar asked with a frown.

"Abby?!" Morian whispered.

Everyone turned to look at Abby and Zoran. Abby leaned back against Zoran when he wrapped his arm around her and smiled. She glanced up at him before looking back at the group and nodding.

"Does this means we won't get to hunt Easter eggs?" Roam asked, staring at the group.

"Not at all! Mr. and Mrs. Easter Bunny have returned and we have eggs hidden all around the palace," Pearl stated with a smile.

"Yay!"

"Thank you, Pearl," Morian murmured.

"It's easy when you have a big ole dragon feeling very guilty. Besides, I could tell Cara would be lucky to make it through the day. Why don't you head on back to the palace? We'll round up the kids and bring them back," Pearl suggested.

"I'll see you soon," Morian said before she brushed a quick kiss across Paul's lips.

"Where's Asim?" Paul asked, watching his mate climb onto the golden transport her symbiot had formed and hurriedly taking off after her son and Cara.

"He was looking for one last egg that was missing. He'll return to the mountains and make sure they are okay. He wants to make sure they are there before Jabir gets home. He loves that little boy," Pearl explained.

Paul glanced over the group. They were all gathering up the items they had brought. Today, there would be one more added to his growing family. A family he had never dreamed he would have. He smiled and knelt down when Morah ran back up to them. Her hands were wrapped around a basket and she had a big smile on her face.

"We found some eggs, Daddy. They are pretty, but the shells broken and makings noises," she said, holding the basket out to him.

Paul gently picked up one of the eggs. He blinked in surprise. He looked up when he felt more than heard the soft chuckles on the wind. Looking down again, he stared in amazement at the soft, yellow chick emerging from its shell. He glanced at the small note attached to the side of the basket.

For Ruby. Even chickens need a happily-ever-after. Happy Valdier Easter ~ Arosa and Arilla.

"Asim and Viper are really going to love this," Paul murmured, staring down at the huge pile of moving eggs.

ADDITIONAL BOOKS AND INFORMATION

If you loved this story by me (S.E. Smith) please leave a review! You can also take a look at additional books and sign up for my newsletter to hear about my latest releases at:

http://sesmithfl.com
http://sesmithya.com

or keep in touch using the following links:

http://sesmithfl.com/?s=newsletter
https://www.facebook.com/se.smith.5
https://twitter.com/sesmithfl
http://www.pinterest.com/sesmithfl/
http://sesmithfl.com/blog/
http://www.sesmithromance.com/forum/

The Full Booklist

Science Fiction / Romance

Cosmos' Gateway Series
Tilly Gets Her Man (Prequel)
Tink's Neverland (Book 1)
Hannah's Warrior (Book 2)
Tansy's Titan (Book 3)
Cosmos' Promise (Book 4)
Merrick's Maiden (Book 5)
Core's Attack (Book 6)
Saving Runt (Book 7)

Curizan Warrior Series
Ha'ven's Song (Book 1)

Dragon Lords of Valdier Series
Abducting Abby (Book 1)
Capturing Cara (Book 2)
Tracking Trisha (Book 3)
Dragon Lords of Valdier Boxset Books 1-3
Ambushing Ariel (Book 4)
For the Love of Tia Novella (Book 4.1)
Cornering Carmen (Book 5)
Paul's Pursuit (Book 6)
Twin Dragons (Book 7)
Jaguin's Love (Book 8)
The Old Dragon of the Mountain's Christmas (Book 9)
Pearl's Dragon Novella (Book 10)
Twin Dragons' Destiny (Book 11)

Marastin Dow Warriors Series
A Warrior's Heart Novella

Dragonlings of Valdier Novellas
A Dragonling's Easter
A Dragonling's Haunted Halloween
A Dragonling's Magical Christmas

Night of the Demented Symbiots (Halloween 2)
The Dragonlings' Very Special Valentine

Lords of Kassis Series
River's Run (Book 1)
Star's Storm (Book 2)
Jo's Journey (Book 3)
Rescuing Mattie Novella (Book 3.1)
Ristéard's Unwilling Empress (Book 4)

Sarafin Warriors Series
Choosing Riley (Book 1)
Viper's Defiant Mate (Book 2)

The Alliance Series
Hunter's Claim (Book 1)
Razor's Traitorous Heart (Book 2)
Dagger's Hope (Book 3)
The Alliance Boxset Books 1-3
Challenging Saber (Book 4)
Destin's Hold (Book 5)
Edge of Insanity (Book 6)

Zion Warriors Series
Gracie's Touch (Book 1)
Krac's Firebrand (Book 2)

Magic, New Mexico Series
Touch of Frost (Book 1)

Paranormal / Fantasy / Romance

Magic, New Mexico Series
Taking on Tory (Book 2)
Alexandru's Kiss (Book 3)

Spirit Pass Series
Indiana Wild (Book 1)
Spirit Warrior (Book 2)

Second Chance Series
Lily's Cowboys (Book 1)
Touching Rune (Book 2)

More Than Human Series
Ella and the Beast (Book 1)

The Seven Kingdoms
The Dragon's Treasure (Book 1)
The Sea King's Lady (Book 2)
A Witch's Touch (Book 3)

The Fairy Tale Series
The Beast Prince Novella
*Free Audiobook of The Beast Prince is available:
https://soundcloud.com/sesmithfl/sets/the-beast-prince-the-fairy-tale-series

Epic Science Fiction / Action Adventure

Project Gliese 581G Series
Command Decision (Book 1)
First Awakenings (Book 2)
Survival Skills (Book 3)

New Adult

Breaking Free Series
Capture of the Defiance (Book 2)

Young Adult

Breaking Free Series
Voyage of the Defiance (Book 1)

The Dust Series
Dust: Before and After (Book 1)
Dust: A New World Order (Book 2)

Recommended Reading Order Lists:

http://sesmithfl.com/reading-list-by-events/
http://sesmithfl.com/reading-list-by-series/

ABOUT THE AUTHOR

S.E. Smith is a **New York Times, USA TODAY, International, and Award-Winning** Bestselling author of science fiction, romance, fantasy, paranormal, and contemporary works for adults, young adults, and children. She enjoys writing a wide variety of genres that pull her readers into worlds that take them away.